To Amy
Enjoy!,
A Kelly

Buying
Time

FORTHCOMING

Borrowed Time

For more information about this series, visit
www.AspenMoore.com

Buying Time

An Aspen Moore Novel

Kelly Cochran

BOOKRISE
St. Louis, Missouri

Library of Congress Control Number: 2012905963

DEDICATION

For Bill, my LSMPM and for Ben,
by far my greatest contribution to this world.

1

TEN MONTHS AGO I began a game of hide and seek. I got a new name, a new city, a new life. The objective was to keep myself alive and I'd do almost anything to win the game. Tonight, anything meant squatting in a bed of mulch with my nose in a juniper bush.

I had approached Max Vanderbur's front door with every intention of knocking. I should have walked away when I heard people arguing, but instead I'd stood there going through the pros and cons. Before I reached a conclusion, someone turned the doorknob and my body heaved itself into the bushes.

When the door didn't open, I turned my attention to an intermittent shadow as it moved across the junipers like a windshield wiper. Cautious, I tucked myself tight against the house and crawled toward the window to assess the situation before popping out from behind the bushes. I took a deep breath then looked inside.

"Holy Sh—" I threw my hand over my mouth to stop my scream.

Max's eyes were wide and he was hanging from the exposed crossbeams in his study wearing nothing but a rope and his tighty-whiteys. The Hostess Ding Dongs I'd snacked on earlier made their way up to my throat as I wondered if the shadow I'd seen had been Max swinging. My throat burned. I couldn't understand why Max would kill himself when he knew I was on my way to see him.

Unable to look at him any longer, I let my eyes wander the room. A leather chair was on its side, suspiciously near Max's dangling body. At first glance it appeared Max had hung himself, but as I continued to survey the room, it was unclear what really happened.

Papers lay scattered across the dark Oriental rug. Two bookcases opposite the desk were nearly empty, the bulk of the books having been tossed, their pages torn. Who rips apart his own room then hangs himself?

Craning my neck, I looked toward the left side of the room. The French doors to the study were closed. Max continued to stare, his body limp. Everything about him was still, even his right eye that had twitched so reliably it could be used to keep time.

I wasn't sure how Max ended up with a rope around his neck, but I needed to do something other than stare back at him through the window. I crawled out of the mulch and into the grass.

The front door opened. *Crap.*

I froze for a mere second then quietly shifted into reverse. I tucked myself back behind the junipers, and prayed my yellow sweatshirt wouldn't give me away.

"I can't believe you did that. I told you we didn't have time," a woman said.

If my situation hadn't been so dire, I would have been tempted to pop out of the bushes and hand her my card. I was in the business of selling my time to people who didn't have enough of their own. As a personal concierge, I did just about anything for just about anybody. In fact, Max had been the first person to hire me. He was a Professor of Urban Development and had asked me to organize his office. Later, to help research a decade old multi-million dollar real estate deal.

No longer able to hear their conversation clearly, I inched up to a small hole in the hedge to get a better view. I watched two sets of legs walk down the sidewalk. One pair covered by pants, the cuffs gently falling atop a pair of tasseled loafers. The other pair bare, anchored into a classy set of black heels.

The man waved his finger in the woman's face as he spoke, then went silent, dropping his arms tight by his side, with fists formed. But the woman continued spewing her words, arms flailing. The hedge's peep-hole limited my view, so I rose until my eyes were just above the brim of the junipers. I couldn't see the man's face, but the woman resembled the photograph Max had prominently displayed on his desk at the office.

My thigh muscles screamed and the ones in my butt were not far behind. Squatting wasn't meant for long term spying, but the tiniest movement and I'd have a lot of explaining to do. I suffered in silence.

When they finally got into a car and drove away, I was relieved but apprehensive. I stood to stretch my legs and ponder the important decision I was about to make. Most people, more than once in their lives, come upon a fork in the road. Last time I'd chosen the high road and lost my life as I'd known it.

Looking back through the window it took only seconds to decide. This time, I was choosing the low road.

I whispered goodbye to Max and scrambled out from behind the junipers. I drove away, leaving Max alone and suspended in air.

———

The morning headline, *Professor Dead*, confirmed what I already knew. I read the article a second time while I waited in a booth at Chubbies Diner. The journalist simply referred to Max's death as a suicide. No mention of the condition of the room or the whereabouts of Max's wife. The article presented his death as a sealed box ready to be placed on the shelf, until I reached the unexpected plot twist in the last paragraph. The police believed Max killed himself, but they continued to look for a person of interest.

My nose caught a whiff of salty bacon as a waitress delivered food to the people in the next booth. Last night's Hostess Ding Dongs had long been digested and deposited on my hips, but I still felt the urge to vomit. It wasn't the first time I'd been exposed to death, but that didn't make the experience any easier. I flagged down my waitress for some coffee, choosing to skip the food. She flipped my cup upright, poured the coffee and dropped a few creamers on the table before heading off to her next refill.

"Aspen. Have her pour me one," my friend Peter Parker yelled as he entered the diner, disregarding the fact that the waitress was now several tables away.

Peter's not like me. At six foot-four, he was not one who could easily hide. Add to his incredible height, his booming voice and it seemed ironic that he owned a spy shop, but he did. He spent his days selling gadgets like smoke detector cameras, wireless video monitors, and tiny microphones disguised as pens.

"Thanks for coming," I said, after he slid into the booth.

Peter ran his hand over his smooth head and down the side of his face, stopping at the soul patch on his chin. He stroked the tiny tuft of hair before he spoke. "Wow. You look awful."

My hair was matted and my eyes stung like lemon juice in a paper cut. I'd spent the evening at my office, disturbed and awake. I looked away trying to hide my red, white, and blues.

"Are you okay?" he asked.

"I'm a person of interest."

Peter winked. "I'm always interested in you."

Normally I'd snap back with harmless flirty banter, because that's what Peter and I did. But flirty was far from how I felt.

"I'm serious. I really am a person of interest! Read the last paragraph." I shoved the newspaper in front of him.

He skimmed the article. "What makes you think they're looking for you?"

"Because I called the police last night," I shouted over the sound of plates and flatware being tossed into a tub by a busboy. I looked around to make sure Peter had been the only recipient of my confession then recapped the events of the previous evening in a quieter voice.

"Damn it, Aspen. Why didn't you call me?"

"I was working through what I saw. It looked like murder to me, but if he did kill himself I didn't want to set off any alarms to the contrary. Plus you would have insisted I go to the police."

A vein in Peter's neck bulged. I took it as a sign he was a little upset. "You do need to talk to the police. If the people saw you behind the bushes, you could be in danger."

I wanted to tell him I knew all about handling danger, but if I did, he'd ask me how. And answering that question truthfully would make everything worse. "If Max's wife saw me she would have come after me, don't you think?"

Peter's eyes narrowed and his brows drew closer, making me wonder what would come out of his mouth next. "Why didn't you tell the police your name?"

"I intended to but they started asking too many questions. So, I hung up."

He smiled and tilted his head back. "Why? You don't have anything to hide, do you?"

Even though he smiled, I suspected he wanted an honest answer. I trusted Peter, but not completely. So, I lied. "I didn't want my company name becoming part of the ten o'clock news. It could be bad for business. Besides, I told them the most important thing and that was where to find Max."

"You know, they're probably tracking your cell phone anyway."

"I called them from a pay phone."

"Now I know you're pulling my leg, nobody has pay phones anymore."

"They do at that little gas station three blocks from here."

"Why'd you use a pay phone?"

"I told you. I don't need the bad publicity."

"You need to go to the police."

"What am I supposed to say? I didn't want to get involved because it might ruin my business?" *Or the truth: I didn't want to get involved because I was afraid they might dig into my past?*

"You panicked. I can call and make arrangements for you to go in."

"You make me sound like a felon negotiating my surrender. I can handle it on my own. I promise I'll stop at the station right after I change out of these stinky clothes."

"Stinky? I think they're sexaaay."

Peter's comment signaled the end of our discussion. He was making nice, attempting to lighten the mood. I knew he wasn't serious because I looked like crap. When Max had called last night, I ran out without changing. I was still wearing my baggy jeans and a yellow sweatshirt with food stains accentuating my two most noticeable features.

Peter tousled my hair then picked up the check. "Call me if you need me."

The waitress came by and poured me another cup of coffee. I mulled over my last conversation with Max. My research into the old multi-million dollar real estate deal had resulted in the mundane until Max made contact with the original land owner. He said he'd found problems with the acquisition of the land and believed he was on the verge of uncovering something big.

Experience taught me how dangerous it was to reveal another person's secret. People had killed to keep their secrets safely tucked away. I should have warned Max, but instead I'd simply told him I'd be right over.

Driving to his place last night all I had thought about was how to ask him for partial payment. My savings had plunged to my self-imposed danger mark and I wasn't due to be paid for the research work until I had completed everything and handed over a report.

I sipped my coffee and watched the diners as they engaged in conversation with only the occasional pause to eat. I longed for my old life, though I knew I'd never get it back. Accepting that fact was easier when I considered the alternative. My life could end tragically like Max's.

The curiosity I felt was unsettling as I picked up the newspaper and read the article again. I should have been hiding from the story. Instead my brain was attempting to isolate the emotion Max had exhibited over the phone, hoping to find an answer. Had Max been killed or had he killed himself? Either way I failed him.

Max had been predictable. Every Friday I'd go to his office, organize for a bit, then he'd pay me for office work. If he had information I could use for my research he'd give me an envelope. The pattern remained unchanged since he hired me, until last night. He had not only asked me to come to his house, he had even offered to give me my weekly check in advance.

My check. He definitely said he had a check to give me. If I didn't pick it up soon, I might never receive it or a single payment for all of my research. My only problem was Mrs. Vanderbur. Had she been staring into oblivion as I hid behind the junipers or directly at my face?

———

Eager to wash off the lingering smell of bacon and dread, I hurried back to my place and jumped in the shower. With each droplet of water my thoughts about packing up and leaving town disappeared. I exited my apartment revitalized, determined to pick up my check from Max Vanderbur's house and get on with my business.

Half a block from my apartment I began to smile when I saw my Jeep – midnight blue, tinted windows, platinum trim – and the only car I'd ever driven for no other reason than to show it off. It was love at first ride. Purchasing something so flashy may not have been my brightest idea, but it imparted a little bit of happiness in my sad little life.

Passing over the dry riverbed of the River Des Peres meant I had left the city of St. Louis and entered South County. Not as affluent as West County, the southern part of St Louis County still had its fair share of great neighborhoods. Max Vanderbur had lived in one of them.

Max's street was lined with large older homes, each architecturally beautiful. In daylight the neighborhood appeared formal and perfect. But I knew the truth and wondered what other secrets lay behind the brick and stone walls.

I neared Max's house catching sight of Mrs. Vanderbur exiting the passenger side of a black Mercedes. She'd barely stepped out of the car when the driver sped off. The Mercedes passed by me and I caught a glimpse of the man behind the wheel, his face angular and tanned, with graying temples. Without seeing his pants and shoes, I had no idea if he was the man I'd seen talking to Mrs. Vanderbur last night.

By the time I parked, she'd gone inside the house. I cut through the lawn to the front porch. Looking over at the junipers, I took a deep breath and knocked on the door.

Mrs. Vanderbur yanked the door open. "What do you want?"

She appeared even more stylish than she had through the junipers. Her suit tapered at her waist and hugged her curves, results not accomplished by off-the-rack clothes. Her jewelry mesmerized me. The earrings and necklace could have been cubic zirconia, but one glance at her watch and I knew better. She wore my dream watch, a diamond, rose-gold Cartier Tankissime. The Tankissime was extravagant for most people, including a wife of someone on a professor's salary.

"First I want to tell you how sorry I am about your husband."

"And you knew him how? You don't look young enough to be one of his students."

I didn't like her tone, but I was too ecstatic about her not recognizing me to throw some clever retort her way. "I'm sorry. I should have introduced myself."

I fumbled through my purse for a business card. The purse slipped off my arm and I tried to grab it before it hit the ground, only making things worse. The folders I'd been carrying scattered across the front porch along with the contents of my purse.

"What do you want?" Her impatience was now officially annoying.

I scrambled to gather my things. "I apologize. I've been meaning to get a briefcase. Here it is." I stood up and handed her my card. "I was working for your husband and—"

"And you're afraid you aren't going to get paid? Is that it?"

My pride took over and I scrapped my crazy idea of asking her for payment. I removed an envelope from one of my folders and held it up. "Did he leave one of these for me?"

"No." She barely paused. At that moment I realized she didn't seem the least bit saddened by the fact that her husband was now teaching at the big school in the sky.

"Would it be too much of an inconvenience to check his desk?"

"It's not in his desk."

"What about his briefcase?"

"He didn't have one. He was a fool, always carrying everything in his arms like a school child."

I ignored her innuendo. She'd made this into a sporting match and there was nothing left for me to do but throw a Hail Mary. "Is there anywhere else you might look?"

"No. Now, if you'll excuse me, I've been locked up in this house all day and I'm getting ready to go out." She slammed the door in my face.

She lied. In my eyes it was as good a sign as any that she was guilty of something. I stood still for a few seconds then turned and walked away. The police had probably already questioned her, but she deserved a second visit, which meant I had to go to the station and tell them what I had witnessed.

A long piece of yellow crime scene tape flapped from the sole of my red sneaker as I entered my Jeep. I couldn't be dragging crime scene tape behind me like an errant piece of toilet paper when I visited the police station. Not only would I look like an idiot, I'd appear guilty, having revisited the scene of the crime. I yanked it off and tossed it into my purse, doing my part to help save the planet.

The clock on my dashboard had me speeding out of Max's neighborhood. My next stop was in the community of Soulard where another client lived. I was late and he wasn't the patient type.

When I arrived, I parked in front of the trendy townhouse and dug around for the house key. Three minutes. That's how long it took me to find the key. Three precious minutes I could have sold to someone else if I were more organized.

I exchanged waves with the neighbor. It had become our daily ritual though we never uttered a word. I made my way to my client's front door hoping I wasn't too late. As soon as I opened it, Mr. P jumped all over me. Lucky thing he doesn't shed.

"Down, Mr. P, down!"

Mr. P, short for Mr. Personality, wasn't exactly a big time client, but he was the dog of a big time client. A Bichon Frise, he was built like a fluffy white slipper you longed to spend a rainy day in.

Mr. Quetzalcoatl, a well-known syndicated radio host, owned Mr. P. He hired my company for a three-week trial and had me sign a multi-page confidentiality agreement covering circumstances I could never imagine and would never admit to if I had. I should have labeled him a wacko and walked away, but money made people do crazy things. What he offered came in way above adequate, but pronouncing his name was a chore, so I dubbed him Mr. Q.

He was currently on a business trip, which required me to spend more time than I normally would on dog duties. I had to walk Mr. P three times a day, feed him and clean up after him when he didn't feel like waiting for me – like today.

I shooed Mr. P out the doggie door onto the screened-in porch and walked back to the kitchen. Reminding myself how much money I was making, I grabbed some paper towels and picked up the mess.

With one end of Mr. P taken care of, I opened a can of dog food to take care of his other end. I heard him bark. He loved the electric can opener. He'd soon barrel through the door like a wild, fluffy, ravenous beast, so I plopped the bowl on the floor and waited.

Silence.

"Mr. P! Mr. Peeeee!"

Still no clickity-click of little paws across the hardwood floors. I went to the porch to find out what was so fascinating that it would trump his chow. The porch was empty.

I checked the second doggie door leading to the back yard and it was still locked. I stood up and twirled around thinking he'd slipped past me and gone back inside. What I found was a note stuck to the back door:

YOU SHOULDN'T HAVE DONE WHAT YOU DID. YOU OWE ME. PAY OR SAY GOODBYE TO YOUR DOG.

Crap. I searched the backyard hoping it was a big joke. But the yard was empty.

What terrible thing had Mr. Q done to cause someone to steal his dog? Poor Mr. P hadn't had a chance to eat. I told myself whoever took him would feed him. I tried convincing myself he would be safe, but my thoughts flashed back to Max's dangling body. I knew I was foolish to think they wouldn't harm a defenseless dog.

Yesterday, a murder? Today, a dognapping? I didn't want to find out what tomorrow would bring.

2

I PUSHED TOMORROW out of my head and walked through the townhouse one last time, calling Mr. P. When he didn't appear, I had to persuade myself to leave. I placed his bowl into the fridge, put the cryptic ransom note in my purse, and called his name one more time before leaving and locking the door behind me.

A new problem had entered my life and I needed to make it go away. I briefly debated reporting the snatching, but Mr. Q's contract clearly forbid police involvement. And no way would I phone Mr. Q to let him know I'd misplaced his dog. He'd fire me and probably trash my company on his radio program. I had to find Mr. P before Mr. Q returned. My best chance was Peter.

The spy shop wasn't Peter's only show. He'd recently launched a small investigation business, but had no clients. This would be a perfect first case. How hard could it be for him to find a missing dog?

"I have a little problem," I said when Peter answered my call.

"Am I sure I want to hear this?"

"Can you meet me at Chubbies?"

"Can't you tell me over the phone?"

"No, I need to show you something and I'm finally hungry. I'll buy."

"Chubbies, again?"

"I've got a hankering for a milk shake."

"A hankering, hey? How can I say no? Victor's due here in a few minutes. I'll leave as soon as he arrives."

Victor helped run Peter's store and he was always on time, which meant I had to go straight to the diner in order to arrive before Peter. Asking him to hunt for a dog was pushing our friendship, so I'd need to make it sound like something he couldn't refuse.

Fifteen minutes later, after maneuvering through traffic, I sat in the middle lane waiting to turn into the parking lot of Chubbies. Some jerk behind me honked his horn. I glanced in the rearview mirror and saw Peter. I did what any hungry self-respecting girl would do, and flipped him off with a smile. My cell phone rang.

"Nice turn signal. Next time hold it out the window." Peter followed his statement with a flirty laugh that made me seriously consider looking for a loophole in our 'just friends' agreement.

We met inside at the hostess stand and waited obediently until they escorted us to a booth. The paper placemats, which earlier displayed hearty breakfast selections, had been replaced with a lunch version. I salivated as I perused the photos of cheeseburgers, shakes, and fries. My appetite had definitely returned.

Peter scanned me from top to bottom. "You look a lot better. Did you go by the police station?"

I fiddled with my napkin, avoiding his eyes. "Not yet."

"The longer you wait, the worse it's going to be."

"I know, but I had to stop by Max's house."

The waitress stopped by to take our order. I welcomed the interruption. As soon as she walked away, Peter continued, "Are you nuts?"

"I wanted to find out if Max set anything aside for me. Besides, I don't think Max's wife recognized me."

"You didn't answer my question."

"No, I'm not nuts." It bugged me when he wouldn't let his rhetorical questions slide.

"Did she give you anything?"

"Nothing. I'm sure she lied about not finding anything. She acted indifferent," I said and then lowered my voice. "How can she be so calm when she murdered her husband?"

"You have no proof she killed him. She's probably distraught. Maybe she didn't even know he was dead. You said the door to the study was closed, right?"

"Right, but why would she be having a hot-looking guy in a Mercedes drop her off at her home this morning."

"So he was hot, was he?"

"Not the point, Peter. The point is she didn't act like a grieving wife."

"We all grieve in different ways." His melancholy tone said please don't ask. I didn't, but tucked the information away for later.

Without any real plan on how to ask Peter the favor, I whipped out the ransom note in order to change the subject. "Here's the real reason I asked you to meet me for lunch."

"A dognapping? I'm not exactly the Ace Ventura type if you haven't noticed."

He had a point. We lived in the same building and whenever our landlady, Mrs. Rippetoe, ventured out with her dog, Peter always kept one eye open.

"The dog, Mr. P, is an important client."

"You have a dog as a client?"

"I cannot divulge my real client's name, but this is his dog."

Peter laughed. "I've never seen your Miss Professional side before. It's sexy, in an uptight librarian kind of way."

"Peter, can you help me?" I asked, shutting down his relentless flirting.

"Okay, okay, I'll ask around."

I continued eating my fries while I listened to Peter describe the new inventory he received for his store. I was fascinated by all the gizmos and envious too. If I owned a spy shop I'd go broke spending all my time playing instead of selling.

The sound at the bottom of my glass when I sucked my chocolate malt through the straw signaled its end. My pants were no match for my expanding stomach. I loosened the button for a temporary fix.

"Thanks for sharing my last supper with me. Now I need to go turn myself in."

"A bit melodramatic, don't you think?"

I enjoyed giving him a hard time. As we both stood up to go I felt a smidgen of guilt for making it sound like I was going to the police station when I hadn't made up my mind yet. To ease the guilt, I smiled at Peter and added a wink for good measure.

"Don't lose your pants." He grabbed the check and ran off to the cashier.

I looked down, and there, in all its glory, was my belly, pooched out through my unzipped jeans. I glanced toward Peter. He was still laughing as he walked out the door.

———

My Jeep idled while I sat in the parking lot exit lane deciding which way to turn. Right and I'd continue on with my concierge duties for the day; Left, I'd head to the police station, which meant I'd need to call Cutter.

The moment I had agreed to testify against my ex-fiancé's murderer, the U.S. Marshal's office had swooped me off to St. Louis and placed me in the care of Marshal Anthony Cutter and his head of copper hair. The only problem with calling Cutter was that he was a man of action and his action would probably include packing my suitcase. The thought of lofting another grenade into my life sounded horrendous, so I turned right and headed to Thomas Brackford's house.

Out of all of my clients, Brackford had the most promising future with my company. He appeared an eccentric recluse, which at first made me wonder if he too were a member of the Witness Protection Program. WitSec always seemed like the best choice when your body suddenly became someone's target. The program offered a chance at a new life, but one which included a constant battle. Hiding from the bad guys wasn't nearly as hard as hiding from everyone.

Turned out when Brackford's story unfolded his life revealed a much sadder version than mine. Five years earlier a bus accident had rendered Thomas Brackford's legs useless. Two years later, his sister, who ran all his errands, had her trip interrupted by a bus on the very same route. She died instantly. Kinda freaky.

I stopped at the post office to pick up Brackford's mail. His box was located in the back of the lobby. I reached inside and plucked out the letters and keys to two other boxes where packages were placed if they were too large to fit into Brackford's regular box.

An avid train hobbyist, two of the three bedrooms in Brackford's home were filled with miniature landscapes and elaborate rail systems. Chances are the packages held model trains or something train related. I grabbed a small package out of the first box. The package in the second box was heavy, so I tucked the small package under my arm, allowing me to pick the larger one up with both hands.

I struggled as I unlocked my passenger side door. My arms hurt and my thighs still burned from last night's squatfest behind the bushes. Listening to my body, I pushed the voice record button on my phone after I settled in behind the wheel. "Check into a gym membership."

A mile away sat Thomas Brackford's home in a quiet, middle class neighborhood built in the nineteen sixties. His brick ranch had been remodeled in an effort to make the house more disability-friendly and for the most part it was easy for him to get around inside.

By the looks of Brackford and his modest home, few would think he could afford a personal concierge to run errands every day. I tried not to nose around in my clients' financial affairs since I'd earned a new respect for privacy. I didn't care how they paid, as long as they paid, and Thomas Brackford always paid on time.

He answered the door before I knocked as if he'd had his eye fixed to the three-and-a-half foot high peephole. "It's about time. Come on in."

"Uh, I, uh, yeah, okay," I uttered, as the man I called a recluse motioned for me to come inside.

I had been in Brackford's home several times, but those had always been planned. Whenever I delivered his mail, I simply slipped the letters through the slot in the door and set the packages on the table behind the evergreen plant.

"I read that Professor Vanderbur killed himself. Did you forget to do something for him?"

"What?"

"I thought you had to have done something terrible. He wasn't the kind of man to kill himself over nothing. In fact, the other day he told me he wa—"

"You talked to Max?"

"Of course I did. You gave me his number."

Brackford wheeled his chair past the dining room and into the kitchen. I assumed he wanted me to follow, so I did. "But I gave you his number months ago for a reference."

"Right. When I called to check you out, he talked about your ability to be detail oriented and I told him you would be excellent with my trains. Turns out he liked model trains too. We even went to the Museum of Transportation one time."

My clients commingled behind my back? Why didn't I know this? "We talked about a lot of things. I wonder why he never mentioned the trains," I said.

"Probably the same reason I don't talk to you about my trains, because you hate them."

"I do not. I've never been much of a collector."

"You don't have a collection of anything?"

"Yes, I do, but model trains are more for men. You wouldn't collect quilts would you?"

20

"Fair enough. Nope, it doesn't seem right that he'd kill himself. I'm not one to gossip, but did you hear Professor Vanderbur had a thing with one of his students?"

Brackford always seemed one step away from connecting. He preferred me to call him Mr. Brackford instead of Thomas, which probably explained why even when disclosing juicy gossip he still referred to Max as Professor Vanderbur.

"No, I didn't." I kept my answer short, so he wouldn't think I was easily titillated by juicy rumors.

"He acted like a teenage boy when he talked about her."

Now my interest piqued. If true then it became an excellent reason for Mrs. Vanderbur to want her husband dead. "Did he mention the student's name?"

"She had a funny name. Don't remember it though. Merrill or something like that. You want some?" He held up the coffee pot then poured some into a cup that had been sitting on the kitchen table.

"No thanks, I need to get back to the office. By the way, one of the boxes I put on the hall table is heavy so be careful."

As I pulled away from Thomas Brackford's home I thought about Max. He hadn't struck me as the type of man to take his vows lightly, but neither had my fiancé. Thinking of my ex-fiancé led to sadness and regret, two emotions that were the epitome of unproductive and something I couldn't afford.

My chances of getting paid for the work I'd already completed were waning and I knew I would soon feel the stress of Max's lost business. Yoga or meditation would help clear my head and keep my stress level low. Unfortunately, my arsenal of de-stressing techniques only included drinking and shopping, both of which had unpleasant side effects.

———

On the way to my office, a heaviness overwhelmed me. A funk worked its way into my mood and I was determined to fight back. I popped in an old classic rock CD I'd purchased at a garage sale, hoping the music would provide an exit out of the pit I'd found myself in. Love Shack began playing. I turned the volume knob as far to the right as I could without shattering my windows and sang like a rock star. By the end, I had almost climbed my way back into happiness. An extra little push was all I needed. I called Stephanie, my only girlfriend in St. Louis, and asked her to meet me at the mall in the food court.

Stephanie was a hoot, a busty redhead with a laugh that could be heard around the world. She worked as a massage therapist, but I'd met her at the St. Louis Zoo in the monkey house where she'd been volunteering as a Zoo Ambassador. She provided visitors with weird facts about monkeys – like how the scream of a howler monkey could be heard almost 3 miles away – sort of like Stephanie.

I pulled into the parking garage, then cut through Nordstrom to the inside of the mall without making a single purchase. As I approached the food court, Stephanie waved.

"What's up, Girlie?" she asked as she adjusted her bra strap.

"I'm playing hooky."

"Wish I could play hooky the rest of the day."

"Hey, why don't you?"

"No way. I'm trying to get Friday off so I can go to Chicago for a long weekend. Wanna come?"

"Can't. Grown up obligations." I didn't go into detail about my chaotic life because Stephanie was just a buddy you went drinking with or shopping with when you should be working, not the type of friend you turned to for support.

"Yeah, I skimmed the headline in the newspaper. Isn't it awful? What did you do to make the professor so upset?"

Why the hell did everybody think I caused Max to kill himself? "What made you think it was something I did?"

"His wife Tracy said he'd been extremely upset about something you were doing for him."

I had referred Max to Stephanie when he'd mentioned his wife had back problems, but it still sounded strange to hear Stephanie call Mrs. Vanderbur by her first name. "She knew I'd been doing work for him?"

"Sure. Every time I went to her house she always spent her time yakking rather than enjoying her massage."

Mrs. Vanderbur had given no indication she was aware of my existence and that was an uncomfortable piece of knowledge.

"I didn't realize you went to her house. I thought she came to the place you worked."

"She's one of my off the book customers. Hey, don't say anything. I'm not supposed to be doing massages on the side. They'd probably fire me if they found out."

"Not my business. Did she tell you what he was upset about?"

"I didn't ask her because my head hurt and I wanted her to shut up. So what are we doing? Shoes? Purses? Makeup?"

My desire to continue the conversation about Mrs. Vanderbur would not be fulfilled because once Stephanie ventured into the topic of shopping it transformed her into a horse with blinders. "None of the above. I need office décor. Oh, and a briefcase."

"Sounds boring." Stephanie added a fake yawn.

"Not boring at all. I need curtains and knick knacks, and maybe a leather executive chair."

"Wow, business must be good."

"You gotta spend money to make money." I flashed my credit card. My credit consisted of a store card and a gas card. I wasn't opposed to major credit cards, but they were difficult to obtain without a credit history. One of the many down sides to changing your identity.

"Now you're talking," Stephanie said as she jumped up from her chair.

We dropped our trash in a can and left the food court. Half way to our destination Stephanie made a detour into Melanie's Accessories.

Until my business provided a dependable income I was trying to be frugal. WitSec had magically transferred my cashed-out 401K into various untraceable accounts, but I needed to save it for my uncertain future. The living assistance they did provide wasn't enough for anything beyond the basics. If it weren't for my secret coffer of cash I stashed without WitSec's knowledge, I wouldn't have any fun.

"I can so see you in this," Stephanie said, holding up a striking belt for my approval.

The antiqued metal flower buckle contained an abundance of yellow topaz-colored crystals and it rapidly increased my heart rate. In my previous life I never felt comfortable in non-traditional clothing, but as Aspen, I relished wearing whimsical items and pretending to be wild and free. The belt would make a perfect addition to my fantasy wardrobe.

"It's definitely gorgeous, but seventy-five bucks?" My practical side wasn't going down without a fight.

Stephanie dangled the belt in front of me like a carrot. "It's called the Aphrodite."

The only words she needed to speak. Who didn't want to be the Goddess of Love? Stephanie and I brought our items to the register.

"Oh, you should get these too." Stephanie held up a pair of yellow topaz-colored earrings.

"Sorry, one frivolous item at a time."

My spirit lifted with the single purchase. We gathered our bags and made our way to the exit.

"Please return to the checkout counter," an automated voice announced.

The clerk waved us back inside the store. "Can I check your bags? I think I might have forgotten to remove a sensor." She found no sensors and we headed to the exit.

"Please return to the checkout counter," the automated voice repeated.

I turned toward the girl hoping she would wave us along, but she motioned for us to return to the counter. My level of irritation rose, but Stephanie's shot up like a rocket.

"Your stupid machine is broken and I have to get back to work, so can't we just go?" Stephanie veiled her demand as a question.

"I'm sorry. If the security triggers more than once my manager needs to check the bags."

A woman walked toward us followed by two security guards. After introducing herself as the manager, she checked our purchases. "No wayward sensors. We'll need to search your purses, please."

"Stephanie's face turned red and she stood with her hands on her hips. "You think we stole something?"

"Purses on the counter, please." A guard pointed to the open space between the registers.

Stephanie plopped her purse onto the counter. I gently set mine down and opened the flap.

"I think they're trying to frame us, Aspen. What other reason would two security guards already be here in the store?"

She had a point. I eyed the guard in charge of my purse.

"We were having lunch with my wife," he said, pointing to the manager.

Stephanie's security guard went through the few items in her purse. "Nothing unusual in here."

My guard looked inside my purse and then up at me. "Where's the kitchen sink?"

The urge to call him a smart-ass was tempered by the thought of getting collared by mall security, so I kept my mouth shut. My guard took out my wallet and a few pieces of paper before pulling out a pair of yellow topaz-colored earrings.

"Oh my God! Where did those come from?" I asked.

"Obviously, they came from this store." The guard stared at me as if I were stupid.

"How do I know you didn't plant them?"

"Right." The guard rolled his eyes.

"Wow, I didn't even think you wanted those," Stephanie said, her eyes wide, "But, they sure would look awesome with your new belt."

Her words were like a guilty arrow aimed directly at me. What happened to her conspiracy theory?

"I didn't take those. They must have fallen into my purse when we tried them on."

"Sure." My guard exchanged glances with Stephanie's guard.

"Honestly, I own my own business. Why would I steal from someone else's?"

"We have a security video."

"I'm late for work. The earrings were not in my purse, so can I go?" Stephanie asked.

I couldn't believe she planned to leave.

"You can go." The guard handed over Stephanie's purse.

"I'm sorry Aspen, but if I'm gone any longer from work they'll write me up." With that statement she was gone.

The gang walked me to the office in the back of the store, a guard on both sides, and the manager in front. We sat down at a table.

"There has been a rash of thefts, so we installed this security system the other day." The manager rewound the videotape and pushed play.

"There, stop right there," said my guard, pointing at the video monitor.

The manager stopped the tape, hit rewind, then play. I watched Stephanie and I laughing. Stephanie held the earrings up to my ears and the smile on my face made me appear happy. I watched as the girl put our items into bags and then I gasped in disbelief.

"Rewind that again," I demanded.

The manager hit the rewind button and played the tape again.

"You've got to be kidding me! Did you see that?" I asked pointing at the monitor. There in black and white was Stephanie pitching the earrings into my purse.

"So, you were teaming up, huh?" My guard acted as though he'd caught a career criminal.

"What? I had no idea she threw those earrings in my purse."

"She does seem surprised," said the other guard, glancing at me.

"You're damn right I'm surprised."

3

EVEN AFTER A GOOD night's sleep my anger hadn't dissipated. The store manager had let me walk with only a warning, telling me I should be thankful Stephanie had left the store. Stephanie's actions didn't qualify for a thank you, if anything, they warranted an apology from her. Even if our relationship wasn't at best friend level, it was the right thing for her to do.

My pajama clad body dragged itself into the bathroom when I realized it was past noon. The day ahead would be a difficult one. I had no idea what to do with myself. I should have been walking and feeding Mr. P, but he was gone. Or organizing and researching for Max, but he was gone too.

I brushed everything that needed it then threw on a pair of jeans and a t-shirt. Fickle temperatures led me to grab a light jacket before flinging my purse over my shoulder and starting my day. A day that normally would have started hours ago.

In less than ten minutes, I arrived at the post office to complete the most important task of the day, my only task of the day. I opened my ashtray to retrieve Thomas Brackford's mailbox key, but the ashtray was empty. I searched the floorboard and the console. Only one task and I couldn't even get it right.

The thought of digging through my purse made me cringe. I tossed my wallet onto the passenger seat, followed by old receipts, a piece of crime scene tape, a spoon, and an old tube of lipstick. Unfortunately, there was no key. How had I been getting paid to organize someone else's stuff when I couldn't organize my own? I pressed the voice recorder button on my phone. "Get key organizer."

My search eventually uncovered the P.O. box key wrapped inside my grocery list along with a piece of Dentyne gum. I popped the gum into my mouth and tossed the gum wrapper back into my purse followed by the items I'd taken out earlier. I closed the flap and tucked the purse under the driver's seat before locking my Jeep and running inside the post office.

Thomas Brackford had more packages. The first had a return address from the Train Enthusiast Collector House and the other was a plain brown box, with only a P.O. box and no name. I couldn't help myself. My thoughts inched their way into the naughty side of my head, picturing a blow up doll. He might be paralyzed, but he was still a man.

"He's got a gun!" someone screamed.

I dropped to the ground. The sound of shattering glass exploded in my ears. Shards skidded across the floor. I didn't move until the screaming stopped.

"Call 911!" a man shouted.

My heart pumped blood in and out at a speed I didn't think it had been built to handle. People ran in all directions, most toward the front door. Someone knocked over a display sending packages of postage stamps and collectible stamp kits flying. I scanned the crowd searching for someone who looked like a gunman, but he was gone.

The plate glass window was on the floor in a thousand pieces. Broken glass crunched beneath my shoes as I made my way toward the door. Outside the commotion continued. I glanced around the parking lot, didn't recognize anyone, so I heaved the packages into my Jeep and drove away. Chaos was following me and I wondered if it was more than just coincidence.

My heart continued to pound even after arriving at Thomas Brackford's home. The topic of Max's death must have lost its importance because Brackford's door remained closed. He amazed me how readily he could go from engaging to disengaging. I dropped his mail through the slot and placed the packages behind the evergreen plant. His curtains were slightly parted, revealing darkness. A vivid picture of Max dangling in air entered my mind once again and I wondered if Brackford had disengaged voluntarily.

Thomas Brackford was a recluse, I reminded myself. Just because he had been outgoing one day and non-existent the next didn't necessarily mean anything was wrong. But still, I found myself edging closer to the small opening in the curtains and peering through the window. It was too dark to see anything. I tore off the bottom half of my grocery list, jotted down a quick note for him to call me, and slipped the note in his mail slot.

I struggled to control the unnerving thoughts entering my head. What if Mrs. Vanderbur had sent someone to get rid of me and Brackford had become collateral damage? Or worse, what if the Witness Protection Program had failed?

I took a deep breath and tried focusing on something positive, but floundered. I wondered if Marshal Cutter would warn me when I'd been spotted or if he would just shake his head and murmur 'what a pity' when he picked up my dead body.

My only task for the day was complete and I was desperate to occupy my time. Too much of it was just as bad as too little. If I couldn't keep myself busy I'd lose myself to paranoia. Grasping for anything, I remembered promising my landlady I'd pick up treats for her dog, Sassy. So once again I turned to shopping to keep from facing the reality of my life.

The grocery store wasn't crowded. I went straight to the inner aisles and picked up the dog treats. I took the list from the side pocket of my purse and proceeded to pick up nutritious people food, like chocolate milk, barbecue potato chips, and a jar of pickles.

I bumped into Peter leaving the store. Avoiding the subject of the post office, I spit out the first thing that came to mind. "You make any calls about the dog?"

"And hello to you too."

"Sorry. I have a lot on my mind. I'm worried about Mr. P."

"I'm sorry too. Finding your missing dog will have to wait. I've got my first investigation job for a paying customer. Why don't you try putting up some flyers in the mean time?"

I worked hard to hide my disappointment. "My client doesn't want any kind of attention drawn to him or his dog."

"I'd spend twenty-four hours a day tracking down your missing dog if I could Aspen, but you know I can't. A first case is always the most important."

I should have been happy for Peter. He was the closest thing I had to a best friend and those were hard to make when you knew you were living a lie. "I know, I'm sorry. Congratulations. What kind of case?"

"I'm doing surveillance tonight. You want to come along? We can talk about the dognapping."

"Can I play your sidekick another time? I've got a lot of things to get done." I had nothing to do, but I couldn't sit in a confined space for hours, not when my head was busy trying to get itself around the pandemonium that was my life.

I arrived back at the fourplex and ran up to my apartment to put away my single bag of groceries, then I ran back downstairs with the dog treats. When Mrs. Rippetoe didn't answer, I ran back upstairs.

Running up and down a couple of flights of stairs left me breathless. My weight hadn't changed much since moving to St. Louis, but my stamina had somehow disappeared. It was time to fight back against Mother Nature and whatever bad juju had gotten hold of me. My computer was at the office, so I went old school, flipping the yellow pages open to the health club section. I jotted the addresses of a couple of places into a small notebook and dropped it in my purse.

———

The first gym I drove to, I had full view of the exercise area from the parking lot. The thought of some stranger on the street watching me torture myself gave me the creeps. A quick scan of the patrons revealed one big blown up guy after another. I passed.

Gray-haired women with baggy t-shirts wandered the parking lot of the second gym. Although I'd always appear youthful next to all the grandmothers, I wasn't ready to give up the fight to be young and hip. If the third gym turned out to be a dud I'd take it as a sign that I wasn't meant to be a gym rat. I'll admit the lazy part of me hoped for a strike out.

All types of people entered and exited the next gym. The crowd seemed to be a perfect mix, an easy place to blend in. The sight of perfectly fit, tall, right-sized, no ring on the finger men going inside didn't hurt either. I took a deep breath and walked through the front door.

A woman around my age smiled. "Welcome to Fit Right. Would you like a tour?"

I nodded.

She handed me a brochure. "Right this way."

Everybody appeared friendly and happy too. The place had a good vibe.

"Do you have a cell phone?" she asked.

"Sure. Do you tweet workout tips or something?"

"No. I need you to check it here at the phone cubby before we go into the locker room. It's a new policy, a precaution so our guests don't end up on the Internet."

I handed my phone to the phone sheriff. He put it in a cubby and handed me a safety pin with a number hanging off it. We walked through a door into the women's locker room. The space appeared clean and smelled more like lavender than Clorox. Most of the women wore white robes.

"The robe service is included in the monthly fee. We also have body gel, shampoo, and conditioner. Bottled water is also free of charge."

I liked a place that provided excellent customer service.

She opened a door exposing a pathway flanked on the left by a stone retaining wall full of plants. "The pathway is circular allowing easy access to the Fit Right rooms."

I followed her around the path going in and out of rooms that contained everything from swim spas to rock climbing walls. With each new amazing item she showed me, the inside of my head was going cha-ching.

"If you don't want to walk around the pathway, you can cut through the inner circle using the doors located on the side with the planters," she said, opening one of the doors.

We continued to walk until she stopped at a door that appeared to take you from the inner circle into the inner-inner circle. I worried I was about to be sucked into some sort of exercise vortex where they'd brainwash me until I purchased a membership.

I grimaced as she opened the door. "And this is The Sanctuary."

A sigh escaped me when the vortex turned out to be the most beautiful room I'd ever seen. The glass ceiling let the outside in. Small clusters of trees and ferns were scattered throughout the room. Soft music played and the trickle of water fountains instantly relaxed me. I wanted to walk over and lie down on one of the wicker chaise lounges strategically placed around a Koi pond. "This is beautiful."

"We are the only gym in the country with a room like this," she whispered. "The baskets on the tables contain complimentary lavender-flaxseed eye masks."

Anytime I heard complimentary I always wondered what the catch would be. I imagined the catch here would be big, big dollars. "The place is amazing. What's the monthly fee?"

"Why don't we go to my office?"

Bingo. She avoided talking price. Continuing the tour, she guided me past the juice bar, the Internet cafe, and finally to her office.

"Would you like something to drink?" she asked.

"No thank you. I would just like to know the membership prices."

"Our fees provide an attractive return on investment by allowing you to realize the healthy person inside you. The All-Fit level is three-hundred a month and provides unlimited access to everything. Free classes, free smoothies, free Internet, free everything."

Free? What the hell was she talking about? It wasn't free. I didn't believe this gym would make me healthy because their prices were already giving me a heart attack.

I tried hard to keep my eyes from expressing my shock. I knew I had failed when she dropped right into the next level. "The Semi-Fit level provides unlimited access to the exercise equipment, classes, and The Sanctuary. All other items are charged on a per use basis. The fee is two-hundred a month."

What did she think this was, Beverly Hills? Hello? The gym is located in St. Louis. "Thanks for taking the time to—"

"Our most affordable option is the Fit-level which is fifty dollars a month."

The monthly fee had become more realistic. "What does that include?"

"Unlimited access to the exercise equipment, eight classes per month, and four sanctuary passes."

"Oh."

"But this month, we are offering a Fit-level special. Pay for six months in advance and you get six months of unlimited access to The Sanctuary."

What I really wanted to find out was if they had a Sanctuary-Only membership. "Do you take checks?"

I completed the paperwork and got up to leave. "I forgot my phone."

"No problem. Can you find your way back to the phone cubby?"

I walked back to the phone cubby, taking in my new purchase of exercise equipment I would probably never use. I handed my safety pin number to the phone guy in exchange for my phone.

The entire drive home I was kicking myself. I had intended to only tour places and then sleep on it before making a decision. In a way, I guess I did get sucked into the exercise vortex.

Passing by my place while on the lookout for a parking spot, I noticed Peter standing on the stoop talking to Mrs. Rippetoe. They were still there when I made my way up the walk.

Not known for her brevity, Mrs. Rippetoe was finally getting to her point. I could tell because Peter had the same relieved expression I'd seen on others who talked to Mrs. Rippetoe.

"So, I looked out the window and caught a man looking in Aspen's mailbox. He stared me straight in the eye, real mean like."

"What did you do?" I asked.

"I stared right back at him, mean like too. I started giving him a scolding, but then I saw the gun."

"What did he look like?" Peter asked.

"He was big. Not just big around, but big and tall like too."

"Do you think he was an undercover officer?" Peter threw a glance my way.

I knew where he was heading with that question. In my eyes, I hadn't quite gotten around to giving the police my statement as a witness. In his eyes, I was still at-large.

She scrunched up her extra large nose, "No, he didn't look like any cop I'd ever seen."

A retired school teacher, Mrs. Rippetoe was still sharp seventy-five percent of the time. The other twenty-five was a mix between, forgetfulness and no clue. I focused on her eyes to see if I could tell whether or not a man with a gun had really been snooping through my mailbox. What I saw was the same sweetness I'd seen the day I answered her ad for a rental apartment. It had been that sweetness along with the pimento cheese sandwich and lemonade she made me that had sealed the deal. I had handed her the deposit on the spot.

"You still need a sidekick?" I asked Peter after Mrs. Rippetoe went back inside.

"Sure. You probably shouldn't be alone tonight anyway, in case what she said is true."

"Let me run upstairs first. Meet me in the hall in five minutes."

When I said five, Peter knew I meant ten. I gobbled down a pickle and took a swig of chocolate milk. I was tempted to sit down for a few minutes, instead I washed my face, brushed my teeth, pulled my hair back in a ponytail and walked out the door.

"Make sure you lock it," Peter said as I started down the steps.

He didn't need to remind me. "Locked up tight."

"Then let's go, Tonto."

4

"JUST BECAUSE I'M NOT looking at you, doesn't mean I'm not listening." Peter kept his eyes on the building across the street.

We sat in his Chevrolet Citation. Receipts, straw wrappers, and lottery tickets littered the floorboard. I found the scattered trash strange for someone who lived like a neat-nick at home.

"Is that the guy?" I asked.

"Nope."

Peter's first case involved a cheater. The wife hired Peter to document her husband's improprieties and he asked me to take notes and pictures. Our goal was to compile a thorough yet thoughtful adulterer's scrapbook.

He kept his eyes on the building as I continued telling him about my day at the post office. As I talked, I admired Peter's profile. I'd never noticed the perfectness of his nose. It reminded me of a summer trip to Italy I took as a teenager where I'd pretended to be fascinated with the nose on Michelangelo's David while all the other students had openly marveled at his lower parts.

40

"Aspen?"

"Sorry. Where was I?"

"You dropped to the ground. I told you I was listening."

"Okay, so the bullet shattered the window and I high-tailed it outside, got in my car and drove away."

"You what?" Peter wasn't looking at the building any longer.

"Why would I want to stay in a place where someone was shooting a gun?"

"But that's twice in two days you've left the scene of a crime!"

"Wait a second. Even you said Max may have actually killed himself, so technically I have only left the scene of one crime. Besides, enough other witnesses remained at the post office. I'm sure nobody paid attention to me."

We sat in silence. Peter's reaction made me want to step out of the confessional. I didn't dare tell him about my quality time with the mall cops.

"You know, I overheard someone describe the gunman as big and tall. What if the guy Mrs. Rippetoe saw was the same guy who shot up the post office?"

"You think the gunman targeted you?" Peter glanced back toward the building.

"I don't know. Maybe I'm being stupid."

"Why would..." Peter started the car. "We're on. Start shooting."

"Shooting?"

"Come on Tonto, start working the camera!"

I grabbed the camera and pushed the zoom button, catching scenes of what promised to be an unfortunate evening. The man opened the passenger door for a pretty blonde. Honestly, she looked half his age and her only interest in him probably centered on his Mercedes and the message the car conveyed about the size of his wallet.

We followed their car as it turned left into traffic. Our hunt for hanky-panky began and I wondered if there'd be foreplay. "Do you think they'll go to dinner someplace fancy?"

"Are you joking? They have an appetite, but not for dinner."

I pointed the camera toward the back window of the car as the sun began to inch its way down. The leggy blonde stroked Mr. Moneybags' head and lord knows what else. "That picture's gonna tick your client off."

"No, the picture will make my client a happy woman."

"Why?"

"Because the pictures we get of tonight's escapade stand to make her a wealthy divorcée."

"Mmmm," I said.

"What do you mean, mmmm?"

"Nothing. It's just a sad state of affairs - no pun intended." Everything seemed to boil down to money, even love.

We had no worries about being discovered. The guy was completely occupied. "Oh my God, they're turning into a no-tell motel!" I spat out, nearly peeing my pants from laughter.

The motel sat on the Mother Road, the famous Route 66. The vintage neon sign, seashell pink buildings, and yellow and white striped awnings made for a postcard moment. Motels like this earned a reputation in their heyday and based on the cars in the parking lot this motel's reputation hadn't died.

"With all his money, why go to a motel like this?" I asked.

"Would you expect a guy like that to be in a place like this?"

"Good point. Where are we going to park so we aren't in view?"

"We're going to park in the parking lot."

"That doesn't seem very undercover."

"No, but checking in as a couple does."

"Wha—"

"Relax. Checking in provides us with the best cover so we can get good pictures. The better the pictures, the better the pay. Besides, I'm giving you a cut for helping."

"In that case, let's go, you animal." I growled and grabbed his collar, pulling him toward me. I was joking, but one whiff and I had to let go. His cologne smelled like pumpkin pie and whipped cream and triggered naughty thoughts involving food.

"You hungry?" he asked.

I nearly choked. "Always."

"Might be a long evening so I brought a bunch of junk food." He patted his backpack that sat between us.

Mr. Moneybags exited the motel office. The blonde pounced on him as soon as he got into the car. Peter went inside to register and I stayed behind. I plucked a couple of miniature candy bars from inside the backpack and watched as the man pushed the blonde aside and started the car. They drove around back, out of view.

I opened my door and skittered to the edge of the front building, poked my head around the corner and caught them walking into a room toward the end of the last building in the back. I worked my way back, conjured up my best lustful look and opened the door to the office.

"Hey, baby! Can we get a room at the end in back? I wouldn't, you know," I said, giggling.

43

Peter's face went blank.

"I mean somebody might hear us!" The high pitch of my voice even irritated me. "Pleeeeeeease?"

"Sir?" Peter pleaded.

"Sure, no problem." The clerk gave him a crooked smile.

The man traded the original key for the key to the room I'd requested. Peter paid the man in cash and turned toward me, his eyes wide. I thought I was a natural at this private eye stuff. Moore Investigations – it had a nice ring.

"What the hell was that about?" he asked after we left the office.

"I thought we'd get better pictures and sound if we had the room next to theirs."

"Hmm, good job." He didn't sound as impressed with me as I was with myself. *Men.*

Our room turned out to be nicer than the image I had created in my head. Nothing fancy, but clean if you kept your eyes off the carpet. Painted white paneling covered the bottom half of the walls and the top half had been covered with a muted grey-blue. Two cottage style nightstands flanked a queen size bed, located across from a basic white dresser with a small television on top. No place to sit but the bed. A lump formed in my throat.

"Now what?" I asked.

"Now, we sit and listen."

I grimaced. "Sit on the bed?"

One television exposé, five years ago, about invisible things left behind on hotel bedspreads had made paranoid about doing anything on a hotel bed, even sitting. And, this wasn't the Ritz. Peter eased my fear by pulling a blanket from his backpack and laying it across the bed. Next out of the backpack, the food.

I was halfway through my second bag of chips when the noise started. It was faint at first, but there was no mistaking the sound. As the volume increased, the words, "Oh baby, yes, yes," turned into primal grunts. I diverted my eyes from Peter to the ground, balancing my embarrassment with my urge to burst out laughing.

Peter hopped off the bed and handed me the camera. While he rummaged through the black case he'd brought in from the car, I checked out the lens. I dabbled in photography, but had never seen a lens like the one he had attached to his camera.

Peter pulled a blonde wig out of the black case and positioned it on his bald head. "Let's go."

"Sure thing, Blondie."

"I can't blow my cover. I might need to approach him again. What's wrong with the camera?"

"Nothing. I'm just not sure how to work the lens."

"It's all set. Work the camera like you normally would."

"I don't think I'll be able to hold my hands steady to shoot in the dark."

"Don't worry. That thing is an AstroScope." He pointed at the object mounted between the camera base and lens. "The scope allows you to see at night and you can shoot without a tripod. I think you'll like it. Brace yourself against a car and remember, the more pictures, the better chance of finding some quality shots."

"Okee, Dokee. What are you going to do?"

"Just be ready."

Peter opened the door and stepped out onto the walkway. I continued into the parking lot and positioned myself by the side of a car a few steps away. I had an excellent but protected view of the adulterer's room. I looked through the lens and my heart raced. I loved Peter's toys. Even though everything looked green, the objects came through clear. I felt like a real spy. I gave Peter the thumbs up.

"Janet, baby, let me in honey," Peter shouted with a slight slur. "Come on baby, I won't do it again, I swear."

He banged on their door. "Janet! You bitch! Let me in!" Peter's voice was so loud I worried the office manager might call the police.

I held the camera steady. The door opened and I clicked away. Mr. Moneybags stood in the doorway practically naked. Even in the dim light, the wrinkles crisscrossing his body were visible. Not a pleasant sight but I had a job to do, so I kept on pressing the button. In the background, on the bed, sat the blonde with no covers. Her legs wide open.

I zoomed in and out, saving the close-up shots for their faces because I didn't know how a close up of a hoo ha could be used as evidence. Unless, of course, it had an undeniable identification mark, like a tattoo. I shivered at the thought of getting a tattoo 'down there', as my mother called it. Peter started yelling and I snapped back to attention.

"Hey man, what are you doing with my girl?" Peter screamed.

"She's not your girl!" the man shouted.

"Yes, she is!"

The blonde finally sat up and pulled the sheets in front of her. "I am not."

Everything was going smoothly until the theme from Mission Impossible began blaring from my pocket. *What the heck?* I grabbed the cell phone. It looked like my phone, but my own phone number was showing up on the caller id. The phone cubby guy must have given me the wrong phone. Nothing I could do except hit ignore.

"What the hell was that?" Mr. Moneybags had stopped exchanging words with Peter. Instead, he surveyed the parking lot and focused on the car I was hiding behind.

"Damn it, Janet. You get out here right now."

"Buddy, get the hell out of here. You have the wrong room," Mr. Moneybags looked around the parking lot again before slamming the door.

Peter turned and walked away. I made my way back toward our room and sidled up next to him. He whispered in my ear, "We need to make this seem real so we don't spook him any more than he is already. Go inside then open the door when I start banging."

I slipped inside our motel room.

"Janet, honey, let me in baby," Peter yelled as he banged on our door.

"No," I shouted, "You don't love me."

"Yes, I do baby."

"You gonna get me a ring?"

"Baby, you know I don't have no job." No rattling Peter, he was playing along.

"You promise you'll get me a ring when you get a job?"

"Yeah, baby, I promise. Come on let me in."

I opened the door and greeted Peter with a wicked grin.

"Funny, Tonto. Why the hell was the theme to Mission Impossible playing?"

I explained to Peter about my missing phone. He acted understanding, though I could tell he was still somewhat upset that I'd almost screwed everything up. We packed our stuff. Our job was done. Peter pulled the curtain aside and peeked out to determine our potential for slipping away unnoticed. All was clear, so we ran out the door and jumped in his car.

"That was exciting," I said.

"You did a good job. And if you agree not to carry a cell phone with you, I just might ask for your assistance again."

The thought of going on another surveillance excited me. I could become addicted.

"Coffee and Danish in the morning at my place?" Peter asked as we pulled out of the motel parking lot.

"Nine-thirty?" I suggested.

"I have a meeting at ten. So you okay with eight-thirty?

"Sure." The excitement of the night quickly lost its punch. The hum of the engine was a fierce competitor, as I battled to stay awake. I knew I'd lost when Peter had to wake me. The five other multi-family buildings on our street created a demand for parking spaces much larger than the supply. We were parked a block away from our building.

Exhausted, I staggered down the road with Peter's assistance. I made my own way up the stairs to my apartment and fell asleep as soon as I hit the bed.

5

JARRED AWAKE by a volcanic eruption in my stomach, I sat up in bed wearing the same clothes I'd had on yesterday. The sun was up. I dragged myself out of bed and hopped into the shower hoping to soothe my angry stomach.

Warm water streamed down my back. I closed my eyes letting images from the dream I'd had flow through my mind. The dreams had been quite vivid. I'd been riding a train filled with leggy blondes and every window was shattered. Guns were being fired, Mr. P was running up and down the aisle barking, and I was selling candy from a tray like a cigarette girl.

The brain, an amazing organ, has been known to invent technological breakthroughs and cure diseases. But mine's a little crazy, especially when left unattended. Awake, it's a serious hard-ass, reminding me Mr. P was still missing. My stomach still felt horrible and a tiny pang twitched near my heart. In my previous life I had worked as a corporate executive. I'd taken care of inanimate things like profit and loss, not something as vulnerable as a life. The fact was sobering. As Aspen Moore, personal concierge, what I did for a living was more critical than anything I'd done before.

I caught my breath and flung the shower curtain open when the spray from the showerhead went cold. I jumped out, dried myself off and tossed on some sweats. My stomach grumbled something unintelligible, which I interpreted as a request for pastry. With only a minute to spare, I ran downstairs and knocked on Peter's door.

"Hello, sunshine. You're right on time," Peter said.

"Where's the Danish?"

"What happened to hello?"

"Sorry, my stomach's a bit vocal this morning." The words barely escaped my mouth when my stomach grumbled again.

"Demanding, isn't it?"

I followed Peter into the kitchen and sat at the table, my eyes transfixed on a plate piled high with the best looking pastries I'd seen in years. Cheese Danish beckoned me with their minimal amount of flaky crust and incredibly large centers full of cheese. Thick strands of white icing zig-zagging across the tops caused me to sigh in admiration.

"They're from McArthur's Bakery."

I stuffed one into my mouth.

"You really are an incredible photographer."

"Oh, ank ew." I took a sip of the coffee Peter handed me.

"I printed these last night. I changed them to black and white in case I need to enhance them, but they were pretty damn good as shot. Check out your handiwork." He laid them out on the table.

Sticky icing covered my hands, so I asked him to move two of the prints closer. "I thought he looked familiar last night. He looks like an older version of the man who had been driving away from Mrs. Vanderbur's home. What's his name?"

"I don't disclose personal information about my clients, but seeing that you worked on the case I'll tell you as soon as I pay you." He winked and slid an envelope toward me.

Now, this was worth licking the icing off my fingers. I opened the envelope and found two one hundred dollar bills and a note indicating payment in exchange for photography services in the Macy Martin case.

"Macy Martin? Is that the wife?"

"Yes. Once she convinced herself I had no dealings with her husband, she hired me. Evidently he's well connected in St. Louis. Name is Samuel Martin, of Martin-Stone Development."

"Are you serious? I was supposed to meet with him today, but his secretary left a message saying he was unavailable. His son John is meeting me instead."

"What about?" Peter asked.

"The work for Max Vanderbur."

"How can you still be working for him? He's dead."

"I know that. Don't you think I know that?"

"Sorry."

"I'm going to keep the meeting. Max stumbled on to something and it definitely had to do with the Martin family."

"But there's no reason for you to go now that Max is gone."

I sipped my coffee and gave much thought to what Peter had said. Was I somehow deficient for disregarding the devastating consequences of getting involved? The answer didn't matter because whether I wanted to be or not, I was already involved.

"The Martins are well connected. If the police believe someone murdered Max who do you think they're going to choose as a suspect? A member of the Martin family or the person who had been squatting outside Max's window?"

"You don't even know if anyone saw you. Besides, what if someone did kill Max? How do you know John Martin isn't the killer?"

"I don't, but I think I'm safe in the middle of a restaurant."

"If you do meet with him, remember, you worked on this case. You are bound by the code of the P.I. Society. Keep everything secret. No talking, no matter who tries to pry information out of you."

"Wow! Do I get a decoder ring too?"

"Smart-ass. Seriously, don't mention a word of this to John Martin or anyone else. Also, make sure you keep your phone on you."

"Oh no. My phone. I have to go call whoever has my phone. Thanks for the Danish."

"So soon?"

"My meeting is at that French restaurant, Le Canard Chanceux. Fancy place means I should probably wear a dress and it'll take me an hour to get into my pantyhose."

"Oh, I see. I get the sweats and he gets the sexy dress and fishnet stockings."

"Pantyhose. Besides, you got an evening with me at a no-tell motel." A quick wink and I closed the door behind me.

I located my telephone number in the log on the mystery phone and hit the call button. "Hi. I think you have my phone."

"Yes, I do. I'll be right over. Where do you live?"

"Could you meet me at my office?"

The guy agreed, so I gave him the address. I chose to work out of an office instead of my home, because it provided me with a way to protect my privacy. Besides, Peter had scored me a deal for my storefront in the building where his business was located.

I dropped the phone on my bed and began my search for a pristine pair of pantyhose. Each pair I pulled out had a run or hole. I gave up. How many women really wore pantyhose anymore anyway? I stuck my sling-backs on and walked out the door, legs stark naked.

My office sat at the end of the red brick building to the right of Peter's storefront. Varriano's Jewelry was at the opposite end and the remaining storefront seemed to have a revolving door. The building also had a second level with two occupied apartments, whose tenants I'd never seen.

Through the front window of my office, any passerby could see the blank walls and an old, gray metal, four-drawer file cabinet. No other items were visible, especially not my desk. I made sure to tuck it back in the corner with easy access to the rear door. My office was insipid. No pictures. No reception desk. No guest chairs. Nothing, not even a simple green plant. It was obvious I had issues.

I poked my head inside Peter's store. "You in here, Peter?"

"He's out on a sales call," Victor answered.

I thanked Victor and swore he didn't need to pass along a message. Walking the few short steps to my office, I pushed the door open and gathered the mail from the floor. I dropped it on my desk then pressed the button on my answering machine.

The first message was from the guy who had my cell phone and had been left before I contacted him. I'm not sure why he didn't just call his own phone to try and reach me. He must have gone through my phone to figure out my office number. The thought was worrisome and I tried to remember if I'd forgotten to delete anything from my phone that I didn't want someone else to find. I skipped forward to the next message.

"Ms. Moore, I was a friend of Max Vanderbur. He asked me to contact you. I'll call you again this afternoon around four o'clock."

I didn't recognize the woman's voice. Perhaps it was Max's affair partner or maybe the work partner he'd mentioned. I'd have to make sure I was back at the office in time to receive her call.

My feet had not adjusted to wearing high heels again because I hadn't worn a single pair since moving to St. Louis. I sat down at my desk and pulled off the sling backs. Despite my discomfort, I loved them. They were smart, sexy, and expensive. I'd purchased them during a business trip to New York two years ago when I was making an exceptional salary and living my life as Amelia Millhauser, Vice President of Information Technology. Now, due to fate, the shoes garnered the honor of being the only pair of Dolce & Gabbana I would ever own.

The crunching, grinding noise from my computer steered my attention away from my past. I flipped through my mail while I waited for the computer to finish booting.

The junk mail got deposited into the trashcan which left me no mail at all.

My email turned out to be the cyber-equivalent of my snail mail. Boring. Three lottery winner notifications, two offers to buy cheap drugs, and an offer to make my big one even bigger. I didn't gamble, had no need for drugs, and the last time I looked I wasn't sporting a big one, so I hit delete.

The bell on my office door jingled. I slipped my shoes back on and glanced toward the door, finding a pair of jeans fitted with glove like precision over a muscular set of legs. My eyes slowly made their way up to his face. "May I help you?"

"I'm Harry Corbitt. Here's your cell phone," he said with a slight British or Australian accent that I hadn't discerned over the phone.

The accent along with his deliberately unkempt blonde hair and rough complexion made him mysterious and not in a good way. I'm glad I hadn't suggested exchanging phones over cocktails.

"Here you are." I held out his phone as I walked toward him, hoping he would take it and leave right away.

"What's Moore Time? Do you sell timeshares or something?"

"No, I actually sell myself. I mean I sell my time. I, uh, I'm a personal concierge, I do things for people who don't have the time, like run errands, things like that."

"Good to know. By the way, you had some calls come in. I didn't answer them."

"Thanks again for coming here."

"See ya later," he said as he walked out the door.

"May I help you?" The maître d' asked as he approached. The black suit, white shirt and maroon tie had been placed on his body with perfection. A hint of snoot hovered in the air.

"I'm here to meet a Mr. John Martin."

"Please follow me." The maître d' glided his hand forward and I moved alongside him. He led me through the obstacle course of tables and chairs with the precision of a dog agility handler.

Except for the maître d', the place didn't come across as cold and stuffy like I'd expected. The atmosphere was sort of romantic. The walls were lined with mahogany panels. Warm ochre and red toile drapes depicting Rubenesque women beneath willow trees fell masterfully alongside each window. Ornate chandeliers with their crystal pendants cast a shimmering glow across the room. The decor was elegant, which meant the lunch would be expensive. I hoped John Martin would be picking up the tab.

The place went from sort of romantic to definitely romantic when I caught sight of the flames flickering inside the stone fireplace. The ambience would be perfect with the right man, but he wasn't waiting for me at the table next to the fireplace. Instead I found Mrs. Vanderbur's mystery man.

"Mr. Martin." The maître d' swept his arm toward the man at the table, triggering John Martin to rise from his chair.

He exuded sexy, though I had to work hard to get his father's wrinkly, naked body out of my head. I extended my hand, keeping my grip firm. "Nice to meet you."

"Likewise, Ms. Moore." The grip of his handshake exuded confidence and his inviting smile immediately put me at ease, but I reminded myself that even a charmer could be a killer.

"I've never been here before. What a wonderful restaurant."

"Dinner is booked months in advance and well worth the wait, but I find lunch to be the real treat. A much smaller crowd, quiet, more intimate."

"A perfect place for an afternoon meeting," I said trying to shake the word intimate out of my head.

The waiter placed a napkin in my lap. I listened as he recited the luncheon menu in French. Nothing but chèvre and escargot sounded familiar. I wasn't sure if I felt lucky enough to pick something at random. When he started to repeat the selections in English I was relieved. I would have been testy had I ended up with a plate full of goat balls.

"Are you ready to order, ma'am?"

"I'll have the chèvre salad, please"

"You, Sir?"

"The croque-monsieur, please, and a bottle of your best white wine."

"Oh, none for me," I protested.

"Nonsense." He waved the waiter away. "Having wine for lunch in a French restaurant is like having a soda with your hamburger at a fast food joint."

I smiled, but had no intention of finishing even one glass of wine. Too much alcohol would strip away my inhibitions and I didn't think I should be stripping away anything in front of John Martin.

The waiter returned with the bottle of wine, uncorked it and poured a little into John Martin's glass.

John sniffed and swirled, gently sipping and letting the wine linger in his mouth before he swallowed. "Superb!" He nodded at the waiter and somehow wine made its way into John's glass and mine.

"Now, what exactly would you like to know about Martin-Stone Development, Ms. Moore?"

"As I told your father when I called, I've been conducting research for Professor Max Vanderbur regarding the history of urban planning in St. Louis. More specifically, the role Martin-Stone played in community development."

"Are you not aware the professor is dead?"

"Yes, but I'm completing the work for his associate." I still had no idea who Max's partner was, but I didn't have to explain that to him.

"Who is this associate?"

Crap.

"Actually, they prefer to remain anonymous," I said, hoping it didn't come across as pompous.

"I see."

"Anyhow, we're not here to discuss my business. "I shifted in my chair and leaned forward. "Yours is much more exciting. I want to learn everything about the Martin-Stone partnership and your planned community, Marston Place. How did your father and Caden Stone become partners?"

"They grew up together. It seemed a very natural progression to join forces."

"Hadn't ground already been broken on the project?"

"Yes, but my father knew Caden would be an excellent asset."

"Was it difficult for them to get past their conflicts?"

"They didn't have any conflicts. My father recognizes a good arrangement."

"So he didn't mind giving Caden Stone a fifty percent share? Even after discovering Caden had tried to sabotage his development deal?"

"Ms. Moore. Please, taste your wine. The flavor is buttery with a hint of raspberry, an outstanding wine."

He had already poured himself a second glass. I indulged in his request hoping to put him at ease so he'd share more about his business. "Delicious. Now, back to Marston Place. Didn't your father stand to lose millions by bringing in Caden Stone?"

A long pause settled between us. I occupied myself by taking another sip of wine.

"Ms. Moore, I am flattered by your interest in Martin-Stone Development and happy to discuss the company's role in developing the community. However, detailed financial information is confidential."

Damn. I had hoped he'd share. The public records only provided a limited amount of information covering the time the company was public, but once they took the company private again everything was locked tight.

"I'm just confused. My research shows Caden Stone worked hard, even spearheading a grass roots effort to block the land from being developed. Why the sudden change of heart?"

"Does anyone know why friends squabble only to make up later?"

"Forgive me, but this seemed like more than just a squabble," I said with a little more attitude then I should have.

He took a sip of water and set the glass down on the table with a thud. "What are you implying?"

Obviously I pushed a button. Like someone who believed they possessed special powers to summon the elevator, I decided to push the button again even though it was already lit. "I'm not implying anything. It's just that your father seems like a keen businessman and it struck me as odd that—"

"Excuse me. I apologize, but I must be getting back to the office. Please stay and finish your meal. Lunch is on me." He stood up, shook my hand and left the table - so much for my special powers.

I watched as he handed the waiter cash and walked away. Unless I was hallucinating, his crocodile tassel shoes seemed eerily similar to the pair I'd seen through the junipers. The Martin-Stone partnership had something to hide. I wouldn't be able to uncover the secret in the public records and John Martin knew it.

His hasty exit made me uncomfortable. I didn't want the waiter to think I'd been surprised by John Martin's departure so I sat alone and continued eating. Plus, I'd never waste a free lunch. After I finished the second glass of wine the waiter poured me, I left. Wobbling a tiny bit on my heels, I crossed the street to the parking lot.

Inside my Jeep, I kicked off my shoes and popped a piece of Dentyne in my mouth. Next stop was my apartment. I had to regain my ability to walk without thinking and my little red sneakers were the answer.

My well-timed departure from the restaurant landed me in sparse traffic. I wasn't inebriated, but the fewer obstacles I faced the better, and the faster I got home, the faster I could get to Mr. Q's house. I vowed to check the house every day in case the creep who stole Mr. P had a change of heart.

Luck appeared to be on my side when I easily found a parking spot in front of my building. I ran barefoot up the sidewalk and through the door of the building, huffing as I took the steps two by two. My forward progress was interrupted when I hit the top landing. Paralyzed, I stared at my open door and the destruction beyond the threshold.

6

I PACED FOR A FEW MINUTES pondering my next move. I had a simple decision to make, but not an easy one. Go inside or run away? Perhaps it was my wine-induced faux bravery or plain stupidity that prompted me to take a deep breath and step through the doorway.

Contents from my small roll top desk were scattered across the floor and the large seat cushions from my geranium red couch had been left leaning against the coffee table. The heirloom quilt my grandmother had made to celebrate my birth lay crumpled in the corner of the living room. I picked the quilt up and wept when I observed a large rip.

I composed myself before entering the kitchen. Canned food, utensils and plates littered the floor. Seeing my brand new jar of pickles reduced to a puddle of juice and broken glass oddly transformed my sadness into anger. I was officially ticked off.

Inside my bathroom, the deep clawfoot tub harbored broken bottles and trash. The tub was the main reason I chose my apartment over the one across the hall. It was symbolic. Every girl needed a place to soak away her troubles. Now someone had defaced my Zen spot and I felt violated.

By the time I reached my bedroom door, all hope of finding a single area of my apartment unscathed had been lost. My mattress had been flipped off its box springs and my clothes flung across the room as if a dog had been digging in desperation.

I was overwhelmed with sadness in the living room, anger in the kitchen, vulnerability in the bathroom and now terror as I looked at my dresser. It had been pushed aside and the door to the attic left open. I crawled through the small opening and traversed the attic space until I reached the far corner. I lifted a section of oak floorboard, grabbed the box it had been hiding, and sobbed.

My knowledge of WitSec, before I entered the program, had come from television. Almost all of it turned out to be true. When they agreed to put you in the system, you agreed to leave everything behind - your job, your friends, and your family. My decision to enter the program had been the most difficult of my life. I had weighed never hearing from my family against the possibility of dying. I couldn't choose, so I didn't. Inside the box I kept a secret prepaid cell phone I used to talk to my family along with precious photographs, and their current addresses, just in case.

I took the phone out then tucked the box safely back in place and crawled out into my bedroom. I reached for the first piece of cloth I found and wiped my eyes.

Whatever force was behind the assault on my life was slowly breaking me. At first glance, nothing seemed to be missing from my apartment, but whatever hope I had of keeping control depended on me believing the break-in was a petty theft. Something must be missing. Otherwise, my mind would convince me the culprit had been Max's killer, or my worst nightmare - the criminals I'd helped put away.

I ran downstairs to Mrs. Rippetoe's place and knocked on her door. She answered carrying her dog, Sassy. "Hi. Did you hear anyone upstairs in my apartment?"

"Why no, Hun, but don't you look real pretty in that dress."

"Thanks, but I need to know if you let anyone go upstairs."

"Sassy and I just returned from the beauty parlor. We had our hair and nails done. What do you think?"

"You both look gorgeous." Honestly, they resembled circus freaks, with their matching black and white polka dot bows and bright red nails.

Mrs. Rippetoe didn't bring to mind the word attractive. Her eyes were dark, the left one bulged out farther than the right and her bushy eyebrows matched her peat moss gray hair. The gracious soul inside was her ticket in life, with an extra chit for her creamy soft, latte-colored skin.

"Somebody broke into my apartment!"

"Oh my," she said holding her hand to her forehead. I expected her to faint so I grabbed Sassy from her arms. When she didn't, I realized how ridiculous it had been to save Sassy when Mrs. Rippetoe could have cracked her head open had she hit the floor.

"Hun, are you okay? Did you call the police?"

Oh, God, here we go again.

"No. I'm okay." I handed Sassy back to her and brushed the dog hairs from my dress.

"Thank the Lord! I'll go call the police."

"No, Mrs. Rippetoe!" I reached for her arm.

"Hun, why don't you want to call the police? Somebody took your stuff. The police can help you get your things back."

"Actually, I don't think anything is missing. My place is just messed up a little bit."

"I think I should still call the police so they know."

I hoped I could get her to drop the subject and that her forgetful side would eventually make this a non-issue. "I have to run right now. Can you please wait to call until I can be here? Also, what I would really like is to get my lock fixed."

"You let me know when I can call the police. And don't worry about the lock. I'll have Toby fix the door when he gets here."

"Who's Toby?"

"My new maintenance man. I rented him the apartment across from yours and he will fix things up around here in exchange for some rent. He says he's real talented."

On that statement alone he registered on my skeptic radar and now he'd be living directly across from me. I wondered if it was a coincidence my place had been broken into the exact day he rented the apartment.

"Can he fix it right away?" I didn't wait for an answer. "I have to run out so I'll check back with you later this afternoon."

I ran back upstairs, sifted through the clothes on the bedroom floor and managed to find a clean pair of khaki slacks and a bright purple polo shirt. My favorite red sneakers were AWOL, so I slipped on a pair of brown loafers.

All I could do was close my front door and hope I wouldn't get any more unexpected visitors. After gathering my thoughts, the logical part of my brain took over and demanded I accept what had happened as an average burglary. It was obvious somebody had been looking for something. The more I thought about the situation the less I worried about the perpetrator being the jerks I testified against. They would have bypassed the message and gone straight for the kill. I suspected my research for Max had caused this mess. I hoped in two and a half hours I'd answer the phone call from Max's friend and be able to put this issue to rest.

Obviously my luck was on the downswing, so I paid extra attention to the cars around me as I drove. The last thing I needed was someone plowing into my Jeep.

———

Plywood covered the gaping hole in the post office where the large glass window had been. They remained open for business - through rain, sleet, or snow. Or gunfire.

I ran in and retrieved Thomas Brackford's mail. The wine I'd had at lunch and the stress of the break-in had taken a toll on me. My head pounded. I tossed the mail onto the passenger seat then dug through my purse for aspirin. Without any water, I popped two into my mouth and swallowed.

The bitter taste still lingered as I arrived at Brackford's place desperate for water. He didn't answer. The packages from yesterday no longer sat on the table, so he either picked them up or someone had stolen them. I knocked on the door again in case he hadn't heard me the first time.

Still no answer. The front drapes remained drawn exactly as they had been yesterday, with the small slit revealing darkness.

Guilt slowed my stride as I walked back toward the SUV. I'd never forgive myself if Brackford had fallen out of his wheelchair and couldn't get up. I turned around and headed to the gate on the side of the garage. A quick peek though the sliding glass door would be enough to ease my mind.

The blinds in back were closed, blocking any view. I hesitated, wondering if I should check for an unlocked door. The fear of what I might find inside intensified as I flashed back to the image of Max. Thomas Brackford was my client and a paraplegic. At the very least I owed him the decency of trying to open the door. Besides, maybe it would be locked. Unfortunately, the door opened. I stepped inside and called his name.

When my eyes adjusted to the darkened room, my stomach lurched like a hijacked train speeding through a winding mountain passage. Thomas Brackford's body lay on the floor, his head surrounded by blood. A large object rested nearby. I figured he was dead and turned to run.

"Mmmppf."

No matter how much I wanted to ignore the barely audible sound and hightail it to my Jeep, I couldn't. "Mr. Brackford?"

"Mmm."

I ran to Brackford's phone and punched in 911.

"Send an ambulance! He's been attacked. He's bleeding. Help!"

"Ma'am, what happened?"

I dropped the phone. "Oh my God. Oh my God."

My response confused me. I was frantic and couldn't seem to hold myself together. I'd seen my share of dead people, so why freak out when the person in front of me was alive? I slapped myself in the face. *Ouch.*

The pain snapped me back and I realized why I was frantic. Another day, another crime and I stood smack in the center of it all. I had to get out before the police arrived. I ran to the front and opened the door wide so the paramedics and police could easily enter after I left.

Thomas Brackford moaned again. I ran back toward him and tripped over the ottoman, beginning my descent to the floor. I stretched my arms out to break my fall and slid into a large locomotive-shaped doorstop, knocking the thing into Thomas Brackford's head.

"Damn. Ow, ow, ow," I screamed. Lowering my voice I turned to him. "Hold on. I called for an ambulance."

The sirens were audible in the distance as I pulled myself up off the ground. If I didn't leave now, I'd land in the middle of this investigation with no way out. Brackford was shaking so I took a nearby blanket and spread it over him, then bent down to move the heavy doorstop away from his head. I lifted the iron locomotive with both hands.

"Drop it! Put your hands in the air, now!" the police yelled, pointing their guns at me.

I screamed.

"I said drop it!" The officer yelled again.

Holding the doorstop far away from Brackford's head, I let go. As I put my hands in the air, I struggle to keep my chèvre salad and wine down.

The police officer walked toward me with his gun still in his hand. "Ma'am, do you have any other weapons?"

"I don't have any weapons."

"Please hold your arms out to the side. I'm going to pat you down just to be sure."

"I swear I don't have any."

"For everyone's safety I need to check you for weapons, ma'am."

I sniffed, trying to keep my nose from running as the tears began to build. "Fine."

The police officer ran his hands along my side and patted my pockets. "We're going to need to take you down to the station."

"Why? I promise I found him like this."

"I understand, but we need to talk with you. You can put your hands down now."

Blood dripped from my arm and I almost threw up again. The officer had to be crazy if he thought I'd go to the station looking like this. My appearance screamed guilty.

"No way. I didn't do anything."

"You can come with me voluntarily or I can make you. Your choice."

"I'm not going." I felt woozy and stumbled. I wasn't a cop, but I knew he couldn't force me to go anywhere if I hadn't done anything.

"You don't look so well," he said, taking hold of my arm.

I was glad he had come to his senses and realized I was only an innocent bystander who needed his help. He reached over and took my other arm.

"Thanks for helping me."

"You're welcome," he said, then cuffed me.

7

"Can I please wash my hands?"

The officer took the handcuffs off me. "Right after we process you."

"Process me?"

"We are going to take a few pictures and swab the blood on your hands. We may have to take your clothes as well."

"Do I need a lawyer?"

"You haven't yet been charged. We're only going to be asking you questions at this time."

"Why do you need my clothes?"

"The blood on your clothes might be needed as evidence. Can anyone bring you a change of clothes? Otherwise, we got a jumpsuit."

He walked me into the processing room where a female officer waited. I displayed my hands just as she asked. She photographed them and the blood on my shirt.

"I need to go to the restroom soon. I'm afraid I might not make it."

"Sure. She'll escort you to the restroom," she said, pointing to another female officer standing by the door. "Oh, but I'm gonna need your shirt first."

"I don't have anything to change into."

"Here, take a jumpsuit."

"Are you kidding?"

"Hold on. I don't think they'll mind. We got a extra shirt around here I think."

She rummaged through a box on the floor. "Here you go," she said holding up a t-shirt.

"Hooters? Really?" I asked, trying not to sound too ungrateful.

"It's this or the jumpsuit."

I pointed to the shirt.

After I changed my shirt in a closet sized room with the other officer watching my every move, the two of us trotted off to the restroom. My reflection in the mirror was straight out of a horror movie. I had blood on my hands, my face, even in my hair. Even after I washed up with a paper towel the blood was still noticeable.

"Can I make a phone call?" I asked the officer as we walked out of the bathroom.

"Sure, but make it quick, they are waiting to talk to you back in the room."

The room. She made it sound ominous. I headed for the phone with my keeper in tow. She stood nearby as I dialed Peter.

"Peter Parker here."

"Hi. I'm at the police station and—"

"Fantastic! I had faith in you. I knew you would go at some point."

I started to cry. "They brought me here in handcuffs and—"

71

"What?"

"Peter, they want to take my clothes. I got the blood on me by accident. Oh my God, I can't believe—"

"Slow down, what are you talking about? What blood?"

"On my shirt. They want someone to bring me clothes. I can't talk now, they're waiting for me."

"Did they read you your rights?"

"No. They said they just needed to asked me some quest—"

"Hold it right there. Don't say a thing. I'm calling you a lawyer."

"I didn't do anything wrong."

"The guy's an old friend. He owes me one. Give me a half hour."

Nervous, I hung up the phone, unsure of what was happening. The death, the break-in, and now the assault totaled up to a little more crime than I could handle. My belief that all the bad stuff was related to Max was waning, but considering the alternative was chilling.

"Miss, if you're finished we should go to the room."

The room. Those two words got on my nerves. Before we entered - the room - I sprang the news on her. "I need to wait for my lawyer."

"Boys, she lawyered up," the officer said as she opened the door. She delivered the line perfectly, like she'd seen it on an episode of Law and Order and had been practicing it ever since.

Twenty minutes passed before Peter and his friend finally arrived. My relief at the sight of Peter's face consumed me. I ignored the attorney and propelled myself toward Peter, embracing him with a massive hug.

Peter pried me off. "Aspen, this—"

"I'm Jack Arbon, pleasure to meet you, Ms. Moore. Peter said you needed me." His eyes were gold, not some cheap 10 Karat gold, but pure 24 Karat.

I was hypnotized. I'd never seen eyes quite like his. Thoughts of looking longingly into them as we removed one another's clothes invaded my mind. What was wrong with me? Disclosure of my real identity seemed imminent, the possibility of facing time in the slammer loomed, and I stood speechless, fantasizing like a lusty teenager.

"It was pure luck I had a cancellation. I advise you to answer all questions unless I instruct you not to do so. Do you understand?"

"Do you understand?" he repeated.

I pulled myself together. "Yes, I do."

The detective entered the room and asked Peter to leave. "Okay then, let's get this underway. I'm Detective George."

Jack and I sat down at the table.

"Where's the other officer? The one who brought me in?" I asked.

"That was Officer Storey, he had other matters to tend to. I'll be the one asking you a few questions. So, ma'am, were you at the post office on Gravois Road yesterday?"

He reminded me of Sergeant Joe Friday from the old Dragnet show, but gruffer and the lines on his face deeper.

"What does the post office shooting have to do with today?" Jack asked before I had a chance to answer.

"We are interested in today's situation and yesterday's shooting as well."

Jack turned to me and nodded. I assumed it meant I could answer the question. "Yes, I was at the post office picking up mail for Mr. Brackford."

"Mr. Brackford? The man whose blood you had on your hands?"

"Don't answer that," Jack ordered.

Detective George continued without a pause, "Did you go to the post office alone or did someone go with you?"

"Alone."

The questioning continued. I tried to focus, but the detective had a wild hair sticking out of his nose that danced whenever he spoke and he spoke a lot.

"That wraps up the post office questions. Now, about Mr. Brackford," he said, while his nose hair did the samba.

The matter under discussion was serious, but I had to stop myself from laughing every time I eyed his nose. I looked down at my nails and the urge to laugh subsided. My brand new acrylics were a wreck. I had chipped them when I slammed into the iron doorstop.

"How long have you worked for Mr. Brackford?"

"He signed up with my company two months ago." I kept my head down, picking at the polish on my fake nails. I'd never had any fake body parts until Stephanie talked me into paying a fortune for nails last week.

The door to the room opened and another officer poked his head inside. "Can I speak with you, Detective?"

Detective George and his wild hair left the room. Glad to have even the smallest break from questioning, I stopped messing with my nails and leaned over to Jack.

"I have another tiny problem. I haven't told them I'm the person they are interested in talking to about Max Vanderbur's death."

"What?"

A word I'd been hearing a lot of lately.

"I am the one who called the police to report Professor Vanderbur's death."

"Wonderful. A serial criminal." He followed his remark with a quiet laugh.

"Very funny." No matter how awesome I found his eyes, he didn't have the right to turn my chaotic life into a joke.

"Do not say a thing unless I signal you. I'll give you the thumbs up if I think you are okay to bring up the topic before we leave."

Detective George entered the room with an annoyed look. "You're free to go."

"Why?" I asked.

"Aspen, the detective said you could go. Does the reason matter?"

"I need to make sure they aren't going to bust into my apartment in the middle of the night and arrest me. So, tell me why I can go now. Please." I hoped being polite might get a better reaction.

"Mr. Brackford regained consciousness and was able to rule you out as his attacker. Like I said, you are free to go."

Jack gave the thumbs up.

"Before I go, I need to let you know I am the anonymous caller you are looking for in regards to Max Vanderbur's death."

He looked too interested in my statement, like a bird dog zeroing in on the mark. "I take back what I said. You're no longer free to go."

I glanced at Jack, wondering if he was a good lawyer.

"Didn't Professor Vanderbur commit suicide?" Jack asked.

"His death is still under investigation. Part of understanding what happened is finding out why she went to the Professor's home that evening."

I think he confirmed what I thought. Max didn't kill himself.

"He was a client and I went to his house to pick up something."

"What is your occupation, Ms. Moore?"

"My company is called Moore Time and I am a personal concierge."

"But, what exactly do you do?"

"Gal Friday?" I served up, figuring him for a bit of a chauvinist.

"Yeah, I gotcha. So was he alive when you got to his house?"

"No, of course he wasn't alive. That would mean I would have had to stand by while he killed himself in order for him to be dead when I called the police!"

"Well, did you?"

In the back of my mind I doubted myself. Had the rope closed around his neck after my arrival? My sanity depended on me believing my own words. "Of course not!"

"Detective, you'll get no more answers if you continue asking questions like that," Jack said.

Detective George rubbed his nose as though he had suddenly become aware of his dancing hair. "How did you get in the house?"

"I didn't. I saw him through the window."

"Do you always go around peeping in people's windows?"

"Look, he asked me to come over." Tears breached my lower eyelids, like a Louisiana levy.

"Did you notice anyone else around?"

The pressure was on. I wanted the police to check out Mrs. Vanderbur and her male friend, but I didn't want to be the one to get involved. I had to find another way to steer the police in their direction. "No. Once I saw him I ran."

Tears continued to flow. "Are we through?" I asked.

"Yes, but don't go out of town without letting us know and if you think of anything else, please contact us."

"Do you think someone killed Max?"

"Ms. Moore. I can't discuss police business with you."

"But you were practically accusing me of murder with your questions!"

"For all we know, you could be an accomplice."

"Hah, so you do believe he was murdered."

"I didn't say he was murdered, you did. Is there something you want to tell me?"

"Watch it." Jack grabbed a square box off the table and passed me a tissue. "Let's go, Aspen."

My chance to point to Mrs. Vanderbur's involvement without getting myself involved had arrived. "Wait! So you're going to arrest his wife?"

Detective George laughed like I'd just delivered the punch line to a joke. "Mrs. Vanderbur is not a suspect."

"Why? Because she volunteers for the policemen's ball?" I cringed as the words came out of my mouth. I knew I should have just thanked the detective and left.

He stood. "I think we're finished."

Peter had been waiting outside the room. The three of us walked out together, keeping quiet until we were outside the station.

"I'm going to get the car. Jack, can you stay here with her until I get back?"

While I waited for Peter to bring the car around, Jack and I exchanged pleasantries. When the conversation lulled, I thanked him profusely for his help, nearly shaking his hand off.

"If you want to thank me properly, have dinner with me." He smiled.

When I figured out I still had his hand in mine, I dropped it. "Isn't there some law against that?"

———

Peter dropped me off at my Jeep. After he drove away, I wished I hadn't told him I'd meet him for dinner, once I cleaned myself up. I wasn't even sure I was hungry. However, by the time I pulled onto my street my stomach was growling and I figured it had known something I hadn't.

When I couldn't find a parking space, I drove back to the main cross street and parked. Walking to my apartment, I kept my head down and folded my arms across my blood-stained shirt. Another thing I wished was that I had taken the policewoman's offer to keep the Hooter's t-shirt.

My apartment lock hadn't been fixed and disappointment didn't even begin to describe how I felt. I swung around and headed back downstairs to Mrs. Rippetoe's place.

"Oh, my Hun, what happened? Are you okay?" Mrs. Rippetoe opened her arms to embrace me. Unfortunately, Sassy dropped straight to the floor. Without a bounce, Sassy let out a shrieking noise I didn't know dogs could make. Mrs. Rippetoe and I bent over to pick her up, knocking our heads and sending us both to the ground.

"Whoa, dudes, are you two all right?" I heard someone ask. I looked up and saw a bright light and a figure standing above me.

"Are you an angel?" I asked.

"Man, you two wiped out," the figure said.

The look and sound of a surfer didn't make sense. We lived at the gateway to the west, the center of the United States, the quintessential definition of Midwest almost six-hundred miles from the nearest ocean. I had to be dead.

"Toby, can you help us up?" Mrs. Rippetoe held up her arm.

Once off the floor, she composed herself while Toby helped me.

"Are you okay Mrs. Rippetoe?" I asked.

"Aspen, this is Toby the handyman." She shooed us inside her apartment.

His blinding white teeth sparkled and his eyes twinkled beneath his pecan brown hair splashed with gold. He was definitely some sort of surfer dude. The color of his skin was not quite like a UPS truck, but any more time in the tanning booth and he'd be close.

"Hey man, what happened to you?" Toby asked.

"Not a big deal, really. I helped out a friend who was hurt."

"Bummer."

Toby was cute, in a no responsibilities, no worries kind of way. He was obviously harmless.

"I hate to jump right into business, but when will my door be fixed?"

"So bogus. I can't believe someone messed up your apartment."

"Can you fix the lock?"

"Yeah, but I worked on a finishing job at those new lofts downtown this morning. After that I had to stop by the new skateboard shop. Won't be fixed until tomorrow. Sorry, man."

What a shirker. "I need to go. Can you make sure the door is fixed tomorrow?"

"No problem, man."

"But what about your shirt, honey? What happened?"

"It's a long story. I promise to tell you about it tomorrow."

"If you're in any kind of trouble, I can help," Mrs. Rippetoe offered.

"Honestly, I'm okay, but thank you." I considered myself lucky to have such a sweet landlady.

"You sure they didn't hurt you?" she persisted. "I've got connections. I can use my martial arts training on whoever did that to you. They never think they're in danger. That's how I get them with a surprise attack."

I laughed silently as I imagined her flying through the air like some Ninja in a martial arts movie. "You trained in martial arts?"

"Oh yes, hun. Sanuces Ryu Jiu Jitsu - street combat."

"What color belt?" I asked.

"Didn't have any kind of belts in my day. It was back in my younger years, but today they'd probably give me one of them white belts."

"Cool," Toby said.

"I'm impressed." I was pretty sure a white belt was the first belt you received, but still, it was a step above the Aphrodite belt.

"Oh Hun, it's not that impressive."

"You should be proud. I'll be sure to ask for your help when I find I need it." If I were ever in a situation where my only chance of survival depended on Mrs. Rippetoe and her JiuJitsu, I'd just have to do the sign of the cross and accept whatever God had planned.

"Sure you don't want to stay and play some Crazy Eights?" Toby asked.

"Sorry, I have to go. But thanks for asking," I closed the door behind me just as Toby and Mrs. Rippetoe sat down to play cards. Maybe he wasn't such a loser.

The mess in my apartment symbolized my entire day. My first inclination involved curling up on my floor and crying myself to sleep, but I'd have to scratch dinner first.

I called Peter, but he didn't answer so I looked for clothes so I could change. I found a pair of faded Levi jeans lying by the window. They had holes in the thighs, but they were comfortable and we were only going to eat Chinese food. By the closet door I found a thin navy blue cotton top with delicate embroidery.

My bathtub remained unusable, still defaced with broken bottles and other junk. I used a wet washcloth to wipe the remaining blood from my face and hair. My dirty-blonde hair appeared dirtier than usual so I tossed on a knit beret. I double-checked myself in the mirror for leftover blood, grabbed my jacket and headed out the door.

8

THE CHINESE RESTAURANT was only a block and a half from my office. A quick check of my messages and I'd be working some chopsticks right on time. I parked next to the street light that illuminated the inside of my office. As expected, the place was empty, no sign of life, plant or otherwise.

Ignoring the light switch, I followed the blinking light on my answering machine and pushed the button. "This is Harry Corbitt. I need to talk to you."

The message sounded like a demand. I had no idea what he wanted because his phone had been in perfect condition when I handed it over to him. I hurried on to the next message.

"Ms. Moore? It's four o'clock. Oh, I didn't think about what I would say if you didn't answer. I'm too hard to reach, so I'll call you back tomorrow around noon."

Her evasiveness irritated me, but at the same time I was curious as to why she wouldn't leave a contact number. Whoever Max's friend was, I needed to talk to her, and soon.

The final message evoked palpitations. It was Mr. Q checking in on Mr. P. Once again I entertained the idea of packing up and leaving St. Louis.

My new life sucked, but there was nothing I could do about it tonight. I locked the door and started my brisk walk to meet Peter. Movement up ahead caught my eyes, as I passed my Jeep. A large figure on the unlit part of the street appeared to be walking in my direction. Mrs. Rippetoe's voice popped inside my head, "He's not just big around, but big and—"

The sound of pounding footsteps cut short her silent whisper. I'd give up almost anything for food, but not my life. I turned around, heading for the closest place of safety. As the footsteps closed in, I pressed the unlock button on my Jeep's key fob. I jumped inside, and slammed the door, pushing the lock button seconds before he grabbed the handle.

I hit the fob's panic button. The inside light came on and I freaked. I knew he was outside staring in. I closed my eyes, breathing with the rhythm of the honking horn. When I opened my eyes the guy had disappeared. An awful metallic taste oozed across my tongue and I wished for something to wash away the fear, something stronger than Chinese tea. Preferably something that would make me numb.

I dug my phone from my purse. "Peter, can you—"

"What the hell is that noise? Where are you?" Peter shouted.

"I pressed my car's panic button!" I yelled.

"Why?"

"I'll tell you later. Hurry down to my office. My head is about to explode."

"It will turn off in a minute or so. Or press the button again to turn it off."

"You don't know what I'm going through."

"Start your car."

I shoved the keys in the ignition. My Jeep started, but the alarm didn't stop. Instead, I ended up on sensory overload with the engine humming, the horn honking, and music blaring. I reached for the radio off button and heard laughter on the other end of my phone.

"Are you laughing at me?"

"No, I'm not. We are. You're making quite the spectacle with your flashing lights and blaring horn."

Through my front windshield, I saw Peter and Jack walking toward me, away from the restaurant where I should have been quietly eating my Mongolian beef. They strolled nonchalantly down the sidewalk as I desperately tried to recover from full panic mode.

Jack shouted into Peter's phone, "Pop the hood."

Once they stood outside my Jeep, I opened my door.

Jack poked his head under the hood. "You got any tools in your car?"

"Do I look like the kind of girl who'd have tools in her car?"

"Actually, you do," Jack said.

"What's that supposed to mean?"

"Let it go, Aspen. The horn is driving me nuts," Peter said.

Jack answered anyway. "You look like a woman who can take care of herself."

"I do have some tools in my office."

Peter rolled his eyes and they followed me inside. A toolbox and tools sat in the office closet, still in the bag, unused. My plan had been to hang pictures in my office, so at the hardware store, I'd purchased almost every tool the salesperson recommended. I never got around to buying pictures. Jack rummaged through the bag and pulled out a wrench and a screwdriver.

Jack and Peter went back outside. I double checked the lock on the back door, locked the front, and walked back to my Jeep. "How long is it going to take?"

Jack was under the hood and a second later there was silence.

"That answers my question. Impressive! How'd you know how to do stop the horn?"

"Unfortunately, experience." Jack ducked back under the hood and re-attached the battery cable.

"You ready to eat?" Peter asked.

"Let me put these back in your office," Jack said.

"I already locked the door. I'll throw them in the back of the Jeep."

"You sure? These are top of the line. You have a good eye for tools." Jack handed them over.

"Enough tool talk. Let's go." Peter turned and walked toward the restaurant and I tried to determine if Peter's tone evolved from anger or hunger.

———

Potstickers, Dumplings, Shumai, Gyozas, whatever they were called, I always called them tasty. Steamed or fried, they're well worth the wait. I knew, because I'd eaten Potstickers in every town I'd ever visited.

"I think I'm being stalked," I said as I mixed the duck sauce with the hot Chinese mustard. "I hit the panic button because a big guy came after me."

"You think it was the same guy who got in your mailbox?"

"Someone went through your mail?" Jack mixed duck sauce with his mustard too. *Freaky*.

"Yeah, and he could be the same one who fired the gun at the post office and attacked Thomas Brackford."

"Are the police aware of this guy? Sounds like something they should know about," Jack said.

"I agree." Peter poured himself some Chinese tea and dumped four packets of sugar in the tiny cup. He amazed me. The man could down a bucket of sugar and still maintain his rock hard abs.

"I don't think they're doing the best job. Besides, Detective George would probably be happier delivering me to the stalker than saving me from him."

"He wasn't that bad. What other choice do you have?" Jack asked.

"I'm not a complete idiot. I'll go on the offensive. Besides, right now I'm more mad than scared." It was hard to tell if they believed me.

"And do what?" Peter asked.

"I'll stalk my stalker."

"Whoa, Aspen. You sound like a complete idiot."

"Cut it out, Peter. The more I know about him the better I can defend myself."

"Why don't you start by having someone else find out who he is," Peter said.

Exactly my plan, but I wanted Peter's help, not the police or the marshals. Ninety-nine percent of me believed the guy who had been following me wasn't tied to the crooks I put away. The stubborn one percent was well aware at how pissed they'd been when I'd turned over embezzlement evidence and testified as an eyewitness to the murder of my fiancé. "Fine. Are you guys going to help me?"

"Count me in." Jack smiled again. His teeth weren't so bright they'd burn your retinas. They were right-white, natural looking, and captivating enough to trigger a fleeting thought about jumping over the table and ripping off his clothes.

Something was seriously wrong with me. All my thoughts about Jack somehow ended up with him wearing no clothes. Maybe the last few days of chaos had triggered some type of delayed post-traumatic stress syndrome resulting from watching my fiancé take a bullet to the head. I probably needed therapy.

"Might be good to have a lawyer assist us," Peter said.

"Aren't good lawyers too busy to spend time on anything but their cases?" I asked.

"Are you implying I'm not a good lawyer?"

"My question didn't come out right. I meant I need someone I can count on. Wait, that didn't sound right either. I guess I want to make sure you have enough time."

"I can't work on the search twenty four hours a day, but if you need me to check a few things out, I'd be more than happy to help."

"Me too," Peter said, with a little less enthusiasm.

"What do we do next?" I asked.

"We need a plan." Jack had taken charge.

I didn't want Jack in control. "Why don't you put together a plan, Peter?"

"Sure." This time his single word held no enthusiasm whatsoever.

"Is something wrong?" I asked.

"I think this might be better handled by the police."

"Like I said, they don't like me. Plus I think they believe Max Vanderbur was murdered and they are completely ignoring the number one suspect. How can I trust them to do the job right?"

"What makes you think that?"

"Yes, I'd like to hear this one," Jack piped in.

"It's a feeling."

"Oh," they both said with an upper inflection. The response sounded like a sarcastic, placating acknowledgement.

"Team members who don't believe in me. What kind of team is that?"

"Who said we didn't?" Peter moved our water glasses to make room for our entrées.

"I can tell by your tone."

"Really? By a tone?" Peter asked.

"I happen to ha—"

"I believe in you," Jack said.

Red flag. I liked Jack but he didn't know me well enough to make such a strong statement or had I become jaded? Perhaps he followed the - innocent until proven guilty - viewpoint in his personal life too.

"Thanks." I looked directly in Jack's eyes and flashed a little half smile. He deserved a chance.

I poked at my Mongolian beef with my chopsticks, wondering if I should bring up the Mr. P situation in front of Jack. I didn't want him to think my entire world was a disaster.

Even if my new life was falling apart right before my eyes, acting like everything was under control wasn't as important as keeping my business afloat. Besides, if Jack hadn't been scared away by my dead client or my comatose client, then a missing client shouldn't even cause him to blink.

"Have you made any progress with my client Mr. P?" I asked Peter.

"You mean the missing dog?"

I kicked Peter under the table.

"Ouch," Jack screamed.

"Oh God, I'm sorry, uh, I had something crawling on my foot."

Peter wrinkled his forehead and stared at me. Seconds later, his forehead was wrinkle-free and the smirk on his face conveyed what I'd hoped he wouldn't discover. I was trying to make a good impression on Jack.

I babbled about a bug on my foot until Peter cut me off. "I asked the guy what type of dog his neighbor had. Told him I wanted to get one."

"And?"

"He said he had no idea. He was wondering if something had happened to the dog since he hadn't seen the dog sitter in several days."

"He called me a dog sitter?"

"Exact words, but they sound more glamorous coming from your lips."

"Do you think he lied?"

"I couldn't tell with just the one conversation. But I don't think so."

"Any other leads?"

"Not yet. Might be another good reason to get the police involved." Peter used his fork to take another bite of his sweet and sour chicken.

"You don't give up do you? I can't call them about this situation. My client has a thing about privacy. We need to solve this on our own. Oh, and before Monday."

"Monday?" Peter asked as if his question might change what I had said.

"Yep, he's coming back Monday afternoon."

"Wonderful."

"Is tomorrow morning a good time to discuss our plan to find the stalker?" I asked, hoping they hadn't changed their mind about helping me.

"Not a problem for me, what about you, Jack?"

Jack pulled out his BlackBerry and punched a few buttons. "I'm free until ten o'clock."

"Seven-thirty, my place?" Peter offered.

Jack and I agreed. The waitress dropped off our dinner check along with three fortune cookies.

"Hope they bring good news." I grabbed the cookie pointing toward me before picking up the tray and offering cookies to Peter and Jack.

I held up the little slip of paper. "You will find the truth," I said, holding back a smile, "in bed." Not my most mature move, but I needed a single moment of fun. Old habits are hard to break. "Your turn, Peter, and don't forget to add 'in bed' to the end."

Peter sighed and cracked open his cookie. "You are a gift to women, in bed."

"It does not say that!" I laughed and made a grab for Peter's fortune. He shoved the paper into his mouth.

"Trust me," Peter said then swallowed.

He was slick. I'd give him that. I turned my attention to Jack. "What's yours say?"

"It's just a bunch of numbers."

"No, that's your lucky numbers. Turn it over for the fortune."

"Seriously, it only has numbers," he said.

"Let me see."

Jack handed me his fortune. It was blank. I'd seen double fortunes, no fortunes, but never a cookie with a blank fortune. How sad was that?

I handed it back. "Fortunes are overrated."

———

"Lock your door when you get in. I'm going to follow you home," Peter said as he pulled up to my Jeep.

"Oh, crap, home. I forgot. I don't have a home to stay in right now. My place was broken into and the lock hasn't been fixed."

"And you didn't tell me?"

"Didn't enter my mind."

"It didn't enter your mind?"

"Are you going to parrot back everything I say?"

"Sorry, just seems like a break-in would be high up on your list of topics of conversation."

"Well, unfortunately, the topic didn't rate as high as skidding through my client's blood, getting handcuffed, and being chased by some stalker who obviously thinks I have something he wants. It's been a busy day."

"You've got a point, Tonto."

"I need to find a hotel room."

"No way. To be safe, you should stay with me at least for the night."

"I don't want to put out, I mean put you out," I said.

"No need to put out for me." A wicked little grin grew across his face.

"What about Madeline? And there really isn't a lot of room at your place, and—"

"Madeline's out of town again and my sofa's a pullout."

Spending the night might lead to trouble especially with all the nakedness that had been on my mind lately. I had been attracted to Peter from the first time I met him and had even kissed him one night after drinking more martinis than a short girl should. The kiss had been awesome for me until he responded by telling me about his girlfriend Madeline. We never mentioned the kiss again and honored our platonic relationship agreement. Still, on occasion, it seemed something hot smoldered beneath our friendship.

When I yawned it was a relief because I was no saint. If I fell asleep I couldn't make a fool of myself.

"Okay, Hotel Peter here we come." I hoped I wouldn't regret my decision.

"So everything is settled. Jump in your car and I'll follow you home."

As soon as we entered our building, I brought Peter upstairs to show him my place.

"You weren't kidding about them creating a mess."

"It's going to take days for me to get the rooms back in order."

"Maybe you could buy someone's time and they could clean it up for you."

"Aren't you witty? Go ahead. I'll be down in a few."

My Rams nightshirt was too skimpy for a sleepover, so I selected a pair of lightweight sweats and a baggy t-shirt. I grabbed my fully stocked travel kit that had miraculously survived.

I knocked on Peter's door. "Want some tea?" I held up a box of chamomile I'd rescued from my kitchen floor. "It helps you sleep."

"Sure, why not." He filled a couple of mugs with water and popped them in the microwave.

"I'm going to change." I darted into his bathroom with my bag.

Peter's place was tidy for a guy and the clean bathroom was like heaven. I brushed my teeth and washed my face without fear of cutting my foot on broken glass.

"You take cream or sugar?"

"Plain, please," I said walking up behind him.

Peter dumped sugar in one of the cups and then handed the other to me. We made our way into the living room, stretched out on the pulled out sofa bed, and watched Monk solve a mystery. The laughter softened my worries and I let myself get lost in make believe.

"Mr. Monk saves the day." Peter clicked the television off. He pulled the covers over me and turned out the light. "Goodnight, Aspen."

I rolled over, puffed the pillows up under my head, and willed myself to sleep. As I dozed off, I entered a twilight dream. Peter and I were standing in my office talking. He had brought me a plant and after setting it down he pressed his lips against mine and gently laid me back on the desk.

Like I said - I'm no saint.

9

THE SOUND OF A KEY inserting into the lock of Peter's front door drew my attention. He had gone out earlier to pick up breakfast while I showered. I stood in his living room putting on my clothes. *Panties. Check. Bra. Check.*

I rushed to finish dressing. *Jeans. Check. Shirt...*

"Well, hello!"

I distinctly heard two voices. I figured one was Peter and the other Jack. My head bobbled inside my shirt and my arms pointed upward. I looked down, relieved to find my shirt covering my bra.

I didn't care about them seeing me in my bra. I cared about them seeing me in *this* bra, the I-haven't-done-laundry-in-a-long-time bra. The only one I could find last night in my disheveled apartment. The dingy-white one with broken elastic sprouting from all directions. I finished wiggling into my shirt. *Check.*

"Hey." I brushed my damp hair away from my face and smiled as if nothing were out of the ordinary.

Peter set a box of doughnuts on the table. I claimed a chocolate covered one, while he poured the three of us coffee. Seven-thirty in the morning and we had a plan. Our plan was to put together a plan.

"This morning it occurred to me that I had no idea what I would be getting into when I offered to be part of the team last night," Jack started.

I cringed and waited for him to complete his thought, anticipating the conclusion. I expected he was about to bow out.

"I think having all the facts is important before getting involved," he continued.

Here it comes.

"So, why don't you start from the beginning? Aspen?"

"What?"

"The beginning. Tell me how Max Vanderbur came to hire you and about the research you were doing for him."

"Please do. I've never heard the entire story," Peter said as though I'd been keeping a secret. I had a secret, but that wasn't it.

"The story isn't all that exciting. I posted a flyer at the University and he called."

"Was there something specific he wanted you to find?" Peter asked.

"Most of his interest centered on the acquisition of the property on which Marston had been built and the merger of the Martin and Stone development companies."

"Did he tell you why he needed the information? And why he chose you when he must have had access to researchers at the University?" Jack asked.

I felt like I was being cross-examined and insulted. "I never asked him outright why he chose me over someone else. I didn't want him second guessing his choice. As far as why he wanted the information, I didn't need to know his motive. He hired me to research and put together a final report."

"Did you ever talk to him about what you found?" Jack continued

"I am great at research and a fantastic organizer despite what you might think."

"I didn't say you weren't."

"Can we get back on track?" Peter asked.

"Most of our discussions were short and involved me regurgitating anything new I came across."

"Had he recently reacted differently to any new information you provided?" Jack reached for a doughnut. The first since we sat down.

I sensed Jack's mind actively processing. I found it sexy. I also found myself imagining Jack and me deep in conversation, which was nice for a change. Sure, great biceps were a turn-on, but add a keen mind, and it sealed the deal.

"I don't think so. He actually seemed excited last time we spoke. He told me he was getting close to uncovering a big story. That was the night he died."

Peter followed up with a question of his own. "Are you sure there wasn't one single instance, during your conversations, where the subject caused you to pause?"

I focused on the first time I met Max Vanderbur and moved forward in time, running through the images like the flipbooks I'd had as a child.

"About a week and a half ago, I told him I found out someone had tried to block the sale of the Obermier property. That is the property on which Marston Place is built. He mumbled 'she knew' and when I asked him what he'd said, he mumbled something again about his student knowing."

"Did he mention the student's name?" Jack asked.

"Merrell, or something like that." My mind played connect the dots as I realized the name Max had mentioned might be the same person Thomas Brackford said Max had been seeing. Until I figured out who she was and whether she was pertinent, I'd keep the information to myself. I wouldn't want to accidentally steer us in the wrong direction.

"That background gives us something to look into. Now, time for the plan," Peter pronounced.

"Go right ahead. Fill us in on our plan." Jack's words came out sarcastically and I wondered what was going on between the two of them.

"Thomas Brackford must hold some key information about the mysterious big guy. I think someone needs to go to the hospital to talk to him," Peter said.

"I don't think they're going to let anyone near him," I said.

"Unless he needs a private meeting with his attorney. Don't you think?" Peter opened his wallet, stared directly at Jack and slid a dollar bill across the table.

"Ah, so you're paying top dollar to hire me as Thomas Brackford's attorney. Unfortunately—"

"It does make sense," I added, happy we were going to be taking some sort of action. I wanted us to find out who the creepy big guy was soon or I'd be buying a gun. I had no idea if I could get a gun legally due to my situation. If not, I'd probably have to get one illegally and that would mean keeping another secret from the marshals.

"One problem. You can't hire a lawyer for someone without the person's permission. Why don't I check in on him on my way to work, as a friend?" Jack glanced in my direction and slid the dollar bill toward me. I smiled at Peter and promptly put the buck in my pocket.

"While you go visit Thomas Brackford, Ms. Doughnut Hoarder and I are going to go upstairs and put her apartment back in order." Peter glanced at my plate.

I looked down surprised to see it topped with three additional doughnuts. I had no memory of grabbing them, but I doubted Peter or Jack had put them there. And the other option, of some impish little doughnut elf lugging those huge chocolate covered delights onto my plate, didn't ring true even to gullible me.

———

"Step away from the panties!" I said, pointing my hand at Peter like a gun. He was swinging a pair of my genuine leather panties around his finger. They were electric blue with black lace trim and the sight of them was bittersweet.

The sexy lingerie had been a gift at my wedding shower. The day after the shower I caught my fiancé Kevin in bed with one of my future bridesmaids. I went ballistic, hysterically crying, and screamed at them to get the hell out. Kevin hadn't argued about it being his apartment, they simply scrambled across the room and out the front door.

Betrayal wasn't what made the panties bittersweet. It's what happened afterward. Sobbing, I had taken his laptop off the coffee table, planning to hide it as some sort of benign revenge. When I heard someone outside I hid in the coat closet. Watching through a crack in the bi-fold door, I saw Kevin enter, followed by a man with a gun. The man demanded Kevin's laptop. Kevin turned toward the coffee table. Looking back at the man, he explained to him that it was missing. The man responded by shooting Kevin twice in the head.

"Okay, no need to shoot! Aspen?"

The sound of my name in conjunction with the word shoot catapulted me back to the present. "Give them to me, pervert," I said, trying to infuse some playfulness back into the air.

"Not so fast. These don't seem to belong here. All the other underwear appears simple and utilitarian. Are you sure the person responsible for ransacking your apartment didn't leave them? I think you should try them on so we can determine if they really are yours?"

"Utilitarian?"

"I mean, even you have to admit the others can't compare to this spicy thing," Peter flung the panties in my direction.

I was getting uncomfortable talking about my panties, but still felt the need to defend my wears. "They're all cute."

"I'm not so sure. Maybe you should model all of them and I'll be the judge."

Peter seemed oblivious to the effect he had on me. Sure, I fantasized about Jack with no clothes, but Peter's the one I'd choose if I wanted a man to hold me close. I changed the subject. "What are we doing after we finish picking up?"

"I can take a hint. No lingerie modeling today, right?"

"I don't think Madeline would approve. Besides, don't you think we need to get cracking on our plan?"

"I think you need to review your research, looking for anything important you might have missed. I'm going to ask Victor to open the shop so I can nose around Martin-Stone Development."

"I want to go! After all, I'm the one who knows the male half of the Martins."

"Precisely why you're not going anywhere near them."

"Fine. I have to be back at my office by noon anyway." I didn't tell him I suspected the phone call I was waiting for might be related to Max's death. If I had, Peter would insist he should sit in on the call and a least one of us should be snooping around Martin-Stone Development.

"I'll call Jack later and see about all of us meeting for dinner around seven-thirty. Danza del Pollo, okay?" Peter had his hand on the doorknob ready to go.

"Si," I said. "Adios," I added as Peter took off down the stairs.

———

Moore Time's filing cabinet sat virtually empty, reflecting my meager number of clients. I removed the Marston folder and read my notes about the community. Nothing caught my eyes, so I pulled out the Martin Development and Stone Development files.

Upon further review, two events stood out. The first was the grass roots group led by Caden Stone that had challenged the purchase of the Obermier property. It demonstrated the friction between the two development companies. The second was the unexpected merger. That action seemed contrary to the original goals of Martin Development.

I read through the scribbles in a spiral notebook I used whenever I talked with Max. On the day I told Max about the grass roots organization, I'd jotted down the word, excited. In hindsight, I could see his reaction had been more of a desperate excitement. A little more than a week later he was dead.

Picking up the handset from the phone, I held it to my ear to make sure I had a dial tone. The mystery lady said she'd call around noon. It was now one o'clock. Jack was probably off being a lawyer and Peter, well, who knew what he was doing, but I should have been doing my job. I put my research files away and made a list of tasks to complete.

The phone rang as I started to lock my office door. I hurried back inside. "Moore Time..." I caught my breath, "Good afternoon, how may I help you?"

"Ms. Moore? This is Harry Corbitt. Can we meet?"

My expectation of hearing the mystery woman's voice on the other end triggered a slight agitation which I tried hard not to let escape. "Is something wrong with your phone?"

"No."

I resisted my urge to fill the silence, as I waited for him to continue.

"Are you still there?" I asked.

"Yes."

To hell with trying to hold in my agitation. "What do you want?"

"I'd like to meet."

"About what?"

"I'd rather not say."

"Look. I have to go. I will call you later. Goodbye." I hung up the phone. Weirdo. He'd be waiting a long time for a call from me.

A white sedan appeared in my rearview mirror and followed me when I turned onto Gravois Road. The car looked exactly like the one that had been parked by the café across the street from my office. The parking spots in front of the café were ten minute, get-your-cappuccino-and-go spaces. The sedan had been there all morning.

I squinted, as I looked in the rearview mirror trying to make out the driver behind the wheel. The sedan was back a few car lengths, but I thought I saw enough to cause my neck to prickle. The driver looked like Harry Corbitt. Whoever it was, I wanted to make sure they weren't following me. I took a quick right turn. A few seconds later, the sedan was behind me. To be sure I wasn't overreacting, I made another quick turn.

The good news? The white sedan didn't follow me. The bad news? I turned left onto a one-way street going the wrong direction.

10

BLOOD DRIPPED on the deflated airbag. My face hurt like hell. Worse than when I was twelve and ran face first into a tree trying to get away from Jimmy Manson, the school bully. At least this time there weren't a bunch of kids standing around laughing.

I coughed, trying to expel whatever particles I'd breathed in when the airbag inflated. I hopped out of the Jeep and made my way to the other car. Thank God the driver seemed uninjured. She appeared to be in her early twenties with her hair pulled back in a ponytail and her face devoid of makeup. She wore sweats, like she'd just finished working out. She looked pleasant enough.

"God damn it! Why in the hell did you turn down a one way street?" she screamed at me from inside her car.

"Ma'am, I'm so sorry, I —"

"Ma'am? Look bitch, you are old enough to be my mother."

Oh, Lord. "I know you must be upset."

"You're damn right I'm upset. I bought this car yesterday."

Where from, a junkyard? The car sported primer gray and the back fender contained several dents - not my fault. A big crack traveled diagonally across the windshield. Now, that might have been my fault, but the cracked window in the back - no way.

"My insurance will cover the damage," I offered.

Sirens sounded in the background. The police car pulled up behind the primered car. Officer Storey, who had handcuffed me at Thomas Brackford's house, stepped out. On one hand, I was happy to see a familiar face. On the other, I didn't think it looked good being in an accident so soon after my first run in with the police.

"Ms. Moore?" Officer Storey approached me without a gun pointed at my face. Still, his light grey eyes and grey hair contrasted with his dark skin, commanding my attention.

"Yes, officer."

"I thought that was you. In trouble again so soon?"

Obviously his question was rhetorical and I was extremely embarrassed, so I kept my mouth shut.

"You need an ambulance? There's a little blood on your face."

"I don't think so. I had a small nosebleed from the airbag. Stopped bleeding though."

"What about a tow truck?"

"That's okay. I'll just drive to the shop."

"I'm not sure that will work."

"I'm not being taken in again, am I?"

"No. Your Jeep's not capable of moving on its own."

Scanning my Jeep, my eyes zeroed in on green water flowing from underneath its carriage. "A tow truck would be nice, thanks."

I gathered my personal items from my Jeep. Officer Storey must have talked to the young woman for a long time because just as he finished the tow truck pulled up.

"You got someone who can pick you up?" Officer Storey asked as he approached me.

"I, well, let me think for a second."

No way would I call Stephanie. Calling Peter was probably not a good idea, just yet. Mrs. Rippetoe didn't drive. I continued to flip through my internal Rolodex, until Officer Storey interrupted.

"Why don't I give you a ride to the station and I'll take your statement when we get there. That will give you time to find a ride home."

"Thanks." I watched as the tow truck hauled away my pride and joy.

Officer Storey opened the passenger side door of his police car. I slid into the front seat as gracefully as I could, my hands full of stuff I'd retrieved from my Jeep. Items fell onto the seat and the floor.

I banged into the screen on the laptop mounted between the front seats. "Oh gosh. I'm sorry."

"Don't worry. These are almost indestructible."

Keyword, 'almost'. "I'm sure you think I'm some kind of reckless driver, but I haven't been here that long and—"

"No need to explain. My daughter moved to Los Angeles and called me just last night complaining about how she is having a hard time finding her way around. She's about the same age as you. I sure miss her."

I turned to face him as he drove. Tiny wrinkles flanked the corner of his eye, revealing him to be a man of many smiles. He wasn't smiling now.

"When did she move?"

"Last month. Her husband got transferred with his job. I miss my grandson too."

Sadness permeated his voice. He seemed like a decent man. Sure, he'd handcuffed me earlier, but he'd only been doing his job.

"How long have you lived here?" he asked.

"Ten months. Well, almost eleven." As I answered his question I realized I had lived in St. Louis almost a year and probably came across as more directionally challenged than new to the area.

"Do your husband and children like St. Louis?"

"I'm not married. I moved here by myself and so far I like the city a lot. The people are friendly."

"Yes, they are. What brought you here?"

"I came here to start my business."

"Why did you choose St. Louis?"

Because my life collapsed around me? Because a government agency thought the Midwest was the best place for me to get lost? If I told him the truth about how my fiancé's involvement with embezzling crooks got him murdered and how I had been the one to finger the killer, he might think me a hero or more accurately a poor judgment of men. None of it mattered. Officer Storey would get the scripted version, the one I had memorized when I walked out the door of my old life and into my new one.

"My mother had been adopted and spent years trying to find her birth family. She believed they might be in St. Louis. My parents were on their way here when they were both killed in an automobile accident. I decided to finish my mom's research so I moved here." I clenched my teeth waiting for lightning to strike. The hardest part of being in the Witness Protection Program wasn't looking over your shoulder, but living every day as a lie.

"I'm sorry your parents passed. That must have been tough for you. Have you made any progress with your search?"

"No. I opened my business thinking I would have some free time, with me being my own boss, but I haven't had much of that lately."

"The guys at the station were talking about your business. Do people buy a lot of time?"

"Business had been going well until my clients started being attacked."

"Sure seems like someone's targeting you."

"I thought the same thing. But if Max Vanderbur did kill himself maybe it's all a big coincidence. I'm still pretty nervous though. If he was killed, I'd feel a lot better knowing who did it instead of being afraid someone was after me."

"Aspen, I have a good sense about people. My sense about you is that you are good people and you're too young to be running around afraid all the time."

"You're good people too," I said, smiling from the true joy of knowing he was kind behind his badge and gun.

"I'm going to share something with you because I think it will put you at ease. But I'll deny I said anything if someone asks. This isn't conclusive, but from what I hear, they do believe someone killed the professor and they're interviewing one of his students."

"Is the student's name, Merry?"

"I believe her name was Merrill. They may be re-interviewing you too."

"Oh." No other words left my mouth because my mind raced. Being an eyewitness in a murder had been hard enough. I didn't think I'd survive a full blown investigation where I was the prime suspect. The marshals would have no other choice but to give the police my real information. If I could find out who killed Max before the police, I'd be able to lead them to the real suspect and save myself from a very public exposé.

"I'll meet you inside after I park my vehicle around back." Officer Storey pulled up the front of the station.

"I can wait out here for you."

"I have to fill out some paperwork and you'll need to sign a few things."

"I don't mind waiting outside"

"Relax. They aren't going to interview you right now. In fact, forget I said anything about it. Might never happen."

Forget? I'm sure he was trying to make the additional interview sound routine, but any interview with the police was far from routine. "Thanks, Officer Storey."

"Call me Eli. If my daughter ever needed anything, I'd be glad to know she could get help from an officer. Here, take my business card. My direct number is on the back. You ever need my help, you call me."

He turned out to be a valuable source of information. I appreciated him sharing things with me in confidence and knew I had found another person in St. Louis who might be worth trusting. "Thanks, Officer Storey."

"Eli, remember?"

———

The station bustled. Two young boys fitted with handcuffs captivated me. I wondered if I were being privy to their future careers. The only part of their conversation

I could make out were the words, 'stolen car'. Nearby a lady in spandex shorts and tight shirt sat in a chair. Her straggled bleached blonde hair with its dark crown covered her face. Uniformed officers paraded through the station while a couple of guys wearing suits stood by the door talking. I was thankful the place hadn't been as busy when they'd brought me in covered in blood.

"Ready, Ms. Moore?" Eli walked past me, heading toward a small conference room.

I followed. "Only fair for you to call me Aspen."

He took my statement. I thanked him over and over for only giving me a warning and promised him I'd contact the other woman to take care of her car. How he managed to let me slide with only a warning I didn't know, and I didn't ask. I walked back toward the front door and sat down in a chair, preparing myself for my call to Peter. With only four numbers punched in, my phone started ringing.

"Hello, you've reached Moore Time."

"Ms. Moore, how are you?"

"I'm sorry, with whom am I speaking?"

"John Martin."

I probably let the silence hang a little longer than I should, but I was shocked. "How can I help you?"

"Yesterday our meeting ended abruptly and I'd like to apologize. As a token of my apology please accept my invitation to accompany me to the Black and White Ball."

"I'm busy."

"I didn't tell you when."

"Going with you isn't appropriate giv—"

"Don't worry. It won't be a date. I thought you might be interested in networking for your business. Many local celebrities will be attending."

Accepting his invitation could be good or it could be inherently bad. I wasn't quite sure how to decide. I began mulling over the possible outcomes when someone called my name. I turned toward the voice and found Jack.

"Thank you."

"Good. The ball is next Friday at 9:00 p.m. Wha—"

"I definitely can't go tomorrow night," I said.

"No, next Friday."

Out of the corner of my eye I watched as Jack closed in. I was confused about how my conversation with John Martin went from me pondering my decision to him thinking I'd accepted. All I cared about was ending the conversation. "Fine. I'll meet you at 9:00."

"I don't mind picking you up."

Jack stood next to me. "I'm sorry I have someone waiting for me. Goodbye."

"What are you doing here?" Jack asked.

"Oh, you know, stuff."

"Are you trying to hide something?"

"Well, uh, you, I uh—"

"It can't be that bad."

Once he found out I wrecked my Jeep, he'd look at me and see a lunatic Tasmanian Devil wreaking havoc on St. Louis and probably run in the opposite direction. I had to say something so I blurted out the truth, "I thought I was being followed and drove my car onto a one way street into another car."

"I see." The calmness in his voice exaggerated the frantic tone of mine.

"They towed my car. I was about to call Peter for a ride."

"I'd be more than happy to give you a lift."

"I don't want to interrupt whatever you're doing."

"Nonsense, I'm all done for now. What are you going to do about a car?"

"I'm going to rent one."

"Why not borrow one of my cars?"

"I don't think that's such a great idea. If you didn't hear me, I just wrecked a car."

"Believe me. You'll be doing me a favor. My old car from college sits in my garage unused. I won't take no for an answer."

Jack put his arm around me as we walked to his car. I found his touch comforting and uncomforting at the same time. The only man who'd comforted me since moving to St. Louis was Peter, but with Madeline in the picture I never dared to act on it and that was fine. It allowed me the semblance of a relationship without actually having to become vulnerable.

I processed what I'd learned about Jack in the last few days. Defined biceps, keen mind, and gentle touch - an enticing trio! One that might be difficult to resist if he turns out to be unattached.

"The police interviewed one of Max's students today. And guess what her name is?" Proud of my investigative work I anticipated a pleased reaction.

"Mirella," Jack said.

"No it's n—"

"I overheard detectives talking about her. Seems you might be right. Max might have been murdered and the student looks like a suspect."

We approached his BMW. He opened the car door for me. I was a little more graceful getting into his car because Eli had given me a brown paper bag into which I'd deposited all my stuff. Graceful, yes. Classy, not so much.

"So, it's not Merrill?" I asked, buckling my seatbelt.

111

"It's Mirella. I didn't get a last name though."

"Why not?"

"I was lucky I got the first."

"It's a start. By the way, how'd your meeting with Thomas Brackford go?"

"He was completely sedated. I gave the young nurse my card and asked her to let me know the minute he seemed more coherent."

Young nurse? Hmm, interesting adjective. I stored the little snippet of information.

When we pulled up to Jack's home in the Central West End, I mentally dropped my jaw because physically dropping it would have been gauche. The castle-like stone façade was out of a fairytale and an upper balcony ran the length of the home. A perfect place to let down my golden tresses.

"Sorry we couldn't pull around back, the city's working on the alleyway."

Curious what the inside of his place looked like, my excitement percolated as we got closer to his front door. I imagined the inside would be just as spectacular as the outside.

We reached the steps leading to the door and Jack took a right onto a stone pathway. "We'll just cut through."

Evidently a tour of his home was not on the agenda, so I filed in behind him and followed him through the garden. The area was more of an outdoor living room. All types of potted plants lined the patio and multiple chairs surrounded a copper fire pit. Continuing on a second path, we reached the garage.

He pressed several buttons on the combination pad. As the door opened, Jack fiddled with his keychain.

"She's all yours." He handed me the key.

Who cared about touring his home, I was stunned. I tried not to lose my composure. Jack's college car was the ugliest automobile I had ever seen. The Fuglymobile.

"Thanks, it's perfect."

11

THE FIRST PLACE I NEEDED to go was home. The first thing I needed to do once I got there was take something for the pain that had begun to emanate from my bones. I drove in silence all the way back to my apartment, no singing, not even a whistle or a hum.

Walking through the door I was elated to see everything still in its place. I popped a single pain killer left over from a run in with an icy sidewalk last winter. It would be strong enough to kick the pain without causing me to drive head on into a car, again.

A few drops of blood from my nose had fallen on my shirt, so I tossed it on top of the other bloody clothes I'd taken off yesterday. An unwelcomed pattern was forming.

I put on another shirt then crawled in bed for a few minutes to let the pill take effect. When I woke up it had been way more than a few minutes.

By the time I picked up Thomas Brackford's mail, I only had time to run by my office before heading off to meet Peter and Jack at Danza del Pollo. Confronting Mr. Q's neighbor would have to wait for another day.

Halfway through my office door, with paper bag in tow, I heard a ring come from the bottom drawer of my file cabinet. My time to chat was limited, but if I didn't talk to her now who knew when we'd be able to talk again.

I had stashed the pre-paid phone I'd taken from my secret box into the bottom of the cabinet earlier. Sometime soon I'd need to toss it and get a new one to be safe. The safest way to communicate was using a pay phone, but life wasn't like that anymore. I hurried to remove the box of file folders from the drawer, then dug through five bags of candy to reach the box of tampons in which I'd hidden my phone.

"Hey Mom!" I ran back to the front to lock the door

"Amelia! How are you honey?"

Hearing my real name filled me with conflicting emotions. I had hated my name growing up, but now I fought off a nagging urge to take it back. "You aren't using someone's cell phone are you?"

"No, honey, I picked up a new pre-paid like you told me to."

"Are you sure nobody is listening?"

"Amelia, honey, I wouldn't risk calling you if I thought either of us would be in danger."

I'd be devastated if something happened to her. I hadn't always cared. At sixteen, she met my stepfather and moved us to another state in the middle of my junior year of high school. I hated her then. Hated how she made me leave my friends, my school, and how she sacrificed my happiness for her own. But the tables had turned. My decision to enter the program had depended on my parents honoring my request for them to move someplace else as well. My mom left behind a life carefully constructed with strong and colorful fibers. A life much richer, much harder to let go of than a sixteen-year-old's life. I loved her more than anything in the world because of what she sacrificed.

"So, tell me how you've been," she said.

I told her all about my accident. When I opened my mouth to tell her about Jack loaning me his car, a burst of laughter came out instead.

"What's so funny?"

"The car is horrendous! I've nicknamed it the Fuglymobile. An orange Ford Fairmont station wagon."

"That doesn't sound so bad. Lots of room for groceries and such."

"I don't think there's a single place on the car where you can see your reflection. Rust has taken over and there are a multitude of dents."

I continued to go on about the Fuglymobile. When I settled down, I told her about Jack.

"Oh, a lawyer. Is he single?"

Before I'd gotten engaged, my mother worked diligently trying to marry me off. She'd spend hours on Match.com and email me possible suitors - GR8DOC seeks perfect patient, YERKNIGHT seeks damsel in distress. I'm not sure who had been more devastated when my fiancé died. I know she must weep at the possibility of never being able to attend my wedding if I do finally fall in love again.

"No, Mom, he's not married."

"Well?" she said, begging me to continue with a detailed description.

"He's intriguing. Good looking, smart, and even nice."

"Sounds perfect."

"Not so sure about perfect. Anyway, he's a friend of Peter's."

"Why wouldn't Peter approve? Didn't you say you two were just friends?"

"We are, but I'm not sure if I'm ready for another relationship and being Peter's friend it could get complicated. Besides even if I think Jack is cute it doesn't mean he thinks I am."

"You are beautiful inside and out. He'd be the lucky one."

Ah, the comfort. She's the one who lifts me up no matter what. We continued to talk about Jack until she was satisfied then she asked if I had talked to Brian.

Brian was my brother and collateral damage. He and my fiancé had started a side business and as Kevin's partner he would have been in danger without the program. We'd conspired to name ourselves after trees because we could. His new name was Birch. WitSec relocated him to New York City. He too had been in the technology field, but now worked as a chef.

"I haven't talked to him lately." The sadness in my voice was hard to deny. Brian and I had been close all our lives and now I spoke with him at best twice a year. "How's Daddy-O?" I asked, changing the subject.

"He's fine. You know, he was talking about getting another motorcycle?"

Daddy-O was the man I thought had ruined my life at sixteen, but turns out he was like a father to me and more importantly he made my mom happy. He'd almost died a few years ago when he wrecked his Harley. It was a miracle the only permanent damage was intermittent vertigo.

"You told him no, right?"

"Not exactly. I said I'd take lessons and he could ride with me. Of course you can imagine how well that went over."

I laughed. The thought of my little mother toting big Daddy-O on the back of a Harley was hilarious. "Mom, I have to run. I love you."

The mom magic worked. She had uplifted my spirit, but my heart still ached for a mother I might never get to hug again.

I removed the tools from the paper bag and threw them into my closet. I quickly filled up the empty space inside what had now become, by default, my new briefcase. I dashed to the Fuglymobile. If I timed it right, I'd hit all the green lights, so no one would be able to get a good look at me inside Fugly.

———

Breezing by the hostess desk, I scanned the restaurant for Peter and Jack. I was twenty minutes late and wouldn't blame them if they'd packed up and left.

Toward the back of the room, my eyes met Jack's. I walked over to his table.

"Hi, Aspen, I wondered if you still planned on coming."

"Hi. Where's Peter?"

"He called earlier and said something came up."

"Oh." I acted like dining alone with him was no big deal. My heart raced and my knees almost buckled. The conversation with my mom had churned up all kinds of ideas about Jack. Clearly I was not ready for anything more exciting than naughty thoughts inside my head.

"This place is one of my favorites. You need to try the PM."

"What's that?"

"Pomegranate Margarita. They are potent and they are addictive."

Jack, Margarita, and me – I didn't think I could handle a three-way. "I'll pass."

"Order one and if you don't like it, I'll drink it."

"We'll both have a PM," Jack said when the waiter approached.

I let him walk away without changing what Jack ordered. I immediately reached for the chips and salsa. If I was going to drink something potent and addictive on top of the pain killer then I had to make darn sure I didn't do it on an empty stomach.

"Let's decide on dinner and then we can relax," Jack suggested.

"Are they famous for anything besides the PM?"

"Two of my favorites are the Chicken Molé and the Carnitas Especial. The Especial entree is excellent. They marinate pork in coriander and cilantro, then slow-roast the meat, place it on a bed of Mexican rice, and top it with grilled vegetables. But get the Chicken Molé if you want something spicy."

"Presented like a professional chef. You sure you don't work here?"

"No, but I eat here enough to keep them in business. Plus, I won a charity auction last year that entitled me to a free cooking class with their chef. Do you want to order both and we can split them?"

"Can we add a guacamole?"

"Sure, let's make it a party." He lifted the margarita our waiter had dropped off seconds before. "Cheers."

I lifted my glass for the toast and took a sip. My taste buds purred as the sweet liquid made its way across my tongue and down my throat.

We chatted about nothing in particular, the weather, the Cardinals, and my Jeep.

"I guess I should fess up," Jack said.

Intriguing. Jack had actually done something naughty and was ready to confess.

"Go on," I said, amused.

"Peter asked me to call and tell you we were canceling tonight."

"He did?"

"Yes, but I wanted a chance to have dinner with you."

"Only two sips and you're already spilling your secrets? What'll you do when you finish your entire glass?" I winked.

Damn. My eye had a life of its own. I couldn't believe it winked at him when I'd almost fainted at the thought of us dining alone. The Pomegranate Magic or Margarita or whatever the drink was called had obviously caused a misfire.

"You really are very amusing. That's one of the reasons I want to get to know you better."

Amusing made me sound like an animal act, as if I were a sea lion balancing a ball on my nose. "And the others?"

"The others?" He looked confused.

"The other reasons you want to get to know me."

"You're sweet, interesting, but most of all you're—"

"Here are your dinners," the waiter announced placing our food on the table.

The plates sizzled and the steam infused with lime and roasted Chile Pepper made its way to my nose. The smell was sensational, but not enough to distract me from Jack's last statement. What was he going to say? I had to figure out a way to get him back on the subject without appearing pushy.

"And you were saying?" I asked.

"I was saying how much of a pleasure discovering more about you will be. Bon appétit." Jack picked up his fork.

"Bon appétit," I replied, picking up my fork with the knowledge that I may never learn the biggest reason he wanted to get to know me.

We both took a few bites before resuming our conversation.

"Do you like running your own business?" he asked.

"So far I love being a business owner, except for the last couple of days. They've been rough."

"I'd have to agree."

I lived my life, so dissecting it wasn't my idea of fun. Somehow I'd managed to jump head first into a turbulent sea from which I could not escape. What I needed was a break. "How long have you known Peter?"

"Since we were roommates in college. We formed an immediate camaraderie when we discovered we both hailed from Virginia."

"Are you from Fairfax too?"

"No. Not far though. I'm from Alexandria. Grew up in Old Town."

While Jack took a bite of food, I offered up something about me. "I attended the University of Virginia."

He probably already knew it because I'd spouted off to Peter one night about where I went to college, never anticipating Peter having been born and raised in Virginia. I'd had to pretend I never graduated, because Amelia did, not Aspen.

"Really? Peter never told me. I had applied to the University of Virginia, but when Washington University offered me early acceptance I couldn't wait to get away from home. I moved to St. Louis a few months before my freshman year. Of course you were probably still in high school."

"Are you trying to flatter me?"

"Honestly, you don't look a day over twenty-nine."

I almost choked on my Carnitas. I loved this man.

"You're close. I'm actually twenty-five."

He choked on his Chicken Mole and his face flushed.

"I'm only kidding, Jack. I'm in my thirties."

He looked relieved. "So how does a beautiful looking woman like you end up in St. Louis as Peter Parker's neighbor?"

The Mariachi band approached our table playing violins, guitars and other instruments I didn't recognize. Each of us smiled politely and played with our food as we waited for the men in their hats to leave. The music faded as the band made their way to the other side of the restaurant.

"Exactly what kind of law do you practice?" I dug my tortilla chip into the guacamole hoping he wouldn't notice I had changed topics.

"Criminal defense, mostly white collar cases."

Great. He'd most likely heard about the case in which I testified because of the involvement of organized crime. The case had been high profile and the reason why both my brother and I were put in the program. "Do you plan on staying in St. Louis?"

"Definitely. I'm shooting for partner."

Jack talked all about his career. He seemed focused and driven, like I had been once. I took one last sip of my second PM and glanced at my watch. Three hours had passed, yet it felt like minutes.

"Sorry to break up our party," I said, "but I have to be heading home."

"Are you okay to drive?"

"Of course, and I probably wouldn't be harmed if I did hit something. Remember, I'm in fug..uh, your iron wagon."

"Yes, she's exceptional, isn't she?"

"The best," I lied.

"I still think I should follow you to make sure you get home okay."

"That's gallant of you, thanks."

The waiter placed the check between us on the table. Not one to make assumptions, I reached for it. Jack was quick-handed, grabbing it and giving the waiter his credit card.

We each picked up a mint on our way and he walked me out to Fugly. The drive home didn't take long. I drove past my building, hoping to find a space. No luck. I parked one block over and Jack pulled in behind me.

"Are you sure you don't mind walking me to my door?"

"It's my pleasure."

I extracted my paper bag from inside the car. Embarrassed, I pointed out the flaw to ensure he didn't think I was a hobo. "Just waiting to find the perfect briefcase."

He smiled, placed his jacket over me, his arm around me, and walked me to my apartment. At my door, he leaned over and gave me the first kiss on the lips I'd had since the night before Kevin was murdered, if I didn't count the Peter faux pas.

My heart and brain began a battle. To tongue or not to tongue, that was the question. Tongue, would he think me too easy? No tongue, too prudish? The margaritas got the best of me and I slid my tongue inside. My temperature rose. Definitely hot.

Jack welcomed me, then pulled back, ending things with a gentle peck. "Aspen, I enjoyed tonight."

"Ditto." The alcohol and body heat had taken their toll.

In my stupor, I'd forgotten Toby had fixed my lock. I handed Jack my paper bag and started digging through my purse.

"I'd like to see you again – a real date," he said.

A date? A real date with Jack? At some point I guess I had to get back on the stud, or the horse, or whatever. "Okay."

"I'll call you," he whispered and handed back my paper bag.

The three words women hated to hear – 'I'll call you.' Nine times out of ten it was a sentence with no meaning, an empty promise, a phrase of convenience. I definitely hoped Jack's was the one out of ten.

12

A FEW RUNAWAY CRUMBS from the sausage-biscuit I'd picked up at the drive-through remained on my shirt. Nothing I couldn't brush away and my coffee cup remained upright between my legs. A successful start to my day.

Stepping inside Mr. Q's house, I headed straight for the espresso machine on the kitchen counter. It did everything, from grinding the beans to squirting out froth. I'd used Mr. Q's machine so many times that if my business ever died – which unfortunately teetered on the realm of possibility - I might find work as a barista.

Before confronting the neighbor, I checked the screened-in porch in case the culprits had returned Mr. P. The porch was as empty as it had been the day he disappeared. I walked back to the kitchen defeated, removed the dog bowl from the refrigerator and cleaned it out. Why someone hadn't contacted me or Mr. Q was a mystery. They should have called by now with a muffled voice, demanding money or something. The lack of a phone call was a bad sign.

I drank my cappuccino and tried to relax as I mentally ran through what I planned to ask the neighbor. Extracting enough information from him to determine his involvement in Mr. P's disappearance, without actually accusing him, would require a delicate hand.

Peeking out the front window, I saw the neighbor fiddling with a bush outside his house, which was a relief. I'd rather discuss Mr. P in public than inside where no one could hear my screams for help. I made my way across the street.

He was writing on a pad of paper as I approached.

"Hey, do you know whose car that is?" he asked. "I bet someone abandoned the junker."

"Actually, it's mine. I mean the thing belongs to a friend. My car's in the shop."

"I'm sorry."

Me too. "Can I ask you a question?"

"Ask away." The neighbor folded the paper and put it in his pocket.

"Did you take Mr. Quetzalcoatl's dog to the park or any place else? I'd been told you sometimes take him for walks." I knew I had butchered Mr. Q's name, but the neighbor didn't seem to mind.

He began clicking his pen. "No. Why? Is something wrong with him?"

"Not exactly. You do like Mr. Personality, don't you?" I asked in order to further read his body language.

In my previous life I'd hired a consultant to teach my employees the art of reading body language. The instructor guaranteed an increase in productivity, but the seminar resulted in my employees acting unnatural for weeks. I, however, found the skill invaluable. Everyone's body told a story.

"I'm Mr. P's uncle. I adore him. I used to own his sister, but she got run over by a car."

"Oh my God, I'm so sorry." I was torn between feeling sorry for him and being suspicious of him. He had lied to Peter about not knowing the breed of dog, but he had lost his pet tragically, and that was terribly sad.

"Took me a while to get over it, but having Mr. P so close helps."

I listened as barking noises came from behind his house. "Did you get another dog?"

"No, that dog lives behind me." He shifted from foot to foot, indicating nervousness.

I zeroed in on his legs. "Eww. You, have—"

"Ouch, damn ant hills. The rain brings 'em out every time." He stomped around.

"Doesn't look like they're going away," I said.

"No shit. I need to go." He continued stomping all the way back to his front door.

His words were worthless and what he didn't say spawned more questions. The biggest one was why he had lied to Peter.

Until that question was answered and Peter came up with some leads, I had to turn my attention to bigger matters. I jumped inside Fugly and headed for the University. I figured only one Mirella could possibly exist at the University and if I asked around, somebody would recognize the name.

I parked in a primo space just inside the campus garage and walked to the student center. If I didn't have any luck, I'd head to some of the computer labs and then the library.

Students filled the center, most with their noses in a laptop. In my day we buried our nose in a book, but I understood the love affair with mobile computing. Before I walked away from my high-paying job and relocated to St. Louis as a pauper, I'd had access to technology every geek drooled over. I knew I'd never have the same setup, but a couple of more clients and I'd be upgrading my computing capabilities.

The students without laptops were eating lunch. I picked up a slice of pizza and headed toward a group who had pulled together a couple of tables. More than a decade had passed since I'd mingled as a student and I wasn't sure what the protocol was today. "Do you mind if I join you?"

A young man in an Abercrombie & Fitch shirt looked up at me. "What?"

"Can I join your group for lunch?"

"Yeah, I guess," he said, giving a what's-with-this-old-lady look to the two guys sitting next to him.

"Thanks. I hope one of you might be able to help me."

"They have an information desk downstairs near the front of the building," Abercrombie-boy replied.

"Actually, I'm kind of trying to solve a mystery and need to find a specific person."

The rambling conversations subsided and I had the attention of every single student at the table, except for the two young girls at the far end. They giggled as they fixated on their cell phones.

"I'm looking for a student. Her first name is Mirella."

A hint of recognition appeared in everyone's eyes, but only a guy midway down the table spoke. "What about her?"

He had thick dark hair that stood at attention with the help of gel. Most of the guys on campus looked as though they'd thrown on their casual shirts after digging them out of the dirty clothes basket. But he was business-like in a neatly pressed button-down oxford.

"Where can I find her?"

"Why are you looking for her?"

"I can't explain the details, but I believe she'd want to talk to me."

"Give me your name and number I'll make sure she gets it."

"I need to get in touch with her today. Do you have her number?"

"Yeah, but I don't think she'd appreciate me giving it out to some stranger, even though you are a girl."

A girl - so much better than being a ma'am.

"Can you call her?"

He punched two buttons on his phone, which told me Mirella was on his speed dial.

"Mir, it's Nick. Some lady is asking for you. Hold on. Hey, what's your name?"

"Aspen, tell her I need to talk to her about Marston," I answered, hoping that bit of information wouldn't spook her.

"Are you with the police?" he asked.

"No, I helped out her professor."

"She had been helping Max. Uh huh. Okay. Sure. Uh huh." Nick kept eye contact with me as he spoke with Mirella. After a long pause he ended the call. "She's at the library and said she'll be here in about fifteen minutes."

"Thanks, I appreciate your help, Nick."

"How'd you know my name?"

"You said it on the phone."

"Oh, yeah, right. So did you know Professor Vanderbur well?"

"Fairly well, I'd been working with him for several months."

By now, most everyone had lost interest and left the table. Nick remained, as well as the student with the Abercrombie shirt who was fixated on a perky brunette sitting next to him.

"A lot of the students thought he was argumentative, but really, he was challenging. He always wanted his students to be the best. I think that made him depressed."

Max was anything but depressed. Nick must not have known him all that well.

"Yes, he was a nice man."

Abercrombie-boy took off with the brunette and left Nick and me alone at the table. I took a bite of my pizza.

"She didn't do it," Nick whispered.

"Didn't do what?"

"Didn't kill Max. They talked to her today, the police did. They aren't so sure he killed himself, but it sounds like it to me. Mirella said Max seemed depressed last time she spoke to him. "

I didn't think Max had come across as depressed, but it worried me that perhaps I just hadn't noticed the signs. "Why'd they talk to her?"

"Mirella didn't agree with one of the grades Max had given her, so she called him on it. A few students overheard their discussion and thought she was actually mad at him."

"What did Max do?"

"Nothing. Mirella's smart. She never took his word on anything and he never expected her to." Nick ran his hand lightly across his hair.

"Did the students go to the police?"

"No, the police listened to a voice mail message Mirella left at his house."

———

I heard what sounded like a woman clearing her throat. I wiped pizza sauce from my mouth and turned around to find the biggest head of pitch black hair I'd ever seen, with curls like Slinky toys gone wild. Each strand stretched just below her shoulders. For such a big head of hair, her stature was small. She wasn't beautiful, but rather bookish and mousy. She set her backpack on the table and held out her hand.

"Hi, I'm Mirella Russo."

She reminded me a bit of myself years ago. My hair had been big and curly too, but blonde and much longer, with wisps of Irish red that only showed in the sunlight. I had tried to be bookish, but too many frat parties kept me out of the library. I guess she wasn't a lot like me after all, but the more I stared at her the more familiar she seemed.

"I have to get going," Nick announced.

That's when I realized she looked exactly like Nick.

"Are you? Uh..." I couldn't get the words to come out of my mouth. "Are you identical twins?"

"Took you long enough," Nick said.

"How can you be identical twins?"

"We're monozygotic. You can find us in the medical journals. I'm the older one." He puffed out his chest.

"Wow." I didn't know what else to say.

Nick turned and walked away.

I finally found more words. "I didn't think identical twins of the opposite sex existed."

"We're rare. The short version is we started out with extra chromosomes, then Nick dropped his X, I dropped my Y and we both became freaks of nature. We like to refer to ourselves as monozygotic simply for the reason you stated."

"Wow."

"Are you going to keep staring at me or did you want to talk?"

Her attitude slapped me across the face and made me acutely aware of the position of my eyes. "Sorry. I need to talk to you about what—"

My phone rang. I hated to stop the conversation, but didn't want to leave any call unanswered in case it was the mystery lady.

I mouthed the word 'sorry' and held up my index finger signaling to Mirella that I'd only be a minute. She seemed displeased.

"Ms. Moore! I am so glad to finally speak with you," the woman on the other end said.

"May I ask whose calling?"

"I've been trying to get in touch with you about Max Vanderbur."

I assumed it was the mystery woman. "Good, it's you. I got worried when you didn't call yesterday."

"Sorry. I'm a nurse. I've been on-call. I have this afternoon off. Can you come over?"

"What did you say your name was again?" She hadn't really given me her name, but I wanted to know who I'd be meeting.

"Mrs. Obermier."

"Mrs. Obermier? Like, in the Obermier property where Marston now exists?" Out of the corner of my eye I caught Mirella staring at me.

"Yes. Can you meet me at my home in an hour or so? I live in West County. I have some things I'd like to show you. Max had planned on giving them to you, but..."

I could tell she didn't want to speak the words. "I know. I can't believe he is gone either. What's your address?" I scribbled down the house number and street name as she recited them to me.

"Was that Sara Obermier?" Mirella asked, the second I ended the call.

"Yes, how did you know?"

"You called her Mrs. Obermier."

Of course I had. I couldn't remember if I called her Sara, but I must have.

"She wants me to come to her place."

"Do you mind if I come along?"

Mirella's role in this mess had yet to be identified. "I'm not sure that's a good idea."

"I spoke with her over the phone several months ago. I was helping Max."

"Do you know Max Vanderbur's partner?"

"I am or was his partner."

I found it odd that Max had called her his partner instead of his student. If she was telling the truth then having her with me when I talked with Sara Obermier would be beneficial. I might even be able to dislodge myself from this mishmash of mayhem by suggesting they work together to come to their own conclusion about the Marston deal.

Mirella waited while I picked up a piece of pepperoni that had somehow escaped my mouth and my boobs and fallen onto the speckled industrial floor. I wrapped it in my dirty napkin and deposited it and my empty cup into the trash before motioning Mirella to follow me.

"Should we take your car?" I asked, trying not to sound desperate. As long as I could keep other people from riding in Fugly I could pretend he didn't exist.

"No, Nick and I share a car and today is his day."

We left the student center and crossed the street to the garage. Someone honked and we both turned around. Nick waved as he drove by in a salsa red VW Beetle convertible. The car gave Nick and Mirella a little added splash of funky to an otherwise dark haired, drab-skinned, set of unusual twins. The car was slick, new, clean, and void of rust spots. I was envious.

"My car is in the shop," I started to explain, when I noticed a large man at the far entrance to the garage. I had to keep cool. Maybe it wasn't the stalker, but then again maybe it was.

"Mirella, I can't explain anything right now but we need to go back inside. So, just turn around and let's walk fast."

"But—"

"Mirella! Now!" I commanded under my breath.

We power walked toward the student center, keeping our pace even, so we wouldn't draw attention. I phoned Peter.

"Peter? I think the big guy is following me again."

"Are you sure?"

"No, but I don't want to take a chance. Can you pick me up? I can't get to the car."

"Where are you?"

"At the University Student Center. I'm with Mirella."

"What's a Mirella?"

"I'll explain when you get here. Meet us on the south side of the building."

"I'm leaving the shop now."

We didn't look back. Each time I glanced at Mirella, she appeared calm.

"Who is this guy?" she asked, finally breaking the silence.

"I think he's stalking me. He was nosing around my apartment and he showed up at my office."

"What does he want?"

"I don't know, but I think he was involved with a post office shooting too. So he's not exactly friendly."

"I heard about that on the news. Are you sure it's him?"

"No, but why take a chance?"

"Why waste time if it isn't him? Let's circle around and come up behind him so you can get a good look."

"Are you crazy? What if he has a gun?"

"I bet I know this campus better than he does, he won't even see us."

"You think we can do it?" I was warming up to the idea because time wasted was a waste of time and it also meant I could call off Peter. I didn't want him to know I was heading to Sara Obermier's house and secondly, I was sure Jack had told him everything that happened last night.

We circled around the garage and kept our eyes on the stalker. Mirella grabbed my hand and dragged me toward a steel door, which led to the stairwell. I followed her up the stairs. When we got to the second floor, she peeked over the railing. She seemed awfully brave for such a little thing and I wasn't about to appear weak, so I got up the nerve and took a look of my own. The man below was definitely the same shape as the shadowy big guy who'd had me hightailing it into my car the other night.

He was dressed entirely in black, Rambo style, his t-shirt tight and pants baggy, with lots of flaps and pockets.

He appeared scary like Mrs. Rippetoe described. We ducked back down to keep a low profile and to figure out what to do next. Peter would be here in another twenty minutes so we had to make our way back to the student center.

A car door slammed.

"Why the hell didn't you answer your cell phone?" a male voice demanded.

"Sir, the phone has been stolen. No chance yet to get a replacement," answered another male with a deep voice. I imagined the words had come out of the big guy's mouth.

"I had to have Simon track your car's GPS to find you."

"Sorry, Boss." And with those two words, Mr. Big Guy became Mr. Small.

"The Obermier problem needs to be put to rest," the boss said.

The ominous statement made me rise so I could catch a glimpse of the boss. I held my breath and urged myself not to make even the slightest sound before peering over the railing. Standing next to the big guy was none other than the adulterer, Samuel Martin. I dialed Sara Obermier's number.

"Sara?" I whispered.

"Who is this? I can't hear you."

"Sara, this is Aspen," I whispered a little louder.

I grabbed Mirella's hand and led her away from the railing into the stairwell and up the stairs to the top of the garage.

"Are you on your way?"

"Sara, we have a problem. Can you leave your house and meet me at the University student center garage?"

"Why? Did your car break down?"

"No, I think you're in danger. I'll explain when you get here. Just leave your house now."

"I need to call my neighbor to watch my son—"

"No, you better bring him. I think he'd be safer with you."

"You're scaring me," Sara said.

"I'm sorry but you need to get out of there now. What kind of car will you be in?"

"A silver Jaguar."

Great. Everyone was driving a nice car but me. "We'll be on the top level of the University garage back by the concrete barriers."

We leaned over the edge to assess the position of our enemy. They were gone. I didn't trust them. They might have stationed a second man to keep an eye on my car.

"Let's head over there."

Mirella and I walked toward the barriers. I dialed Peter. "Change of plans. It wasn't the big guy after all," I said. I added a light laugh so he wouldn't catch the terror in my voice.

"What?"

"I'm sorry, the guy left."

"So you don't need me to come get you even though I am more than halfway there?"

"No. I'm really sorry, Peter. I'll make it up to you."

"You will? Anything I want?"

Oh God. It amazed me how fast he could slip into horndog mode.

"Nope. Dinner or nothing."

"What about seven o'clock at Danza del Pollo since we didn't get to eat there last night?"

Was this a trick? I would have bet my stash of Hostess Ding Dongs that Jack would have already made the obligatory conquest call to his buddy telling him all about our secret rendezvous. Perhaps Jack was more complex than I thought.

"I'm not much in the mood for Mexican, what about Pho Mo?"

"Vietnamese it is then. See you at seven."

I often wondered why Peter never asked me a lot of questions. His gadget shop contained an abundance of products with the specific purpose of finding out information about other people, yet he never seemed to delve into the details of my life. Even though I didn't want him to probe my past, I still felt a little jilted.

"Do you think they're going to kill Sara Obermier?" Mirella asked.

I'd completely forgotten she was by my side. I had no reason to deliver my thoughts camouflaged in less definitive words. "Yes."

13

THIRTY MINUTES LATER a car made its way up the entrance ramp. I immediately recognized the hood ornament and I stood up from behind a concrete barrier where Mirella and I had been hiding.

The Jaguar pulled into a parking space near us. Sara Obermier stepped out of her car, her hair salt and pepper gray, long on the top, but tapered short around her neck. She looked more like a grandmother than a mother. "Aspen?" she asked, walking toward Mirella.

"No, I'm Aspen, this is Mirella Russo."

"Hi," Mirella said, extending her hand.

"You're the one who was working on the paper for your school project right?" Sara asked as she shook Mirella's hand.

"Yes ma'am."

"We need to get going. I thought we'd go to my office so we can talk," I offered.

Sara directed her attention toward me. "Can I talk to you in private?"

"Umm. Sure." Excluding Mirella was awkward, but Sara had only wanted to meet with me. I glanced at Mirella. "Do you mind giving us a second?"

Following Sara to the rear of her car, I noticed her son buckled up tight in the back seat.

Sara glanced back at Mirella before she spoke. "I'm not sure why Max would kill himself. It doesn't make sense to me, but I trusted him and he trusted you. He told me to contact you and only you if something happened to him," Sara said. She glanced at Mirella again. "Do you trust her?"

"I think so. She helped me find out that Samuel Martin wants to put an end to your questions about Marston, but if you aren't comfortable we don't have to bring her along."

Sara's eyes remained on Mirella. "If you think she can be trusted then it's fine with me." Sara looked around the parking lot. "Where's your car?"

"Might be safer if we all went in yours." It wasn't that I hated Fugly, I actually believed it wasn't safe to go to my car. I waved Mirella over.

"If you want we can go to my place. It's close by," Mirella said.

"It might be safer than my office," I said to Sara. "What do you think?"

Sara looked at her son inside the car and then back at me. "I'm not sure what's going on, but if you all think the safest place is Mirella's then let's go."

Eyeing Sara's son in the back, I claimed shotgun. It wasn't that I didn't like kids. In fact, I loved kids. But I didn't think I was up to offering goo-goo noises in order to keep him entertained.

"I live with my brother on Russell, near Soulard."

We turned left out of the parking garage and I caught a view of Fugly as we drove away.

"I'm almost afraid to ask, but why did I need to get out of the house so fast?"

After explaining to Sara my close encounters with the big guy and how I'd finally linked him to Samuel Martin, I thought she might stop the car and tell me to get the hell out. I wasn't the best person to be hanging out with at the moment. When I continued my story, I could see she was visibly nervous during my description of the danger she might be facing.

"Take a left," Mirella screamed.

Sara jammed on the brakes and made an erratic left turn, complete with squealing tires. I reached for the grab handle above the door as my body flew to the right. My hand missed and whipped back into my eye.

"Is everybody okay?" Sara asked. Her hands gripped the steering wheel and her eyes focused on the reflection of her son in the rearview mirror.

"Sorry, I wasn't paying attention. I'm up on the left. Go to the alley behind the house and we can park in front of the garage," Mirella said.

She sounded unusually perky and I wondered which Mirella was the true Mirella, this one or the stern one I'd first met in the student center.

"Why don't we park in the garage?" I asked.

"Can't, our landlord rents it out for storage."

The detached garages for the other homes backing to the alley appeared in good shape, but this garage had peeling paint and more than half the shingles missing from the roof. A quick peek inside the window on the garage's side door confirmed it was filled with boxes and old furniture.

We entered Mirella's home through the back door, which led into a kitchen with vintage blue metal cabinets and white appliances. Mirella placed her backpack on the Formica countertop. "Let's go in the dining room."

The dining room was smaller than the kitchen, separated from the living room by a set of half-sized built-in bookcases fronted with glass doors. The shelves were filled with paperback romances.

"I'll get us something to drink."

I listened to Mirella clinking around the kitchen and watched as Sara settled her son on her lap.

"What's his name?"

"Mitchell, after his father."

"Does he look just like him?" I asked making polite conversation.

"Yes, as a matter of fact. More now, since he turned two."

"I bet his dad is proud."

"He disappeared before Mitchell was born."

"Oh. I'm so sorry."

"Here we are." Mirella placed a tray on the table with a pitcher of water and three glasses of ice.

"Would you hold Mitchell for me while I run out to the car?" Sara shoved her son into my arms.

As soon as she walked out the back door, he began crying. I tried to soothe him by talking softly, but he continued to cry and point in the direction Sara had gone.

"Hi. Booga. Bugga. Bo. Bo," I sang in my highest voice with a big smile. Mitchell responded by crying louder.

I tried even harder to get his attention. "Uh, Bu bubu bu."

He stopped crying and I smiled, which sent him right back to crying again. I turned him toward me with his legs straddling my knee and bounced him up and down. He giggled. I bounced him faster and he giggled louder.

Sara came back into the room carrying a box. I was sure Sara would be impressed with how easily her little boy and I had acclimated to one another.

"You might not want to do that too much because..."

Large amounts of liquid loaded with chunks exited Mitchell's mouth and landed on my shirt.

"...I just fed him before we left," Sara finished, setting the box on the table."

"Oh boy," I said.

"I'm sorry Aspen, I should have warned you."

"My fault. I'm the one that took him on a wild bronco ride."

Mirella went into the kitchen and came back with some wet paper towels. I wiped off the barf the best I could. "Shall we get started?"

Sara reached into the box she'd brought in from the car and handed me a few pieces of paper. "I had planned on giving these to Max. These are some emails from my husband's computer. I printed them all off after he went missing."

"Went missing? I thought you meant he walked out on you. He's missing? That's terrible."

Mirella poured us some water. While Sara fussed with her son, I skimmed over what she'd handed me. The emails were between Mitch and others who were interested in buying the property that he and his brother had inherited from their father.

"Your husband didn't want to sell did he?" I said.

"No, he was trying to keep it in the family like his dad wanted, but his brother was pressuring him to sell."

"How long has he been missing?" Mirella asked.

"He disappeared over ten years ago."

I was no math wizard, but if her husband disappeared over ten years ago, then his son would have to be at least ten, not two.

"But Mitchell's only two," I said, almost daring her to come up with a viable explanation for the discrepancy.

"Let me explain."

"Please," Mirella requested, sounding as though she too had figured out the math.

"Mitch and I had been undergoing fertility treatments without success. We still had five embryos frozen when he disappeared. So I used them."

"Why did you wait so long?" I asked.

"I thought perhaps Mitch might be found, or God might bless me again with someone to love the way I loved Mitch. But one day I woke up with gray hair and an even deeper yearning for a child."

"It's wonderful you made a conscious decision to become a mom. Kids are blessings," I said, disregarding the throw up stain on my shirt.

"Am I going to be able to go home?" she asked.

"I don't know, Sara. I'm thinking you should stay at a hotel for a couple of days until we figure out what's going on."

"Why don't you stay here," Mirella offered, "Your car would be out of sight in the alley."

"That might be a good idea, Sara, so you won't be alone," I added.

"Are you sure? I think if someone is trying to kill me maybe I should go to the police."

"The police won't be able to do much. It's not like we have a recording of Samuel Martin threatening to kill you and I don't think they'd arrest him with no proof the conversation took place."

"You're probably right. The police weren't much help when Mitch disappeared."

"Stay here. My brother, Nick, won't mind. He loves kids," Mirella said.

Sara staying at Mirella's house would be better than her staying at a hotel. Mirella and her brother Nick could keep a watchful eye and perhaps Mirella could get some useful information out of Sara. But, Sara looked nervous.

"Could we have a moment alone, Mirella?" I asked.

Mirella headed into the kitchen. Once Sara said she'd be okay staying with Mirella I felt more relaxed. Between the three of us we surely could figure out why Max was dead, and maybe even figure out what happened to Sara's husband.

"Take this box with you, Aspen. Max was planning on giving it to you for your research. Most of the papers are legal documents about the property and communications between Mitch and his brother and the Martin Development Company. I never even went through all of it."

Mirella entered the dining room. "Why don't you keep the box here and we can go through it together?"

She must have been listening to our conversation. I returned the papers to the box and replaced the top. "No, I think I'll take it with me."

"Hey, you home?" Nick called out as he walked through the front door. When he looked up we all waved.

"Oh, I didn't see you all. Who's the little guy?"

"That's Mitchell and this is his mom, Sara. They're going to stay with us for a few days," Mirella said.

I took out my phone. "I better start making some calls to get a ride."

"Nick or I can take you," Mirella offered.

"I'm going back out anyway," Nick said. "I just came home to get a book." Nick ran upstairs and Mirella followed.

"Here take this," Sara said, handing me a note. "I was going to send this to you if I wasn't able to get in touch with you."

I opened the note and started to read.

"Put it away," Sara whispered when Nick and Mirella started back down the stairs.

Without hesitating, I crammed the thing into my pocket.

"Really appreciate the ride, Nick." I stood and picked up the box.

"What's that smell?" Nick asked.

"Uh, me. Mitchell threw up on me."

"Yuck."

"I'll call you all later this evening to touch base after I talk to Peter," I said.

"Who's Peter?" Sara asked.

"I thought I mentioned him before. He's my neighbor and dabbles in private investigations."

"I hope he'll be more help than the police. The only thing the police focused on when Mitch disappeared was the state of our marriage. They were convinced he just ran out on me."

"Bye. Bye." I waved at Mitchell as I followed Nick out the door.

I placed the box in the back seat of the VW before plopping down in the front. Tonight's dinner with Peter was going to be taxing because I was already exhausted.

"Why don't you take me to my car at the University?" I figured we could drive by Fugly and keep on going if someone was watching.

"Whatever."

"How well did you know Max Vanderbur?" I asked.

"He came over to the house to visit Mirella a few times."

"Were they working on her paper?"

"Well, sure if that's what you want to call it," he said.

Although I was curious about Mirella and Max's relationship, I didn't want to make Nick spill details about his sister's indiscretion. I switched subjects, asking him about himself.

Nick wasn't low on words. He answered every question in detail, providing a picture of a young man who thought highly of himself. He told me about pledging for a fraternity, getting a date with a girl in his Psych class, and blatantly boasted of being in possession of a brilliant idea that would make him a million dollars.

"The car's parked around the other side," I said, pointing.

When we turned the corner into the next parking section I didn't see Fugly. "I parked my car here. I know I did. Right there, in the third spot from the front entrance."

Nicked pointed. "In one of those spaces with the signs that say permit parking only. Violators will be towed?"

14

NICK APOLOGIZED for being unable to give me a ride home when he realized he would be late to his class. I called Peter for a ride while Nick parked. We crossed the street to the campus entrance. Nick apologized again and gave me a half hug goodbye. As his arm left my body, I noticed Peter pull up to the curb.

"Wow, that was quick," I said as I got into his car.

"I was in the neighborhood. Picking them kind of young now, aren't you?"

"More stamina!" I licked my finger and marked an invisible scoreboard - one for the home team.

"Did you call the towing company?" Peter asked, ignoring my witty comment.

"Yep. Do you have time to drop me off?"

"What smells?"

"Puke," I said. "Don't ask."

"I'll do you one better than dropping you off. The owner is a friend. He might be able to bring the car to us."

"You sure do have a lot of friends."

"You'll owe me one of course." He winked then punched a few number on his phone. "Mark, Spidey here."

I snickered. Some of Peter's friends called him Spidey because Spiderman's real name was Peter Parker, but I'd never heard him refer to himself that way. Once he finished explaining the situation to the person on the other end of the phone, he handed his cell over to me. "He needs to talk to you."

"Hi. I parked the car in the north garage. Yeah, that's the one." The guy on the other end was laughing. I gave the phone back.

"So, Tonto, what's the mystery?" Peter asked after he said goodbye to his friend.

"What mystery?"

"First you think the big guy is waiting for you at your car then you don't. I catch a young boy embracing you. You get in my car smelling like puke. And what's in the box?"

"He's not a young boy. He's at least in his twenties so that makes him a man."

"A young man."

"Okay, he's young," I conceded.

"Yes, he is. What's in the box?"

"The information Max Vanderbur had wanted me to have."

"That's a bit bigger than an envelope."

"I can't wait to review the contents." Yesterday I'd thought about unloading the whole research job, but my curiosity had taken over.

"Why didn't he just tell you Sara Obermier had the information?"

"She gave me a letter and in it she said he thought his house was being bugged."

"Why?" Peter asked, always interested in anything spy related.

"Her letter said John Martin was privy to information discussed in private conversations at the Vanderbur home."

"Or if they'd been sleeping with his wife," Peter added.

I reached into my pocket. "You're probably right. I do think John Martin was the man she was with the night Max died. I guess I can scratch that possible motive off the list."

"What list?"

"My Ten Reasons Why Max Vanderbur's Wife Killed Him list. Obviously he hadn't suspected his wife of having an affair with John Martin, so that wouldn't be her motive for killing Max."

"What if right before you got to Max's house, he discovered his wife's pillow talk had been the source of the leak and not a bug?"

I put the note back in my pocket figuring I could finish reading it later. "Good point." Motives needed to be eliminated or I'd never find the perfect one to give the police as proof of Mrs. Vanderbur's guilt.

Peter shook his head. "Never-ending theories. Now, speaking of bugs, are you ready for a surprise?"

"I can't stand anticipation! Hmm, what could it be?" I played along with Peter, though I was sure it was some new device at his store. He was always showing off new gadgets.

"I'll show you after we eat."

"Well thank God we aren't eating bugs for dinner."

Peter parked a half block from our building. "You should leave the box in the car," he said.

"What do you think about ordering pizza and rummaging through the box," I said.

"As interesting as that sounds, I think you'd be unhappy if you didn't get the surprise tonight."

"But you said the surprise was after dinner."

"I know you. Once you start looking, you'll never want to leave your apartment."

Damn, he did know me. I begrudgingly agreed to leave the box in the trunk of his car. We walked in unison. When we reached the front of the building, we talked in unison too, "Hi, Mrs. Rippetoe."

"Don't you two look cute?" She held a grocery bag in one hand and Sassy's leash in the other. The dusk lighting must have kept her from seeing the puke stain on my shirt.

"Let me help you with that." Peter kept one eye on Sassy and reached for the bag.

She'd gone to the small store down the block. A great place for the basics or a convenient alternative if someone were in a crunch, say her car was in the shop and the car she'd borrowed had been impounded.

"You are such a gentleman. Would you all like a glass of iced tea?"

"No," Peter and I said. Had she been facing us, the force of the single word leaving our mouths might have caused her face to appear as if she were pushing some serious G's.

"Thanks, but we have somewhere we need to be," I added, hoping we hadn't hurt her feelings.

"Have either of you seen Toby lately?"

"No," we answered. Our perfect timing had become obnoxious.

"He told me yesterday that he'd come over this morning, but he never showed." Mrs. Rippetoe finally stopped fiddling with her keys and opened her door.

"I'm sure he just got busy."

"Let me know if you see him," she said.

"Okay," we both said, once again perfectly synchronized. *Freaky.*

———

"Want to split an order of spring rolls?" Peter asked.

"Are you crazy? I can eat an entire order by myself."

"We don't have all night."

"Okay, we can split those, but I'm getting my own bowl of beef noodle soup." The restaurant was affordable and casual. Even so, the beef noodle soup had obtained the same level of stardom as caviar.

"Yes, ma'am," Peter said, giving me a mock salute.

The waiter took our order and quickly returned with our beers. Music seeped through the walls from the adjacent lounge as we waited for our food. I tried getting Peter to spill everything about his surprise, but he wasn't budging.

"Here's your food. Your waiter had to leave unexpectedly. My name is Jack, let me know if you need anything."

Great. Jack. I hadn't had time to think about him. But now, looking at my watch, I realized he never called, and it was already seven-thirty. Soon he'd be crossing the line into the group of guys who didn't keep their promises.

"So, tell me about your new boyfriend."

I flinched thinking he had been asking about Jack. "What?"

"Your young boy."

"Oh, you mean young man."

"Right. Who is he and where did you meet him?"

My soup smelled delicious and I took a few bites before answering. "He's Mirella's twin. Mirella's the student they interviewed about Max's murder."

"So the police declared his death a murder?"

"No, not exactly, but that's just a formality. All their actions point to a murder investigation."

"What were you doing with your boy toy?"

I rolled my eyes. "Jack had provided me with Mirella's name. I went looking for her but found Nick first."

"So you talked to Jack today?"

"No, yesterday. At the police station."

Peter stopped eating. "What did you do now?"

"Why does it have to be something I did?" I snapped.

"Stop being defensive, I figured you wouldn't go to the police unless you had to."

"I wrecked my Jeep and it's in the shop. Is that what you wanted to hear?" I shrunk back into my seat when the other diners began staring at us as though we had entered into a full-fledged lover's quarrel.

"Then whose car got towed?"

"I was driving Jack's car, Fugly."

Peter laughed so loud the waiter came by and asked if we needed anything else, or more likely, he wanted to shut Peter up.

"Not funny," I said.

"Yes it is. I can't imagine you driving around in the orange bomber."

"How did you know I was driving that car? Maybe he loaned me his BMW."

"After you wrecked yours? He may be a lawyer, but he's not stupid. Besides, you called his car Fugly."

"Don't tell Jack I named the thing Fugly."

"He doesn't care. He thinks the car's ugly too."

I slurped up some more soup. "Why does he still have the stupid thing? With all his money he could buy a new one."

"In case he needs an extra and because he'd have to pay someone to take it away. What makes you think he has a lot of money?"

"His house is huge."

"You went inside his house?"

"Well, no, I was just by the garage."

"There's a good reason he didn't let you inside."

My imagination ran wild. He was probably married. Or better yet, his parents owned the house and he was living in their basement. I wasn't sure I wanted to know, but I cut my agony short anyway. "Why?"

"Outside, his house looks like a million bucks, but the inside is another story."

"So he isn't rich?"

"He's not poor, but he's not exactly a millionaire. A few years ago he bought the place in a foreclosure sale. The money ran out after he started fixing up the outside"

"I feel better. I mean it would be terrible if he were loaded." I had no reason to blatantly admit to Peter that I secretly hoped Jack would whisk me away to some tropical island. I wasn't a gold digger, but every girl has a dream.

"Funny. You're good at getting me off track. Let's get back to Mirella and her brother."

"Now, don't get mad at me, Peter."

He let out a big sigh. "Did you know when you preface something by telling a person not to get mad, the effect is the exact opposite?"

"Seriously Peter, please don't get upset. You promise?"

"I promise."

If he lied I couldn't tell. "I tracked down Mirella at the University this morning. The two of us were on our way to meet Sara Obermier when we came across the big guy—"

"Wait, you told me it wasn't the big guy."

"You promised."

He crossed his arms over his chest. "Go ahead."

"While we spied on the big guy, Samuel Martin drove up and started talking to him."

"That doesn't make sense."

"None of this makes sense."

I continued to give Peter the details about the events at the garage. The more I talked the more agitated he became.

"What if they had seen you?" he asked, clanking his spoon on the side of his soup bowl.

"They didn't, and we found out they're planning to kill Sara Obermier."

"Are you sure you didn't misunderstand? You weren't exactly standing by their side."

"Samuel Martin said the Obermier situation needed to be taken care of."

Peter looked amused. "That could mean anything. An overactive imagination is what you have."

Every now and then I'd gotten things a little mixed up, but my intuition was right this time. We sat in awkward silence, except for the slurping noises we each made as we sucked the soup up from the bottom of our bowls.

"I think I'm right on this one. I bet Mrs. Vanderbur had John Martin hire the big guy to kill her husband to get him out of the way. Or she could have overheard Max talking with Sara Obermier and told John Martin."

Peter put his spoon down. "I can't believe I'm going to bother saying this, but if you believe you are right, you should get the police involved."

"No. Not yet."

"Exactly the response I expected."

Once again I found myself rolling my eyes. "I need to find credible evidence first or they'll laugh at me like the first time, when I asked if they were going to arrest Mrs. Vanderbur."

"Will you at least keep me involved? Don't do any poking around on your own. Call if you think you're on to something and we can check it out together, promise?"

Peter's concern was touching, but he was crazy if he expected me to risk missing a perfect opportunity by waiting for him to show up. Besides, I had pepper spray. I crossed my fingers under the table. "I promise."

"You ready for your surprise?"

"Can't you give me a little hint?"

"Just one. It involves listening and music."

"A concert?"

Peter shook his head. I tried to pick up the check, but he swatted my hand and put a pile of money on the table. I followed him out the door. He turned to the left. I expected him to go through the lounge's door but he continued walking.

"I guess clubbing is not the surprise."

"No."

We got back into Peter's new Cadillac, all shiny and blue, the identical color of my once unblemished Jeep. The

Chevrolet Citation he'd driven the night of the surveillance was nicer than Fugly, but still a clunker. Tonight we had the sweet ride which meant we weren't going on surveillance.

We went East on Arsenal Street toward the river. I got excited when he made a left on Gravois. I couldn't hold my excitement any longer.

"You found Mr. P! Peter, you're the best. Of course, listening to music, Mr. P's owner is a DJ! God, what a relief." I leaned over and placed a thank you kiss on his cheek. He didn't look appreciative.

"I wish I had."

"You're pulling my leg now. I'm not that gullible."

"Seriously, Aspen, I didn't find him."

"Oh." I sat back in my seat.

"I'm sorry."

I was crushed. "It's not your fault."

"Mr. P's owner is a DJ?"

"I shouldn't have let that slip, he's extremely private."

"If I wanted to know what your client did for a living, I'd already know. I do own a security and surveillance company and I worked on investigations for another firm, remember? I promise you my lips are sealed."

We pulled into the parking lot of a commercial building located across the street from Martin-Stone Development. Peter parked the car behind a construction dumpster.

"What are we doing here?"

"Surprise!" Peter screamed and threw his hands up.

"I thought my surprise had to do with listening to music?"

"No. Listening, and music."

"What's the difference?"

Peter turned on the radio. "This station plays music."

Jazz infused the air. I started getting into it before he tuned to a different station that played nothing but a beeping sound.

"This is a radio station which could play music, but it doesn't."

"Okay," I said, but didn't quite understand his point.

"We are still going to listen to it, can you figure out why?"

"Not really."

"Because, outside is not the only place bugs live."

"What does that have to do with anything?" I was tiring of his guessing game.

"Buuuuugs, in the building," he said.

"Bugs? Oh, Buuuugs."

"Yes. And tonight's show, I clearly saw marked on Samuel Martin's assistant's calendar, includes an eight o'clock meeting between Samuel Martin and Caden Stone."

"Holy Smoke!"

"I love it when you talk dirty."

"Are bugs legal in Missouri?" I asked, curious as to exactly how he'd bypassed the issue.

"Sure, look at all of those flying around free?" He pointed to the streetlight where hundreds of bugs were busily doing what bugs do.

"You know what I mean."

"The skin of my hand never touched a bug in their office. Let's leave it at that, okay?"

The beeping on the radio vanished and was replaced by the sound of a door opening, footsteps, then gibberish. The reception had to get better or it would be a painful evening.

"Macy, dear, I'm going to be late. Caden and I are wrapping up some business." Samuel Martin's voice was loud and clear.

"Samuel and Macy Martin are still together? Didn't you give her the photographs," I asked.

"She has them, but she's a patient woman. Getting what you want takes time."

Samuel Martin talked with his wife for a few more minutes about nothing spectacular and said goodbye as soon as the sound of more footsteps became audible.

"Come in, Stone."

"Sam, what's the emergency?"

"We have a problem with Marston."

"Can't be much of one. The project was completed so long ago," Caden Stone said and I imagined him waving off Samuel's comment.

"We need to survey lot 48."

I took notes using the small spiral notebook I had tucked into my purse.

"Look, the situation is getting complicated. I met with Rocco today and sent him out on a special project. She wasn't there," Samuel said.

"Must be the big guy's name," I whispered to Peter.

"You don't need to whisper, they can't hear us. Talking might make us miss something though."

"Who wasn't there?" Caden asked.

"Sara Obermier. We checked her work. She's out due to a family emergency and won't be back for a week, but our background check showed no family, except the elder Mrs. Obermier and that son-of-a-bitch son. But there are no emergencies in their family."

"Tell me what situation is getting complicated and why you are so concerned about Sara Obermier?" Caden Stone asked, sounding a little impatient.

"She's renewed her interest in the Obermier property transaction. She's been talking to a Professor Max Vanderbur."

"What's the worry, isn't that the guy who killed himself?"

"He's dead, but the person he hired to help is still alive."

I hoped he wasn't talking about me. If he was, I didn't like the direction this conversation was heading.

"Sam, don't tell me anything else. Just do what needs to be done."

"Look, Stone, you're just as responsible as I am."

I wasn't quite sure what Samuel Martin was taking responsibility for, but whatever it was didn't sound innocent.

"Sammm-my, I never touched anything, not even the money. So, I'm not the one with dirt on my hands."

Several minutes passed before Samuel Martin spoke. "We need to find out exactly what triggered Sara Obermier to start poking around again. I'm calling Rocco off Ms. Moore for now because I think she's clueless."

Oh my God, they were talking about me.

"Like I said, do what you need to do."

Noise from a chair scraping across the floor exploded from the speakers.

"Stone, don't forget this is your life too."

Caden Stone didn't respond, but the sound of his footsteps became fainter the longer we listened. Peter turned the radio off and started the car.

"We better take off now," Peter said.

"What a fantastic surprise! I didn't like the part about me though. I'm smarter than they think I am."

"You should be glad they're calling off your stalker. I still think being alone is a bad idea until we figure out what they're up to."

"That's just not practical. Besides, I bought pepper spray the other day." I scrounged around in my purse and pulled out the container. "See?"

"You'd be in a chokehold before you found it. Why don't you put the thing on your keychain?"

"Thanks for the vote of confidence." I took out my keys, pried the little ring open and hooked on the pepper spray.

"I'm not kidding. This sounds dangerous."

"I can take care of myself. I'll keep you on speed dial."

"Fine. But you better call me the minute you feel something's not right."

"I promise." I didn't cross my fingers this time.

"Make sure you stay away from Sara Obermier and Mirella."

"I need to call them."

"Okay, but that's all you do."

Peter had turned into a microscopic splinter – not large enough to cause serious pain, but big enough to effectively deliver irritation. "Why does everyone think I'm stupid?"

"I'm worried about you."

A tiny pitter-patter bounced around my heart, reminding me how sweet he could be and the splinter-like irritation faded.

"Can you research the Marston plat map?" he asked.

"Sure, lot 48?"

"Exactly. Call me as soon as you find the information. I'll drive by and identify a good surveillance point."

"Super. I'll go with you."

"Sorry. I'm making a couple of sales calls for my new Bioscan-3 system and I'll be swinging by Marston sometime in between them."

"Maybe I could swing by your spy shop and ride along with you?"

I watched him squirm as I called his store a spy shop.

"First, as I've told you a billion times, it's not a spy shop. It's an advanced security and surveillance technology co—"

"Yeah, well, spy shop sounds cooler."

"And second, the meetings might run for hours."

"Rats."

"Don't worry, I'll fill you in and if you're good, I'll even let you join me on the surveillance."

"Now, you're talking!"

"I'm not promising. You won't be able to come along if I decide it's dangerous."

"But Danger is my middle name."

"Right. What's your middle name, really?"

"Eloise." I sat up straight, proud of the middle name I'd had since birth. The one part of my name I hadn't changed.

15

DESPERATE TO PUT A SMILE on my face, I clicked the remote searching for cartoons. Why didn't the networks run the classics like Bugs, Wylie Coyote, and Foghorn Leghorn?

Yesterday had been taxing. I was taking a mental health day, hanging out at home and doing nothing but eating junk food and watching TV. I licked BBQ chip seasoning off my fingers and took a big sip of chocolate milk. One more day of unhealthy food wouldn't hurt my aspirations of getting in better shape. I needed something to comfort me until I began actively visiting the gym.

The doorbell rang as my hand explored the inside of the chip bag scavenging for the crunchiest ones. I muted the television and pulled my hand out of the chip bag hoping whoever it was would go away.

The intruder persisted. I didn't answer and they stopped ringing the bell. I thought I was in the clear until the knocking started. I ran to the bedroom, grabbed my robe, and hurried to the door before the person pounded a hole through it.

"Who is it?" I asked. I had no intention of opening my door to a stranger.

When there wasn't an immediate answer I flipped out, imagining Harry Corbitt on the other side of the door. "Who's there?

"Toby."

Even though my Saturday plans hadn't included talking to anyone, I was relieved it was Toby. I cracked the door open. "What do you need, Toby?"

"Cool man, ten o'clock and still in your pajamas, right on."

"What's up?"

"Some dude dropped this off last night. I didn't think you'd want someone ripping you off so I took the box over to my place."

I opened the door wider and he handed me a rectangular box with a big red bow on top.

"For me? Wait, who delivered the box?"

"He wore a uniform."

"What kind of uniform?"

"Actually, I'm not sure, man. I was drawing and heard a noise, poked my head out and only caught part of the dude. At first I swore the guy was a cop but then it coulda been a mailman or just a delivery guy."

I hadn't initially wanted to engage Toby in conversation, but a new question popped out of my mouth. "You draw?"

"Oh, yeah. I'm a skateboard artist, just breaking out. I design under the name T. J. Starch."

Another thing I hadn't left behind when I started my new life was my love for creative people. I was an artist groupie. My brain leaned heavily to the left. The logical side knew if there was any hope for symbiosis between my

164

left and right brain, I needed to latch on to creative people. Writers, singers, painters, fire-eaters, it didn't matter.

"Wanna check out some of my designs?" he asked.

"Sure." I placed the box on my breakfast bar, tucked my feet into my slippers, and followed Toby over to his place. I had no shame.

"This is my latest." Toby handed me a skateboard.

The colors were reminiscent of Peter Max: gold, blue, red, and green – bold. A montage of skateboarders skating down the St. Louis Arch stood out on the brilliant background. Every detail, down to the eyelashes.

"You're very creative." I handed the board back to him. Even if I wasn't creative, I understood what creativity looked like.

"Thanks. All my designs include The Gateway Arch. It's my signature. Starch stands for – St. Louis Arch."

"Pretty clever, Toby."

"Here's the sketch for my new design I'm working on."

I took the sketchbook. "This is going to be a true piece of art. I can't wait to see the finished work."

Toby showed me a few more drawings unrelated to skateboarding. A couple of minutes later I snuck back to my place, thankful I didn't live on the bottom floor where someone coming down the steps might catch me in action. The thought of having to explain why I'd come out of Toby's apartment in my robe and slippers caused me to chuckle.

I caught sight of the big red bow as I entered my apartment. I couldn't imagine who had dropped off a gift for me. My birthday was several months away. I took the package and sat on the couch.

The box wasn't wrapped or taped, and it wasn't ticking, so I lifted the lid. Inside was the most beautiful red

165

briefcase I'd ever seen. I would have purchased a cheap, utilitarian one. The briefcase I held in my hands far exceeded my expectations. The softness of the leather and the quality of the stitch told me it was expensive. Best of all, red was my favorite color.

I searched the box for a card, but found only classy designer tissue paper. Stephanie could be trying to make up for the mall incident. Or Toby did say it might have been a cop who dropped it off, perhaps Officer Storey felt sorry for me. The only problem was how either of them would have been able to shell out that kind of money on me.

My day off in my pajamas came to an end because I couldn't stop thinking about who gave me the gift. I hopped in the shower and lathered my body with lavender-scented gel to quiet my thoughts. Unfortunately, aromatherapy was no substitute for psychotherapy. When I finished showering, I towel-dried my hair, deciding to go with a natural, just-got-out-of-bed, look.

The red briefcase lured me over when I walked into the living room. I unloaded the mountain of items from my purse and paper bag, spreading everything across the table in preparation for filling up my new briefcase. I couldn't give it back because I didn't know who gave it to me. Besides, refusing a gift wasn't polite.

The soft-sided case had two clasps used to fasten shut two large storage sections. I opened the first clasp and peeked inside, hoping I would find more compartments to organize my stuff. Instead, I found an envelope with my name typed on the outside.

I opened it and pulled out a map with a note attached. "Come join me this Saturday in Tower Grove Park for a nice surprise," it said. "Meet you at one o'clock at the Old Playground Pavilion."

Jack popped into my head. I bet he'd planned a romantic picnic at the park to make up for not calling. If so, I might actually consider dating him.

My pendulum clock struck the half-hour mark, informing me I had exactly thirty minutes to get to the park. I swept everything off the table and into the briefcase, grabbed the map and the note, and flew out the door.

Walking the short distance from my door to the car, I created an entire fantasy. I envisioned Jack sneaking by late last night replacing Fugly with a brand new Mercedes, whose key I would find in the other compartment of my new red briefcase. Unfortunately, Fugly was right where the tow truck had dropped him.

———

According to the map, the Old Playground Pavilion was close to the entrance off Grand Boulevard. I reached Tower Grove Park in less than twenty minutes.

The tall white columns on either side of the entrance were joined together by a black wrought iron fence with several sections embellished in gold. The entrance lived up to the street name. Lions adorned the top of the two front columns and I spotted griffins on the other two as I drove into the park.

Rain had fallen overnight with abandon, creating a muddy mess. I pulled alongside an area near a blacktop trail. A few cars passed by on their way to the center of the park. The sound of birds singing when I exited the car lifted my spirits.

I walked along a trail parallel to the road then veered onto an old gravel path, leading me past a small building hidden by a patch of evergreen bushes. The path allowed me to avoid the mud and led me straight to the Old Playground Pavilion with its pale yellow arches and dark blue scrollwork.

The pavilion's architecture was playful with an ornate cupola and horse-shaped weathervane topping the blue metal roof. I grabbed one of the bright red columns and stepped up onto the concrete foundation. Jack had yet to arrive so I sat on top of a picnic table beneath the pavilion and waited.

A light breeze rolled in and I pulled my jacket tighter. I was amazed the torrid rain hadn't caused the vibrant orange, red, and yellow leaves to drop. They flickered in the sun. It was like I'd been dropped into the scene of a romantic movie. Fifteen minutes later when Jack hadn't shown up, I gave up on romance and headed back toward the car to give Romeo a call.

A noise came from behind the old building and I was ecstatic that Jack had finally arrived. I turned to greet him, but he wasn't there. Someone yanked my hair hard from behind. I screamed like my ass had just been branded with a cattle iron.

The person's massive body made it difficult to escape. I couldn't afford to be afraid. I kicked my leg up behind me hoping it would land in his crotch, but willing to settle for any body part. I took my key chain and blindly pressed the button shooting pepper spray all over the goon. Within seconds, I was free. I ran through the grass, ignoring that my favorite red sneakers were sinking into mud. I didn't look back; afraid he'd be right behind me.

Fugly didn't have remote entry, so I steadied my hand and put the key in the door. I pushed down the lock and prayed the damn car would start on my first try.

When the engine turned over and I was confident the door between me and my attacker remained locked, I took a peek. I hoped the guy would still be agonizing in pain, but he was gone.

If I wanted to know why Jack was a no-show, I'd have to call him. I didn't want to alarm Peter, but he was the only person who could give me Jack's phone number.

Peter answered my call. I could tell he was busy because he rattled off the number without asking a single question. I wrote down the telephone number and took a deep breath before punching in the first digit. My phone rang before I even got to the second number. I hit the answer button.

"Hello, Aspen. Peter said you—"

"Where are you? I've been waiting at the park. Why didn't you show up?"

"What park? What are you talking about?"

"The briefcase and the map."

"Aspen, are you okay?"

I actually took a second to think about the question. "No, I'm not okay. Someone just attacked me in the park. My shoes are all muddy and I thought you were going to be here, but you—"

"Slow down. Take a deep breath."

I took Jack's advice and breathed in, paused, then exhaled, shutting down my hysterical tirade. "I found the note in the briefcase you gave me and—"

"I didn't give you a briefcase."

"You didn't?"

"No, I didn't. What did you say about a note?"

He listened without saying a word as I explained everything that had happened, minus my artist addiction and the trip to Toby's apartment.

"I called to see if you'd like to go to lunch with me today, but you should probably call the police. We can do lunch another time or I can pick up something and meet you at your place."

I'd rather eat pizza than go to the police. "How about Imo's?"

"What kind?"

"Pepperoni, please."

"You bet. And Aspen?"

"Yeah."

"I'm glad you're okay."

I pulled the rearview mirror toward me. My hair and face were not in bad shape for someone who'd literally been running for her life. My favorite red sneakers had been the only victim to not make it out unscathed.

In my eyes, pizza wasn't pizza without an ice-cold beer, so I stopped to pick some up. By the time I made it home, my stomach was in conversation mode. I trekked my way up the stairs with my briefcase and six-pack in tow. When I reached the top, I found the sexiest pizza delivery guy I'd ever seen.

———

"Here, let me help you," Jack said.

The man looked awesome in his jeans and leather bomber jacket. It was a rougher version of Jack, but just as sexy if not sexier than Jack in a suit. But, I imagined, not as sexy as Jack in his birthday suit.

"Could you take the beer?" I handed the six-pack over and stuck my key in the lock. "No comments about my housekeeping. I haven't quite gotten everything put away since the break-in."

"Don't worry, my place isn't the showplace I imagined either."

I didn't let on that I already knew his place wouldn't qualify for a spread in Architectural Digest. It was best to keep my conversations with Peter, about him, to myself. He set the pizza and beer on the breakfast bar while I ran back to tidy up and change my shoes.

"I'm starving." I walked back out to the kitchen.

"Good thing because I ordered a large. Why don't we have a little appetizer first?"

"Sure, what'd you bring? I don't see anything but a pizza box."

"Come here." He wrapped his arms around my waist.

His breath was hot, but darned if it wasn't minty fresh. Our lips met with an electric shock. We both jumped back, caught off guard by the static that had built up from walking across the rug.

"You're dangerous, aren't you?" Jack asked.

"Well, some might say Danger's my middle name."

"I bet it is," he said, giving me a quick wink. "Let's get you fed."

He opened the box to reveal an Imo's, saliva-inducing, thin crust pizza, cut into squares. St. Louis style pizza was usually covered in Provel cheese, an acquired taste, and not generally found in other parts of the United States

"Yum." I moaned as I took another bite.

"I talked to Mr. Brackford today." Jack grabbed a second slice of pizza. "The nurse called me early this morning and told me he was alert."

"What did she say? I mean he say."

"He had no idea who attacked him. Said the man came through his back door and demanded the information you'd given him."

"I just dropped off his mail, that's all."

"That's what Mr. Brackford told him."

"Did he say what he wanted?"

"Mr. Brackford handed him the boxes of trains when the guy insisted Brackford give him what you dropped off. The guy got mad and hit him over the head."

"Would he be able to recognize him?" I picked a few pieces of pepperoni off the pizza and popped them in my mouth.

"Thinks he might."

"Hey, I don't think I told you that I found Mirella."

"Already?" Jack ran a napkin across his mouth.

"Surprised myself at how quickly I located her."

Jack and I continued to chat about Mirella and my trip to the University. I neglected to mention the part about Fugly having been taken against his will.

"And the big news is, the person who had been trying to get in touch with me called."

"What did she want?"

"She gave me a box full of information. Oh damn. I was so tired this morning and then the briefcase fiasco occurred, I completely forgot I left the box in Peter's trunk."

"Peter's trunk? Why didn't you put the box in the Fairmont?"

The thought of having to tell Jack one more story about something bad happening to me, stressed me out. Pain began radiating from my neck toward the top of my head. Panic set in. "I've got a bit of a headache, I'll be right back." I dashed into my bedroom.

I sat on the bed, hyperventilating. My life was a freakin three-ring circus and I was locked in the trunk of the clown car. It was as if I had no control. The purpose of relocating to St. Louis was to start a new life, a simple, uncomplicated, go to work and come home every day, life. Instead, it was getting more complicated by the minute.

"Aspen? Are you alright?"

I continued holding my head in my hands.

"Why don't we lie down," he continued.

When I looked up I felt more at ease. I saw a thoughtful guy. Resting and having him hold me in bed sounded wonderful, but I knew getting into bed with him would turn into having sex with him. At this point, sex would complicate an already complicated situation.

"I'm better now. Why don't I show you the note?"

Out of the bedroom and into the safety zone, we sat on the couch and looked over everything, including the box the briefcase had been inside.

"Tell me why you thought the briefcase was from me."

"I'm so embarrassed. Honestly, you're the only person who was aware I needed a briefcase who might also be able to afford something this expensive."

"The brown paper bag definitely needed replacing." He laughed.

"Whoever gave me the case was obviously aware of my need."

"Do you think it was the big guy who attacked you?"

"Maybe. Of course anyone would appear massive while they were attacking me."

"You should call the police. They might be able to dust the briefcase for fingerprints."

"Monday. I'll call on Monday. The officer who helped me out with the car accident gave me his card." I retrieved it and slipped the business card into the pocket of my black blazer, so I'd remember to call in the morning, or at least remember to think about calling.

"I know this is such a cliché, but I've never met anyone quite like you." Jack reached over and brushed my hair away from my eyes, so I took his statement as a good thing.

He pulled me toward him, the aroma of pepperoni and Provel wafting from his mouth. Not as appetizing as minty fresh, but I didn't complain. I opened my mouth wide. Not dental patient wide, but wide enough he'd be able to figure out I liked the way he kissed.

A moan escaped from my mouth and I hoped it sounded to him like an I-can't-get-enough-of-you moan. Because to me, it sounded eerily like the moan I'd let slip when I was munching on my pizza.

Brushing my hair back, he ventured away from my lips, kissing my face and neck. He gently laid me down on the couch. *Ouch.* I felt something hard and it wasn't between Jack and me. The object pressed into my back. I said nothing because I didn't want to ruin the moment.

When he ran his tongue along my neck, I no longer cared about the object. I listened to the only sound that mattered, his anticipating breath feeding mine. *Wait. What was that noise?*

"My phone!" I said, trying to lift Jack off of me.

"Let it ring," he encouraged.

"Uh, well, it's underneath me."

Jack popped up. "Why didn't you say something?"

"I was kind of busy." I grabbed the phone and pressed answer. "Hello."

"You sound out of breath, are you okay?" Peter asked.

"Yeah, I had to find my phone."

"What are you doing right now?"

I said what I could. "Jack and I just finished a pizza."

"Really."

The inflection of his voice was a bit off and I wasn't quite sure what to make of it. The tone was similar to the tone he'd had after Jack complimented me on my tools. But Peter had Madeline and we had an agreement – he knew it and I knew it.

"Yeah, Imo's. Where are you?" I asked in an effort to stave off his uncomfortable pause.

"I called because I have news about Mr. P."

16

"ASPEN. WAKE UP."

I opened one eye and looked over at Jack in the driver's seat. "Why'd you let me fall asleep?"

"I didn't realize you had, until I asked you a question and you responded with a snore."

Oh my God, a snore. I snapped to attention and sat up in my seat afraid to imagine what other kind of noises I'd made. I raised my arms above my head, pretending to stretch, then ran my hand across my mouth to check for drool. "So what time is it?"

"A little after nine."

Almost five hours had passed since Peter called and told me he was hot on the trail of Mr. P. We were on our way to Kansas City because Peter had a plan to get Mr. P back.

I called Peter. "Keep an eye out for us. We're in Jack's Beamer."

"Jack's with you?"

"Yeah, I wasn't about to drive Fu..., the Fairmont three-hundred miles by myself."

Peter didn't comment, he simply instructed me where to park and hung up without saying goodbye. "Peter said to pull around the back of the hotel," I said.

Jack parked the car by some bushes and we grabbed our bags from the trunk. I pulled my black nylon carry-on bag and its wobbly wheel behind me as if I were in an off-road dune buggy. Jack, on the other hand, pulled his tan leather Hartmann bag across the hotel parking lot like a speed skater on virgin ice. I'd never felt so mismatched.

Peter opened the back door from inside the hotel. "The place is sold out because of a couple of conventions going on in town. I snagged the last room."

The hotel had an elevator close to where we entered. Peter pushed the up button.

"We're in room 2069."

"One room?" I asked.

"The room is a suite with a kitchenette and a living room."

"I'm sure it's plenty big, but, how many beds?"

"One," Peter answered with a straight face.

"I, uh..."

He laughed. "Stop sweating it, Aspen. There are two beds and a sleeper sofa."

"I wasn't. Just wanted to make sure everyone had a comfortable place to sleep."

Peter turned left out of the elevator.

The carpet was thick and barely worn, with a pattern of diamonds, bordered by acorns and leaves. Ornate gold-framed oil paintings hung above each console table we passed. I admired the wallpaper. "Wow, this is ritzy."

"You haven't seen anything yet." Peter took a key card out of his pocket.

When he opened the door we were met with a spectacular panoramic view. The lights in the city buildings twinkled. I'd never visited Kansas City before and I was excited to find out what the city had to offer. I hoped our plans included time to check out more than the view.

"So where is the dog?" Jack asked.

"The hotel only allows pets on the first floor." Peter grabbed a soda from the refrigerator.

My cell phone rang and I answered without thinking. "Hello." My heart sank when I heard Mr. Q's voice on the other end.

"I'm sorry I didn't call you. I had a few things to take care of."

Mr. Q confirmed he'd be back Monday afternoon. While I paced around the room and half listened to him, I overheard Peter telling Jack he could sleep on the couch.

"Mr. P? He's at a resort for the night." Technically I was telling the truth. Some people might consider the hotel a resort. I picked a placard off the desk that showed the hotel's indoor pool, Jacuzzi, and sauna. I flipped the card over and discovered an entire menu of massage and spa treatments. I caught Peter rolling his eyes.

"I wanted him to have a little day of pampering since he seemed down. I'm sure he misses you too. No problem at all. Talk to you Monday." I pushed the end call button on my phone and plunked down in the nearest chair.

"You're pretty good at that, Aspen," Jack said.

"At what?"

"Bending the truth. I'm impressed."

On the one hand I was flattered I had impressed Jack, but the fact that he had been impressed by someone not telling the entire truth worried me.

"No need to be. So what's our plan?" I asked of no one in particular.

Peter responded first. "Your client's neighbor is here for the Comi-Con convention. I expect him to go out tomorrow and leave Mr. P in the room."

"What good does that do us?" My faith in Peter's ability to get Mr. P back began to wane.

"He'll be alone and we'll snatch him back."

"How do you expect us to gain access to the room legally?" Jack asked.

"Legally?" Peter half laughed.

"It wouldn't look good if I were caught in someone's hotel room without permission."

Jack's use of the word 'I' bothered me. His concern over getting caught extended only to himself. Spending time with someone in close quarters created an excellent opportunity to get to know them better, which reminded me that I didn't know all that much about Jack.

"My plan is to use the two of you as lookouts while I go in and snatch Mr. P from the room. Aspen, you'll have to be near the door because Mr. P knows you."

"That sounds good. Anything we need to do before tomorrow?" Jack asked.

"Not until later," Peter said.

"Let's go see what this town is all about." Jack looked directly at me.

I was up for a night on the town. "That sounds like a—"

"I brought the box in for you, Aspen. I thought you might want to check out the contents tonight," Peter said.

Check out the city or go through the box? There was no need to consider my options. "Why don't we order in?"

Jack seemed irritated. I picked up the room service menu off the desk, flipped through the pages, selecting a basic burger and fries. After I let Peter know what I wanted, I went into the bathroom to wash up. I was in for the evening, so I changed into a pair of sweats and a t-shirt.

I grabbed the box from the bed and walked back into the living room. When I bent over to place the box on the coffee table, I noticed both Peter and Jack staring at my chest. I looked down, wondering what was wrong. My nipples were the problem. At full attention, they were working diligently to poke their way through my t-shirt.

Blessed with the curse of the D cup, my breasts had helped me get my way more times than I could count. But on the flip side, they were disruptive to the male population and the backaches were enough to drive me to drink.

Someone knocked on the door. "Room service."

Peter got up to answer it. The room service guy deserved a gigantic tip for alleviating an awkward moment. If I had to spend the entire evening thinking about Peter and Jack looking at my boobs, I wouldn't get any research done. I snuck back into the bedroom while the two of them transferred the food from the cart to the table.

I didn't want to strap the girls in again, so I went to the closet for a robe. When I came back out of the bedroom, Peter was staring at me. I instinctively lowered my head to get a visual of my breast, wondering what the heck was wrong this time. Everything looked okay to me.

"Why didn't you tell me you were attacked at the park today?" Peter asked. He was definitely mad.

"Did I really have an opportunity? You called and then we had to get on the road."

"The drive to Kansas City was four hours," Peter batted back.

"I'm sorry, but what's the problem? It's over and I'm safe." Peter was starting to sound like my step-dad, Daddy-O.

"The problem is, you could have been seriously hurt or killed. Did you even think about calling me before running off to meet some stranger?"

"I thought I'd be meeting Jack!"

The room fell silent. I glanced over at Jack who was busy eating his food. He had the same expression on his face people get when they're in the midst of a married couple quarrelling, a forced disinterest in the conversation.

"Let's just eat," I said, trying to put us out of our misery.

"Not so fast. Let me see this briefcase and note."

Like a little girl in trouble, I hung my head and shuffled back into the bedroom. I grabbed the briefcase from inside my suitcase, where I'd thrown it during the pandemonium of packing. I shuffled back out to the living room, handed the case to Peter, then sat down and bit into my burger.

"Macy Martin has one exactly like this."

I took another bite and swallowed before speaking. "I'm sure there's more than one."

"Not many. She made a point of telling me all about her expensive limited edition."

"Is that Samuel Martin's wife?" Jack asked, finally coming up for air.

"Yeah, Peter talked to her about security equipment for her home." I glanced at Peter.

"You think that's Macy Martin's briefcase?" Jack didn't wait for an answer. He finished his beer and got up to put his dishes back on the room service cart.

"I didn't say that. But I don't think having one show up on Aspen's doorstep that is exactly like Macy's is a coincidence."

"Finish your meal, Peter, before it gets cold." I dropped my dishes on the cart then walked over to the box and lifted the lid.

Each time I removed something, I inspected the item thoroughly. In addition to the printouts of the emails between Mitch Obermier and Martin Development, I found copies of letters to the court. Each letter had been written by Mitch and protested his brother's attempt to have him removed from the property title.

Collectively, the papers read like one big saga. I even came across nasty handwritten letters from Mitch's brother. They accused Mitch of trying to rob his brother of his inheritance.

The last item was a manila envelope. I emptied the contents onto the table and unfolded a few of the papers. One set was a copy of the will for Mitch Obermier's father. I scanned the content and then turned my attention to the other stuff from the envelope.

Another paper indicated the land had been left to Mitch and his brother equally. I'd owned a home in my old life and had knowledge of property titles. Joint tenancy with right of survivorship meant each of them owned an equal share. But if one brother died his share would go to

182

the other brother, not the dead brother's heirs. The father must have wanted to make sure his property stayed in the family.

I picked up a photograph of two men. One had the same smile and curly brown hair I'd seen on Mitchell yesterday. The other guy I'd never seen, but figured he must be Mitch's brother.

"Anything interesting?" Peter asked.

"Lots of information about Martin Development's aggressive pursuit of the Obermier property. You know, if Mitch Obermier hadn't disappeared, Samuel Martin might never have gotten that property. Makes you wonder."

"So you think a prominent real estate developer is responsible for this guy's disappearance?" Jack lifted his bottle of beer to his mouth.

"No, I just said it makes you wonder."

All of the information painted a tumultuous picture of the brothers' relationship. I couldn't help wondering if Mitch's own brother had somehow been involved with Mitch's disappearance. When I started putting the papers back into the manila envelope, I noticed something taped to the inside.

"So, do you think Samuel Martin killed this guy for his land?" Jack persisted.

"I don't know what I think right now." Actually, I was thinking I wanted to pull out the item secured inside the envelope, but I didn't want to share my secret find until I knew what I'd found.

"We'll be back in twenty minutes. You ready, Jack?" Peter grabbed the keycard off the table and shoved it in his pocket.

"Where are we going?" Jack asked, tossing his beer bottle in the trash.

"We need to scope out the first floor and establish our positions for tomorrow."

The second the door clicked shut I ripped the taped item out of the envelope. It was an index card with the handwritten words Creek Boulder Flat 86927. My brain hurt the minute I began thinking about what it could mean. The five digits made me think of a zip code.

I piled all the papers back into the box, except the cryptic note. I took the box back to the bedroom and slipped the index card into the side pocket of my suitcase. Pulling down the covers, I plopped on the bed nearest the window, grabbed the remote, and channel surfed, until I found the news channel.

———

"You asleep?"

"Wha..who is it?" I asked.

"Peter. Sorry I woke you."

"That's okay, how long were you all gone?" I sat up and turned the television off.

"About forty-five minutes. We had some technical difficulties we needed to resolve. I'll fill you in over breakfast in the morning."

"Sounds good." I pulled the sheets over me.

"I'll let you get back to sleep." Peter turned off the light and closed the door.

When I woke up, the room was dark. The last thing I remembered hearing was Peter leaving the room. I turned over to check the digital clock which glowed 3:15 in my favorite color. I glanced at the other bed. Peter was asleep under the covers. I had to pee and I was wicked thirsty.

After I went to the bathroom, I tiptoed out to the kitchen. I'd stashed a dark chocolate candy bar in the fridge next to a bottle of water in case I got a craving for something sweet. I stuck a small section into my mouth.

"Hey, midnight raider."

My bottle dropped to the floor and I clutched my chest. "Crap, you scared the hell out of me, Jack."

"Only reason to be startled is if you had been doing something bad. What's that in your hand?"

Amazingly, I hadn't dropped the chocolate bar. The top to the bottled water remained intact. I bent over to pick it up.

"I didn't mean to wake you." I took a bite of chocolate. "Want some?" I waved the bar in front of him.

"Let me do a taste test first." Jack grabbed me and pushed me up against the wall.

"Jack, wait," I whispered.

"Shhhh." The heat from his breath reached my neck's nerve endings, prompting them to bark off orders. My nipples were the first to obey.

He licked the chocolate from my lips and I licked his in return. *Mmmm, hot chocolate.* We continued to kiss and lick. When his hand worked its way between my legs, I went from hot to flash frozen.

"I don't think this is such a good idea," I said, removing his hands from my body.

"Shhhh, don't worry. I'm sure we won't wake Peter. He always slept through the night no matter what activity took place in our dorm room."

My mind filled with images of Jack fooling around with an assortment of drunken college girls while Peter snored away on the top bunk.

The sound of shuffling feet caught my attention. Jack's and mine were planted firmly on the floor. The kitchen light flicked on and I stiffened up like an iron rod.

"Well, well," Peter said.

Guilt set in and I didn't understand why. "We were just having a late night snack."

"A snack huh." Peter folded his arms across his chest.

I grabbed the chocolate bar and inched closer to Peter. "Want some chocolate?"

"It's really tasty." Jack winked.

The wink got lost in delivery and could have been aimed at either of us. I slapped the chocolate bar down on the counter and turned my back to both of them. "I'm going to sleep."

I shut the door and crawled into bed embarrassed and fuming. If Jack had been winking at me I found it kind of sexy, but if he'd been winking at Peter I wanted to throw up.

Neither of them followed me into the bedroom. I listened while they engaged in conversation. The closed door made it impossible to decipher their muffled words, but their tone clearly indicated the discussion had become heated.

At some point I'd fallen asleep, because when I opened my eyes a faint light shone through the sheers. Peter wasn't in the room, so I jumped out of bed to catch the panoramic view of Kansas City in the daytime. Instead of something breathtaking, I discovered a drizzly landscape and raindrops racing down the window.

My body called out for coffee, but I didn't want to show my face outside the bedroom yet. I took a hot shower and volleyed solutions to the cryptic note around in my head.

By the time I finished showering, I hadn't come any closer to solving the puzzle. The thought of a zip code superseded every other thought I had. I took my time getting dressed and replaced the thoughts about the note with the words I was going to say when I saw Jack and Peter this morning.

Stalling, I thumbed through the HBO booklet. All the good shows had started a half-hour earlier. I used up a little more time by packing my bag.

My body was clothed, my hair was dry, my makeup was applied, and my bags were packed. I had nothing else to do, but walk out the bedroom door.

17

"GOOD MORNING!" I stepped through the door acting as though nothing awkward had happened the previous evening, but the room was empty.

A note leaned against a basket of baked goods, next to a carafe of coffee. Peter had gone to the store to get some supplies and Jack left to go back to St. Louis last night. The note didn't mention why Jack left, but I suspected the reason had to do with the argument they had. Whatever was the case, it sounded like Jack wasn't going to be here to participate in the re-napping of Mr. P.

I hoisted a monster blueberry muffin to my mouth, poured some coffee and moved to a chair near the window. The silence gave me time to think. Again, I juggled - Creek Boulder Flat 86927 - in my head. Each time I landed on the numbers representing a zip code. I had to wait until I got home to research the code because I'd neglected to sign up for an unlimited data plan on my phone.

"Honey? I'm home." Peter walked through the door with a paper bag and his black case. The same case he'd pulled the blonde wig from at the no-tell motel during our surveillance. I was positive he'd be playing dress up today.

"What's in the grocery bag?"

"Food." He dropped the bag into my lap.

"Dang, that's heavy." The grocery bag contained a five-pound bag of dog food, a dog bowl, a liter bottle of water, a dog leash, a pack of beef jerky, and two chocolate Yoo Hoos.

"I found out the maids will be nearing Mr. P's room in about thirty minutes."

"And?"

"They're the key to the room."

"No maid is going to let us into a room we can't prove is ours. They'll just tell us to go to the front desk," I said.

"Ah, now this is the point at which I question how you ever became an entrepreneur."

"Ouch."

"C'mon Aspen, use your imagination." Peter opened his identity case as if he were a magician. "Would you like to be a redhead or brunette?"

"Hey, I thought I'd be taking on the position of lookout."

"We're one man down," he reminded me.

"Then, maybe this isn't such a good idea."

"No sweat. It's not my business." He shut the case and snapped the levers closed.

"Wait. At least let me hear your plan."

Peter re-opened his case. I fiddled with the wigs and makeup kits as he ran through his entire plan. Jack's absence had escalated my role in our little caper to headliner. A much larger role than I preferred. Peter's plan sounded solid though.

"Get yourself ready while I take our things to the car. Once we get the dog we need to be ready to roll." He handed me a wig and a makeup kit.

Although I looked feminine, with my long hair, full lips, and killer lashes, I wasn't extremely girly. My regular routine included a little eye shadow, mascara, and lip-gloss. Peter's expectation of my transformation, in only ten minutes, created a big challenge.

I pulled my hair into a ponytail, wrapping the long strand around until I'd formed a small bun on the back of my head. Holding the bun in place, I maneuvered the red wig over my hair. Once I got the wig situated not even a wisp of blonde was visible.

The eyebrow pencil wasn't sharp enough and I ended up with a pair of lopsided, bushy brows. My fight against time gave me no other choice but to leave them crooked and move on to my lips and cheeks. By the time I finished, I had created the perfect 'before subject' for an extreme makeover show.

"Holy crap." Peter's voice boomed from behind me as I stood in front of the mirror. "I take back all the times I said you were cute."

"Shut ufff." The fake teeth flew out of my mouth.

Peter leaned over and picked them up off the floor. "Here, don't bite me."

The teeth had collected some dirt. I rinsed them off under hot water, reinserted them then scrutinized them before agreeing with Peter. My appearance was incredibly unattractive and incredibly un-Aspen. If I were caught on camera even my mother would have a hard time identifying me.

Peter tucked the makeup kit in his backpack.

"I'm ready." I grabbed the bag of dog food and the small paper folder that once held our keycard.

My head remained lowered as we walked to the elevator. In what could only be explained as a gift from the Great Provider, not a single person stepped into the elevator when we did. The blessing continued as our car descended and didn't stop until we reached the first floor.

I followed Peter at a distance. He passed by the maid, in the hall, and stopped when he was several doors away. He coughed, signaling 'Operation: Pinch the P' had been cleared for takeoff.

"Excuse me. Can you help me?" I rested the bag of dog food on my hip.

"Que? Hablo muy poco ingles," the maid replied.

Shit. Peter's plan had no contingency, other than running like hell all the way down the hall and out the door without Mr. P in tow. I had no intention of using that plan after getting this far.

"Me. Nooooo Keeeey." I held up the empty keycard holder.

"Si." She smiled and nodded.

"Gracias." I couldn't believe how easily she agreed.

"Si," she said, pointing toward the lobby. "Go, desk."

I reached down into the bottom of my foreign language trashcan and scrounged around for some high school Spanish.

"Uh, Hambriento. Quiero comer un perro."

An expression of horror appeared on her face and I knew I should have paid better attention in Spanish class.

"No. No. Perro. Dog. Comer. Eat." I patted the bag of food and pointed to the hotel room. "Woof, woof." I pretended to bring a utensil to my mouth. "Por favor?"

"Si." She waved me over to the door and slid her keycard through the slot.

"You first say you hungry and want to eat dog." She laughed and I got the impression she understood more English than I did Spanish.

"Gracias." I gave her a huge smile, making sure she got a good look at my crooked bucked teeth before she went down the hall.

I wandered around the room until Mr. P's bark led me into the bathroom. An animal crate had been tucked into the closet alcove. I put the bag of food on the vanity and knelt down to let Mr. P out. My hand barely had hold of the latch when the handle on the hotel room door clicked.

I hoped a paramedic walked through the door because I was having a heart attack. My next thought was, hide!

I grabbed the food and jumped into the bathtub. The shower curtain had been halfway open and it didn't completely cover me. I pulled it closed a little more and tried not to breathe.

"Yeah, I've got him with me." I recognized the voice. Mr. Q's neighbor must have been talking on his cell phone. "I'm leaving in a few hours, after the conference. Hey, I'm about to take a dump. I'll call you later."

Shit, literally. I weighed my options. Follow the contingency plan - No Mr. P, lose my client, and get sued. Or, stay put and deal with the smell. I clamped my nose between my index finger and thumb and waited.

He entered the bathroom and Mr. P started whining.

"Hey, little guy. You want to get out?"

No. No. No. Letting Mr. P out of the crate would end in disaster. He'd run straight for the tub, hop inside or continue to bark, until he forced the guy to take a look behind the curtain.

"You have to wait little buddy."

If I could have sighed, I would have let out a big one. He opened a book or a magazine. I hoped whatever he planned to read wasn't dirty or interesting. If he decided to turn the bathroom into a library, I didn't intend to handle it like a librarian. He flipped a page and laughed. *Great.*

The sound of my breathing escalated the longer I had to breathe through my mouth. Too loud and I'd not only be caught, I'd be embarrassed, so I unclamped my nose. When the toilet flushed, I almost jumped up and shouted "hallelujah." A few minutes later, I heard the hotel room door click shut.

Not wasting a second, I jumped out of the tub and unlocked the crate. "Come here, Mr. P, baby."

I turned my cell on and called Peter. "Is the coast clear?"

"What happened?"

"I'll tell you later. Is it clear?"

"Ready to roll."

The heavy hotel door made it difficult to exit with a five-pound bag of dog food in one hand and a ten-pound dog in the other. I used my elbow and foot to maneuver the thing open. When the door latch clicked behind me I knew my mission was complete.

———

Peter laughed so hard after I told him what happened in the hotel room, I thought he was going to drive into a ditch. "Are you kidding me?"

"I swear on the porcelain throne." I started laughing too.

Mr. P was on my lap and I slipped him a tiny piece of beef jerky. I ate a larger piece, handed the bag to Peter, then opened our drinks and sat back for a smooth ride.

"So, what do you think is going to happen when the neighbor discovers Mr. P gone?" I said, then took a big gulp of my Yoo Hoo.

"I bet the shit will hit the fan."

My attempt not to laugh failed and I sprayed my drink everywhere. Any secret wish I had about Peter wanting me disappeared. No man could be sexually attracted to a woman after he'd seen her shoot chocolate Yoo Hoo through her nose.

He had a look of amusement scrambled with a side of horror. "Napkins are in the glove box."

"Can we stop at a gas station? I need to remove this makeup and wash off." I tossed Mr. P's Yoo Hoo covered body in the back seat and mopped up the mess.

At the next exit, we spotted a gas station-slash-convenience store-slash-Dairy Queen. While Peter topped off the gas tank, I walked Mr. P over to a grassy area.

"Want anything from Dairy Queen?" I asked Peter as I put Mr. P back inside the car.

"No, I'm good."

I went into the bathroom, washed my hands and tried to rub off the makeup with a wet paper towel. When I finished, I stood in line and ordered a small vanilla cone.

"Now, that's hot," Peter said when I came back to the car.

"Cut it out. My crooked eyebrows won't come off." The wet paper towel hadn't worked and my eyebrows were now large brown smears.

"Sorry, I forgot to bring the special remover."

194

"Thanks a lot. As long as you've got the remover at home I'll let you live. Want a lick?" I held out the ice cream cone.

"I'm not even going to touch that one." He licked the cone a couple of times and then handed it back.

We had over two hours until we'd be back in St. Louis. I was eager to find out why Peter and Jack argued last night, but I didn't want to talk about me and Jack. I chose a ride filled with pleasant conversation, rather than finding out the scoop.

"I might never have found Mr. P without you," I said.

"Not a big deal. That's what friends are for, right? Besides, you were the one who suspected the neighbor."

"Yeah, but I'm lucky to have someone like you to prove me right. I'm going to pay you back for the hotel room and gas."

"What I would like, is to talk to you about Jack."

Last night my imagination had caused me to think Peter might be jealous. I'd even suffered from a bout of guilt. But he'd had no idea what was going on in my head. I suspected he was going to tell me about their argument.

"What about Jack?"

"Are you really into him?"

"I'm not sure. I'm attracted to him, but I need to learn more about him."

"He and I go way back. Over ten years."

"So, is he worth getting to know?"

"Honestly?"

"Of course, honestly." My ears perked up and I readied my invisible shield. Sometimes honesty hurts.

"He can be a decent guy. But I thought you should know that he has a girlfriend."

The hum of the engine and the sound of Mr. P scratching his head filled the car. I was speechless. The image of my bridesmaid's naked body next to my fiancé flashed through my head. I knew my wounds had not yet healed, but now they felt infected. Disloyalty was all around me, politicians, celebrities, Samuel Martin, Max Vanderbur. Who hadn't cheated? Trust issues were not an easy thing to cure.

"Aspen?"

"I don't want to talk about Jack anymore."

Peter let the silence linger for a while before turning on the radio. I appreciated him choosing not to pursue the topic.

An hour outside of St. Louis my phone rang. "Hello, Mr. Q." For the first time in several days I was happy to take his call.

"Aspen, I have a real problem. Mr. Personality is missing."

"No he's not. He's right here with me."

"You can cut the charades."

"What are you talking about? Hold on and I'll put the phone next to his ear."

"Aspen, I know he is not with you. I had my neighbor take him and now someone has stolen him from my neighbor."

"You did what? I've been going insane trying to find him. Why would you do such a thing?"

"To test you. I needed to make sure you wouldn't go public with anything, no matter what the circumstances. Now I need your help finding him."

Somehow I acquired an immense willpower that stopped me from hanging up on him. The money he paid me was good, but not good enough to put up with this crap. Even if I didn't continue to provide services for him, I still had to foster my reputation. I remained calm. "Mr. Q, I'm the one who stole him from the hotel room."

"Mr. Personality's with you?"

I finally convinced him Mr. P was in the back seat, and then admonished him politely for not trusting me. He had agreed to reimburse us for our time and expenses.

"You did good," Peter said, "but what a nut."

"I was thinking the same thing. Hey, I'm sorry I clammed up earlier. I just didn't think Jack would turn out to be an ass."

"I didn't want you to get involved with him and get hurt. Right now it seems like your life is way too fragile for someone like Jack. You should stay focused on keeping yourself out of danger. There is a murderer running around."

"Thanks for reminding me."

Peter's smile conjured up the emotions I secretly harbored for him. My radar seemed to be locked on to men with girlfriends. At least Peter had been up front about Madeline. Even though he flirted a little, Madeline was well aware and knew it was harmless.

"So did you glean anything important from the papers in the box?"

Peter had already spent enough time fixing my problems, so he didn't need the mysterious note taking up more of his time. If he didn't take care of his own life, it might turn into a web of chaos, like mine. "Not much."

18

SOMETHING WET TOUCHED my face. I opened my eyes to a furry white ball hanging out next to my pillow. The minute I moved, Mr. P dove in for another kiss.

I admit, I wanted to wake up pissed. Pissed at Mr. Q. Pissed at Jack. Pissed at life in general. But when Mr. P started twirling around in circles and bouncing up and down on the bed like a Super Ball, I couldn't help but laugh.

"Okay buddy. I know. I need to pee too."

I threw on some sweats after my trip to the bathroom. I hooked Mr. P up to the leash Peter had purchased yesterday and walked him outside. Rather than risk someone involuntarily removing Mr. P from his home again, I decided to ask Mrs. Rippetoe if she would take care of him for the day.

"Isn't she adorable," Mrs. Rippetoe said when she opened the door.

I didn't bother to correct her about Mr. P's sex. Fluffy white hair and a girly bark, didn't exactly shout macho.

"I wanted to ask you a favor. Would it be possible for you to watch Mr. P today?"

"Oh my Lord, yes. You're the cutest thing. Oh Hun, she is so cute."

"I'll bring down the dog bowl and food."

"Oh no, I have everything here."

I'm sure Mrs. Rippetoe's doggie junk food would be a sinful treat for Mr. P. "Thanks. I'll be back later this afternoon."

"Oh, Sassy, look here. This is Mrs. P. You got a little girlfriend to play with." She swept Mr. P into her apartment. I figured she'd discover his little surprise later in the day.

My phone rang as I entered my apartment. The voice was soft, but unmistakable. I should have hit the ignore button. "What do you want, Stephanie?"

"I wanted to tell you how sorry I am about what happened. I didn't call earlier because I went to Chicago."

"What exactly did happen?" I asked, bracing myself for some wild ass explanation.

"Well, I...I'm a recovering kleptomaniac. I don't know why I did it. I haven't taken anything in almost five years. I'm so embarrassed."

She's embarrassed? If only she could see my face. What should I say to a recovering kleptomaniac? Okay, I forgive you, but I'm going to need to strip search you every time you leave my house?

"I'm sorry, Stephanie. I didn't real—"

"Can you forgive me? I swear, I won't do it again."

Everyone deserved a second chance, unless they committed first-degree murder. Stephanie's transgression was way down on the list of bad things in the world. I was more worried about finding out who broke into my apartment, and who killed Max. "It's okay, really."

"Oh, thank you, thank you, thank you. I swear I won't disappoint you. I want to pay you back though, so you can come into the spa anytime and I'll give you a free massage."

"I need to get going," I said.

Fifteen minutes passed before I finally got her to hang up. My list of things to accomplish today was long. On the personal side I had to find out the status of my Jeep and exchange Fugly for a rental car. Then I had work to do, not to mention an impromptu murder investigation. If anything else came up, I seriously had to consider buying someone else's time.

I stuffed the list into my purse and headed out to visit Brackford.

———

The automatic doors opened, leading into the hospital. I took a deep breath to stave off a panic attack and made my way up to the seventh floor. The last time I'd gone to a hospital to visit a friend, I'd gotten shot. My mother had held me in her arms until medical help arrived. The vision of her in blood soaked clothing had been the final push I needed to enter the Witness Protection Program.

"I'm a friend of Mr. Brackford. How is he?" I aimed my question at the only nurse who had been polite enough to acknowledge my existence.

"You're just in time."

"For what?"

"He's been released. He told us to call a cab, but I'm sure he'll be glad you're here to give him a ride."

"I didn't re—"

"He's in 732."

I wanted to help him, I did. Except, I found myself on overload, and giving Thomas Brackford a ride home wasn't on my list.

Relief hit me when I poked my head through the doorway. He looked ninety percent better than he had when I found him bleeding on his floor. "Good morning, Mr. Brackford."

"Hello, Aspen. Thank you for helping me out the other day. Make sure you bill me."

"I can't charge you."

"Yes you can."

"We'll talk about it later. So you're going home?"

"Yes. The nurses are calling me a cab."

The bandage on his head might as well have been my guilty verdict. I sentenced myself. "Nonsense. I'd be happy to take you home."

My life is what caused him to end up in this mess and I had to make it up to him somehow. A ride home seemed too small an offering. A hospital volunteer helped me load Thomas Brackford into Fugly's passenger seat. Brackford's legs and face were thin compared to his upper body, which had become overdeveloped from years of doing double-time.

"You need to raise your rates," Brackford said, as we pulled away from the hospital.

"Why's that?"

"This car. It's not exactly the state of the art in modern transportation."

I knew he was serious. Thomas Brackford's disgust with Fugly gave me one more reason, other than Jack cheating on his girlfriend, to trade Fugly in for a rental. As soon as I dropped him off, I was calling the rental car agency.

When we arrived at his home, I retrieved his wheelchair from inside and positioned it next to the car. He began lifting his body, but his full strength hadn't yet returned and he dropped back into the passenger seat.

"Okay, on the count of three," I said.

A few seconds later he landed in his wheelchair and I went into spasm. I clenched my teeth and visualized the pain leaving my body. My nerve endings paid no attention because they were too busy holding a union meeting smack dab in the middle of my lower back.

"Good Lord. Is that my blood?" he asked when he caught sight of the irregular brown spot, the size of an extra large pizza, on his hardwood floor.

"Yeah, you sure got whacked."

The room was exactly as it was the day they took me out in handcuffs, except for the dead flies. I didn't think he needed any details.

"Would you like me to find someone to clean up this place?"

"Doesn't your company do anything for anybody? Isn't that your slogan?"

"I think you'll want a special company skilled in cleaning up after crimes. They know exactly what cleaning solutions are best." I had to add crime scene clean up, right under sexual favors, to the list of things my business won't do. "I'll find someone for you."

I eased myself out of my chair, after jotting down a long list of additional jobs Thomas Brackford wanted me to do over the next few months. One small step after another, I made my way back to the car. A single giant-sized whimper and I was in the driver's seat.

Convincing myself I had no other choice, I picked up the phone and made the call. "Hi Stephanie, I have an emergency. Can you fit me in for that massage you promised?"

"All booked up today. I can bring my portable table and meet you at your place, but I can't meet you until seven because I got a client at my house at five-thirty."

I didn't hear anything after 'meet you at your place.' I was too busy wondering how long it would take me to hide everything so she wouldn't get the urge to steal my stuff. "Why don't I just come over to you?"

"Even better, see you at seven."

My plan to go to the county records building would have to be put on hold. Lifting plat books and rummaging through microfilm didn't seem possible with my back in trouble. Instead, I'd have to do some work in my office.

Pulling away from Thomas Brackford's place, I had every intention of heading straight to my office. But when I reached my first red light, I glanced across the road at a black Mercedes. Inside, Mrs. Vanderbur and John Martin were happily engrossed in conversation. The light turned green and they drove through the intersection too busy to notice me staring. I couldn't stop myself. An empty road was all the permission I needed to hang a u-ey, so I whipped my car around and headed after them.

Whoop. Whoop, whoop. Whooooooooooooo. "Un-f-n-believable." I obeyed the siren and pulled over to the side of the road. Looking in my rearview mirror, I begged God to have Officer Eli Storey exit the patrol car.

The stranger behind the dark sunglasses and badge took out his bad news tablet. As I sat waiting for my punishment, an awareness came over me. God must have enrolled me in his distance-learning program designed for people like me who had stopped going to church. What other explanation could there be?

I thanked the officer as he handed me the ticket. When I read the amount, I realized I was an idiot. Who thanked an officer for giving them a ticket equaling twenty-two Starbucks Vanilla Lattes?

———

I placed my briefcase and purse on my lap, swung both legs out the car door, and placed my feet on the ground. A few choice words escaped my mouth as I stood up and hobbled slowly to my office.

Peter had been talking with a customer when I passed by his store. A quick trip to the bathroom and I'd head back to ask him for a loan. Not a monetary loan, but an electronic gadget loan.

"What are you doing?" I asked when I finally entered Peter's store. He stood at the counter as Victor walked around dusting the displays.

"Why are you walking so funny?"

"Just a little muscle cramp. Got an appointment with Stephanie later."

"Oh, the redhead from hell?"

"That would be the one. I wondered if I could borrow a gadget."

"You mean an expensive security or surveillance device?"

"Yeah, a listening gadget."

No matter how much he wanted me to view his company as a professional security and surveillance business, I couldn't. The place overflowed with cool items and most of the stuff was used to spy on people - spy on spouses, spy on neighbors, spy on employees - the possibilities were endless.

"Should I even ask who you want to listen to with this expensive equipment?"

"Will you quit telling me how expensive the equipment is because you're making me nervous. I don't even want to touch a thing."

"Maybe that's the point."

"I want to listen to someone while I stay in my car. Do you carry anything like that?"

"A portable parabolic listening device. Allows you to hear sounds up to 300 feet away."

Well aware of my inability to estimate distance, Peter tried to help me get the picture. "It's not quite equal to a football field."

"How far in girl terms?"

"Let's see. Well...it's like from Nordstrom to the food court."

"Wow, that's a pretty good distance. That should work."

Peter opened a display case and pulled out something resembling a satellite dish. For the next twenty minutes, he explained the finer details of the HEAR 300.

"Let's do a quick test, okay? I'll signal you when we're ready," Peter said. He and Victor walked to the back of the store.

I put the headphones on my head and pointed the contraption in their direction. Sure, he hadn't given the signal yet, but what good was a covert listening device if you didn't use it covertly?

"Why don't you tell her you like her?" Victor asked.

Victor's voice was so clear, had my eyes been closed I would have thought he was standing next to me. A truly incredible device.

"What are you talking about?" Peter asked.

"It's obvious. You talk about her a bunch and you seem to spend a lot of time with her. And you got to admit, she's hot."

My ears perked up. I wondered what Peter would say. The chance of anything happening between us was zilch. He respected Madeline and I respected myself, but it was always good to know what someone thought of you.

"Yes, she's hot, but we're friends. Have you forgotten Madeline?" Peter turned around and gave me the thumbs up.

I returned the thumbs up and smiled.

"So can you hear me?" Peter asked.

"Wow," I yelled, "Any better and I'd be listening to your thoughts."

A rush of red made its way across Peter's face. Or maybe my imagination had gone into overdrive again. After all, he had no idea I heard what he said. Peter headed in my direction, leaving Victor in the stockroom.

I held up the HEAR 300. "This is fantastic, thanks. I promise I'll return it to you in the same condition."

"Don't be getting into any trouble, but if you do, you know who to call."

"Since when have I gotten myself into trouble?" I looked up from the HEAR 300 just in time to catch the expression on his face. "Never mind, don't answer that."

"Don't let your guard down."

"I'm not worried. The stalker has been a no show lately."

"It doesn't matter. You still need to watch out for yourself. Would you like me to get you a stun gun?"

"No thanks. Pepper spray, remember? Besides, if I'm going to carry a gun it's going to be a real one."

I left Peter's store and placed the equipment in the back of Fugly before returning to my office. Preoccupied at Peter's, I hadn't paid attention to the pain. Once inside my office I gave in and sat down at my desk to call Mirella.

"Mirella? It's Aspen."

"No, it's Nick."

"Oh, sorry. Is Mirella in?"

"Nope. She ran to the store. Where have you been? She got tired of waiting for you to call."

He sounded irritated, but with no time to explain, I gave him the short version. "Finding a lost dog. Is Sara available?"

"Yeah, but she's still pretty upset. I think she wants her box back. You want me to come get it?"

"Can I talk to her?"

"Sure."

Minutes passed before Sara got on the phone. "Hello? Aspen?"

"Sara, are you okay?"

"I want to go home."

"You can't go home yet, but I may be on to something. Hopefully you'll be able to go soon. Does Creek Boulder Flat 86927 mean anything to you?"

"No. Why?"

"The phrase was written on an index card I found in the box."

"I have no idea what it means. I never came across a note like that, but going through the box was painful so I didn't look at everything. What do you think it means?"

"I'm not sure, but I plan to find out. Can I speak to Nick again?"

"Hey, it's Nick."

"Can you do me a favor and stay with Sara until Mirella gets back?"

"Sure. So what did you find in the box?"

"Not much."

"Why don't you tell me? I am pretty good at deciphering things."

Clearly he had eavesdropped on our conversation. At this point I was keeping the information between Sara and me. "Not really sure what it is."

"What do you mean you're not sure? Can't you just read the thing to me?"

"Sorry, the note isn't in front of me. Look, I need to run. Tell Mirella I'll call later."

I hung the phone up for a second then called Mrs. Vanderbur. Other people might think it insensitive to call a widow and ask for the name of the company used to clean up after her husband's death, but I didn't care. A talk with Mrs. Vanderbur gave me an opportunity to get her to trip up and perhaps tell me something she didn't want me to know.

"Vanderbur residence."

"May I speak with Mrs. Vanderbur please?"

A few minutes passed, allowing my imagination to run wild about whether the person who'd answered the phone was a relative or hired help. I personally knew hired help wasn't cheap.

"Hello," Mrs. Vanderbur chirped. She seemed in a good mood for being a week old widow.

"This is Aspen Moore. I hope you won't think I'm being insensitive, but I needed to ask you a question."

"What is so important you call up a widow, in the midst of mourning the loss of her husband?" Once again, Mrs. Vanderbur's tone had turned nasty.

"I'm trying to help another client."

"Are you looking for money again?"

"No. I thought you woul—"

"Just go ahead and ask your damn question. You're wasting my time."

"I was wondering what company you used to clean up after your husband passed away."

"I didn't take care of the mess. Sandra did. Ask her."

"Wait. One more question."

"What now?"

"Could I come over tonight and speak with you, privately?"

"Impossible. I have a guest coming. Now, here's Sandra." She drew out the first a in Sandra, making her sound a bit like Zsa Zsa Gabor.

A guest was coming to visit. Hooray. I couldn't wait to use the HEAR 300. I asked Saaandra what company she called.

"Crime Undone." She hung up the phone without a goodbye.

I hopped on the cyber highway, stopping at the website of Crime Undone – the affordable crime cleanup company. They had an open slot so I booked them for tomorrow.

My next stop, Google, where I finally searched for the 86927 zip code and discovered none existed. I popped in and out of web sites, reading anything remotely relating to the cryptic note. Not a single thing I read covered everything in the note.

Three hours of searching passed before I remembered to call the car rental company. "Hello. I'd like to rent a car."

"Do you have a reservation?"

"No. Do I need one?"

"Normally you don't, but everything is booked. The World Series game is tomorrow night. It's been a madhouse."

I couldn't believe I'd forgotten the Cardinals were playing in the series. The red banners blanketed downtown. "When will one be available?"

"Probably not for another two days. I can put your name on our list and call you as soon as one becomes available."

The guy took my information and I mentally whacked myself upside the head for not calling earlier. The thought of another day in Jack's ratty car reminded me of the rat. He'd already called once today and I'd sent him to voice mail. Any man who cheated on his girlfriend didn't deserve my time.

I reviewed some of the emails I'd gotten requesting quotes. A few wanted me to track down some season tickets for the Cardinals in the prime seating areas. Fat chance on that one, especially with the Cardinals in the series, but I told them I would look into it. They'd pay me a twenty percent commission. The others included planning a kid's birthday party, two months of grocery shopping for a woman going through surgery, and some personal organizing. None were ready to commit, so I placed the information in my leads folder.

The phone rang. When I answered, it was Harry Corbitt on the other end.

"Mr. Corbitt. I'm very busy. If you can't tell me why you'd like to meet then I will have to respectfully decline."

"I want to hire you to finish planning my wedding."

The thought of a new customer thrilled me, but Harry Corbitt was a little creepy. "I don—"

"My fiancée had an unexpected business trip out of the country and won't be back until a week before our wedding day. I haven't the foggiest where to start," he pleaded.

All of a sudden he was filled with words, so different from how he'd acted over the phone earlier. "Did you call a wedding planner?"

"Yes. An entire list I found on the Internet. They were either out of business or booked."

I wanted to tell him he had the wrong person. That my only experience with planning a wedding had ended tragically with death and debauchery. "Is it possible to postpone your wedding?"

"It's too late. Bucks night is set and my mates already purchased airline tickets."

"I'm sorry did you say Bucks night?"

"Oh yes. Sorry. It's the Australian version of a bachelor party. My mates are flying in from Australia. Can you help? Invitations have gone out. Several remaining details need to be taken care of and I am short on time."

That was all he had to say. I was in the business of selling time, how could I refuse? If he wanted me instead of a real wedding planner, then so be it.

"Consider me your wedding planner," I said, not quite believing the words coming out of my mouth. I scribbled down the information.

"Can we meet?" he asked.

"I'm pretty sure I have enough to get started."

"I'd really like to meet."

I'm just saying, the guy was creepy. "I'm busy today. I'll call you in the next few days."

We finished our conversation. I reviewed my notes, making a few calls to the venue he'd indicated they'd already booked for the wedding. It was the only tasks besides the wedding invitations that had been completed. No reception hall had been booked, so they didn't include it on the invitation. I had my work cut out for me. I filed away the information before heading out to Stephanie's place.

19

STEPHANIE LIVED IN THE CENTRAL WEST END, not too far from where the rat lived. I parked in front of the mid-rise building and made my way from the road to the sidewalk and up the steps without cussing.

The brick courtyard, lined with bronze, three-lantern light posts, reminded me of New Orleans. The outside was beautiful and quaint, which meant the inside had to be a dump because I didn't think Stephanie could afford something super elegant.

"Hey, Girlie, come on in. I need a second to get the room ready. The guy only left fifteen minutes ago." Stephanie's dangling earrings brought back memories of mall guards.

"No problem. I'll look around your new place if you don't mind."

Stephanie walked down the hall. I perused the living room and the kitchen. Granite countertops. Hardwood cherry cabinets. This puppy was even decked out with Viking Professional appliances. I either needed to get a job as a massage therapist or Stephanie had to be selling extras.

"Come on back," she yelled.

"Nice place." I hoped she'd elaborate on how she came into this fabulous condominium.

"Thanks."

"Business must be great."

"Yeah, I'm busting it."

She didn't give an inch. I took the light robe she handed me and changed in the bathroom. When I came back in, the lavender aromatherapy oil filled the room. Stephanie continued mixing oils and I got a whiff of eucalyptus.

"That's strong, but smells wonderful."

"I'm blending a special relaxation and muscle pain relief formula."

"Exactly what I need."

"Hop up on the table. Face down. I'll be back in a second."

Stephanie left the room and I disrobed, easing myself onto the table. I rolled my hipster underwear down a bit so she'd be able to massage my lower back. I wiggled my head back and forth until I found a comfortable position on the head support, then reached back and pulled the sheet up over my body.

The stress left my body as soon as Stephanie began working her magic. She could be loud and boisterous, but when she gave a massage she stayed silent. For the next thirty minutes, I drifted in and out. I may have even snored.

"Aspen? Go ahead and turn over." Stephanie's voice was soft like a sportscaster covering the PGA tour.

I kept the sheet over me so my Big D's wouldn't fall out. As I turned myself over, I froze in mid turn. Across the room, on the floor, leaning up against the wall, was a gorgeous red leather briefcase exactly like mine.

———

"Where'd you get that briefcase?" I eased myself into a sitting position, wrapping the sheet around me.

"Oh, that. Nice, isn't it?"

"Yes, but where'd you get it?"

Stephanie fell silent. Every muscle in her face appeared to have lost its power. She hung her head. When she looked up at me, her eyes were moist. "She was such a bitch to me."

"Who?" I asked.

"Tracy Vanderbur."

Bitch was too tame a word in my opinion. Every contact I'd had with Mrs. Vanderbur reminded me of a spider eating its prey. I held my words and waited for Stephanie to explain the briefcase.

"Tracy always treats me like her lit—"

"Stephanie." My voice remained calm. I reached out and placed my hand on hers so she wouldn't become more agitated. "What does that have to do with the briefcase?"

"After I gave her a massage, I packed up my stuff and put it in my car. I went back in to get paid like I do every week. She was furious. And do you know what she said?"

"No. I don—"

"She said she didn't think a little tramp like me deserved such an exorbitant amount, but she wanted to make sure I stayed away from her man. She handed me two thousand dollars and told me to get the hell out of her house and never come back. I took the money and the bitch's briefcase too."

Stephanie had admitted to being a kleptomaniac, but I was beginning to think she was a compulsive liar too. "When did this happen?"

"Yesterday."

"Her husband died a week ago."

"Not her husband, her man. John Martin."

My intuition had been right; Mrs. Vanderbur had been cheating with John Martin. The questions materialized faster than I could spit them out. "Are you sure?"

"In my business, people tell me a lot of things. They think of me as their friend. I have a reputation."

I cleared my throat to stop a radical snicker from escaping. I understood what she meant, but I couldn't help think – reputation? I bet you do.

"Was she right about you seeing John Martin?"

"No. I slept with him twice, if that's what you mean. It sort of just happened. It wasn't planned."

Sleeping with him once might be a case of it just happening, but sleeping with him twice meant she wanted it to happen. An image of Stephanie and John Martin on the massage table prompted me to jump off the table and grab my clothes to get dressed.

"Can I see the case?" I asked when I came out of the bathroom.

"Sure. Feel how soft. You're going to love it."

"Very soft." I opened the case up trying to find anything interesting. "What happened to all the stuff?"

"Oh. The only thing inside was a bunch of junk, mostly papers. I threw them out."

"Are the papers still in your trash?"

"Why?"

"You don't want any evidence lying around."

"Right, glad I tossed my trash in the dumpster. They pick up tomorrow."

"Thanks for the massage. You are gifted. Not a single pain left in my back."

Stephanie opened the fridge. "Take some water for the road. You need to wash all the toxins out of your body," she said, handing me a bottle.

The minute I walked out the front door of the building I scanned the area looking for the dumpster. Even though I was in my thirties, I was an experienced dumpster diver from way back. Surely it couldn't be that much more difficult at my age.

I retrieved my flashlight from the car and walked around to the back of the building. The dumpster sat in front of a three foot retaining wall. I carefully climbed on top and shined my flashlight inside. Bad move. The dumpster was at maximum capacity filled with what appeared to be a month's worth of trash, the grossest of which had not been placed inside plastic garbage bags.

A scratchy voice blurted out from a window on the second floor. "Gladys! Someone's out near the dumpster again. Call the police."

The gross trash was enough to make me question taking a dive, but the added threat of another run-in with the police had convinced me I should pass. My chance of finding the papers before I passed out from the smell was slim anyway. I turned off my flashlight, eased myself off the wall, and skedaddled.

Disappointment set in as I drove. I'd not only lost my chance to get Mrs. Vanderbur's papers, I now had two other people with a briefcase like mine. I was more confused than ever. Did one of them send the case to me and hire someone to attack me, or could they be innocent victims too?

I checked my watch. Mr. Q hadn't called, but I was sure his plane had landed. Mr. P couldn't go home tonight if I wanted to listen to Mrs. Vanderbur and her guest. I placed a call to Mr. Q to let him know I'd drop Mr. P off tomorrow. My call went straight to voice mail, so I left a message.

I knocked on Mrs. Rippetoe's door when I got home. "Can Mr. P spend the night with you?"

"Of course. The girls played all day long."

I thanked her and waited to roll my eyes until I was walking up the steps. If she hadn't figured out Mr. P was a boy by now, I didn't have the heart to tell her.

Mrs. Vanderbur's guest should have arrived at her house by now. I hustled out to the car with a few munchies and my briefcase. The car door creaked as it opened and reminded me Fugly wasn't the best choice for a surveillance vehicle in an upscale neighborhood, so I called Peter.

"Hey, I know this is short notice, but do you want to go spy with me?"

"Surveillance, not spying. Sorry though, I can't. Madeline will be back in a few days and I want to make sure I'm caught up on my paperwork at the store."

"Oh."

"Don't do that, Aspen."

"Do what?"

"Make me feel guilty."

"I didn't do anything. I just said, oh."

"It's how you said it."

My spirit was broken. I couldn't risk using Fugly to spy on Mrs. Vanderbur. The thought of asking to borrow

Peter's Cadillac was fleeting since I'd already wrecked my Jeep and gotten Jack's car towed.

"Okay. Your place, thirty minutes," Peter finally said.

"Yes," I whispered and pumped my fist.

"I heard that."

"You're the best. I'm at home. Pull up front and I'll come outside."

I ran back up to my apartment, hauling my spy paraphernalia along with me. I took my to-do list out of my purse and marked off each item I'd accomplished, which didn't take long.

My cell phone vibrated across the table. Jack's number popped up, but I didn't answer. My first inclination was to delete the message he'd left without listening to it, but curiosity got the best of me.

"Aspen, I've tried calling you four times. Please call me. Whatever Peter told you is incorrect. He doesn't have the story straight. At least give me an opportunity to explain." His recorded voice came across softer and deeper than his real voice.

I deleted the message. My stomach fluttered and my heart picked up speed. The whole situation had gotten out of control. I didn't have a lot invested. A quick sharp cut would produce less residual pain. But what if Peter was wrong?

A knock on the door interrupted my thoughts.

"Shit." I looked at my watch and ran to the door.

"Meet me outside. Isn't that what you said?"

"Yep, sorry." I gathered my things and Peter and I set off down the steps.

"Who are we trying to listen to?"

"You actually brought the Cadillac?"

"I figured you wanted me to come along because you didn't think a bright orange Ford Fairmont station wagon was exactly the perfect surveillance car."

"You picked up on that, did you? You are an excellent investigator. I'm sure the PI side of your business will do as well as your spy shop."

Peter shook his head and started the car. "Where to?"

"Mrs. Vanderbur's house."

I cringed, waiting for his reaction.

"You said you were going to stop focusing on her? She's done nothing to make anyone think she had anything to do with murdering her husband. Sure, John Martin dropped her off, but you have no idea why they were together."

Without evidence, passing on the information from Stephanie as fact wouldn't win the debate. I formulated another approach. "I saw her with him today too. She is guilty of something. She could be responsible for the person attacking me in the park. Don't I have a right to try to find out who's after me? Don't I have a right to go after whoever it is, instead of waiting for the person to get me?"

"Whoa. Down girl."

"Well, geez Peter, I mean...if I don't try to protect myself, who will?"

"I will. The least you could do is let someone help you instead of hiding things. Why does it always seem like you're hiding something?"

My heart responded to his question with an ache. "What makes you think that?"

"Oh, I don't know. Maybe the way you got all excited after you went through the box Sara Obermier gave you and then said nothing was in the box."

My head swung around and I tried to keep my eyes from morphing into gigantic moon pies. "How did you know about that?"

"Hah. So you did find something."

"You tricked me?"

"How else am I going to get you to share information with me?"

"Fine. You win. Come by my office tomorrow and I'll fill you in." I hoped by then he might lose interest.

"Finally. You can be so stubborn."

As we drove to Mrs. Vanderbur's neighborhood, I caved and told Peter about Stephanie's confrontation and the briefcase sighting. I also confessed to my aborted dumpster dive.

"I think we should go back to the dumpster tonight. Either we prove Stephanie right or wrong. You game?" Peter asked.

"Seriously?"

"Sure. You'll find out if Stephanie was lying. If she was telling the truth then the papers might be important. Even if they don't contain information we need, we might be able to use them to get what we need."

"I never thought of that. Dumpster diving by moonlight, what a perfect date."

"Yeah, well don't tell Madeline. She'll be jealous that I've never taken her."

"It's our dirty little secret." I winked at him and finally relaxed. Having his help to figure out who killed Max Vanderbur probably wasn't a bad idea after all. At this point, I would do almost anything to get my life closer to normal.

"We need to park on the street behind the Vanderbur house," Peter said as we circled around the cul-de-sac.

We drove back to the cross street and over to another development under construction behind Mrs. Vanderbur's place. Irony smacked me in the face. "Did you see that? Oak Farm Estates, a Martin-Stone Development."

Peter laughed. He turned left onto a street where two new executive homes had been built. All the other lots were vacant, including the lot right behind the Vanderbur home.

"Not a spot much more perfect than this." Peter parked the car in front of the empty lot and turned off the lights.

I reached into the back seat and grabbed the HEAR 300. "Too bad we don't have more than one set of headphones."

"Check this out." Peter pulled a small headphone set from the pocket on the side of his door then reached over into the glove box.

A sizzling tingle ran up my thigh when the back of Peter's hand brushed across my leg. My need for sex had ventured way past the due date because I didn't normally react to Peter's touch with such electricity. He had no idea his touch had caused a reaction inside me, but I still couldn't stop the embarrassment from rising.

"You okay? You look a little flushed."

"I'm fine. So, now what?"

"I'll plug this adapter into the HEAR 300 and then our earphones into the adapter. We should both be able to hear everything."

I placed earphones on my head and pointed the part that resembled a satellite dish toward the house. A vague figure of a woman was visible through the attached viewfinder. She stood on the patio talking with someone whose back was to me. They sat down next to a stone pit, brimming with fire. I lodged the contraption between the window and tip of the door and sat back to listen.

"Have another glass of wine, Tracy."

"No. I want a kiss, not wine."

"Guess we got here at the good part," Peter whispered, after pulling the earphone away from my left ear.

I swatted his hand away.

"I've waited a long time for us to be together," Mrs. Vanderbur said.

The man sounded like John Martin. I'd seen them in the car earlier and Stephanie had verified what I suspected.

"Oh, Samuel, kiss me all over."

I flung my head around to look at Peter and he looked as shocked as I felt. Father and son? Uggh.

"Yes, yes." Mrs. Vanderbur moaned softly.

Buttons popped, zippers zipped, patio furniture scooted and then the all too familiar sound Peter and I heard at the no-tell motel began. I took off my headphones and stared at Peter until he obeyed my silent command and removed his. The two of us had been listening to a lot of sex lately – other people's sex.

"We should put these back on. We might miss something important." Peter picked the headphones up out of my lap and started to put them on my head.

"Pervert."

"You love it." He let the headphones snap to my head.

We listened to a few more minutes of grunts and groans. I was surprised the neighbors hadn't turned their lights on with all the noise.

"Thanks, baby," Samuel said.

I could sort of see them moving around the back yard. I heard glass clink.

"Samuel?"

"Yes." Samuel's tone oozed disinterest.

"I've misplaced my new red briefcase. I can't find it anywhere."

"How many of those have you lost now?"

"I'm not sure. I'd really like another one in case mine doesn't surface. If I do find mine, I can still use the new one as a spare."

"I'll ask my son if he can get another one."

The conversation implied John Martin was the source of the briefcases. Mrs. Vanderbur had lost more than one briefcase. Stephanie had one, which meant the other one Mrs. Vanderbur lost might be the one I had received in the box.

"Samuel?"

"What now?" He sounded impatient.

"Are you leaving Macy?"

"I don't want to talk about this again. I told you I can't leave Macy."

"When I told you I was leaving Max you told me you were trying to leave too. Do you think she'd stay with you if she knew you killed Mr. Obermier?"

"What are you talking about?"

My heart beat faster. I hadn't expected to uncover another murder. Samuel Martin's tone indicated he knew exactly what she was talking about.

"I know you murdered him and I don't care. But I bet Macy would. I hope she doesn't find out."

"For God's sake, Tracy, spreading a rumor like that will land you in a lot of trouble."

"You can't deny it," she persisted.

"I'm leaving. No need to show me out."

"Are you still getting me another red briefcase?"

Samuel didn't respond, so I assumed the answer was no.

"Bastard," Mrs. Vanderbur screamed.

The outside lights on the homes flanking Mrs. Vanderbur's house lit up. Peter started the car and we drove away with our lights off. I lowered my window and pulled the HEAR 300 into the car and placed it in the back seat. At the main road, Peter turned on the lights.

"Holy crap! Did you hear that? The whole damn Martin clan is turning out to be bad news," I said.

"Definitely some explosive information. Too bad we can't give any of that information to the police, unless we want to risk being arrested for listening and watching them without their consent. Which way to the dumpster?"

"You still want to go?" I asked.

"Now more than ever."

———

I was still in my black sweats and black t-shirt, but Peter wore a long sleeved, red madras shirt under a light tan cotton sweater with dark jeans. We approached the dumpster with our flashlight off.

"You're going to have to take the dive," Peter whispered.

"Why me?"

"Because you're dressed appropriately."

"Thanks for pointing out that I've clothed myself like a dumpster diver."

"Shhh. Keep your voice down." Peter jumped onto the brick wall and gave me a hand up. He shined the flashlight into the dumpster. "Disgusting."

"You thought I was lying? Are you sure you want to make me jump in?"

"Why don't we start with you plucking out a bag and handing it to me?"

"That sounds a little better."

"You said she just threw the bag out, so it's bound to be in one of the bags on the top." Peter tossed me the flashlight.

"Yuck. Here, take this." I handed him a bag.

I gave him two more bags and the flashlight. If we didn't find Mrs. Vanderbur's papers in the first three bags, I'd actually need to take a dive.

"Does Stephanie own a dog?" Peter asked.

"No."

"I can pass on this one." He handed the bag back to me and I placed it on the wall.

"What's in that one?" I wished I'd been the one rummaging. You can learn a lot about people by looking in their trash.

"Found some papers." Peter held them up, shaking them back and forth.

"Well, what do they say?"

He flashed the light on them. "Damn. Just kids coloring book pages."

"Wouldn't be Stephanie's garbage."

Peter opened the third bag. "Another set of papers. Oh yeah."

"What?"

"I believe we've found what we came for." He removed a few more papers.

I scooped up the first bag and aimed at the dumpster. My throw wouldn't land me on a basketball team any time soon. The bag overshot the dumpster and went crashing into the parking lot. Lights blinked on in the upstairs window of the scratchy voiced apartment dwellers.

"Hurry, turn the flashlight off," I yelled under my breath.

"Wait. There are a few more papers in here."

"Peter, the old man upstairs is currently commanding his wife Gladys to call the police."

"One more minute."

The extra minute turned into five. Peter finally tossed the other two bags into the dumpster – perfect rim shots. "Here, take these."

I rolled the papers up and held them in my left hand while Peter took my right arm and helped me down off the wall. We walked back towards Peter's car until we heard the siren.

20

"RUN!" I TOOK OFF at full speed.

"Hold on, Aspen. Slow down." Peter's footsteps echoed behind me. His voice was muffled and getting farther away.

Torn between saving my ass and helping his, I turned around. He looked pathetic. He was doubled over and breathing hard.

"Are you okay?" I asked, hoping the answer would be 'yes'.

"Got a cramp."

I made my way back to him and grabbed his arm. "Either you move or I'll make you explain to the police why I'm dressed in black and reek of garbage."

"Can't. Go ahead." Peter handed me the keys.

"I'm not leaving you like this. Honestly, we don't even know if they're coming to get us. I should call for an ambulance."

"No. I'll be okay. It's only a cramp, but I need to lie down for a few minutes. Get the car and circle around." Peter stretched out on the sidewalk.

"I'll be back." The red and blue flashing lights were visible.

The police car passed me when I was halfway down the block. My eyes fixated on the rearview mirror as the police stopped next to the spot where Peter lay sprawled on his back. The stress of another possible police confrontation gave way to worrying over Peter. He hadn't been sick the entire time I'd known him, not even a cold.

In order to circle around, I turned left at the light and ended up behind a little blue car having convulsions. Forward. Stop. Forward. Stop. I didn't have time for the driver to figure out how to use his clutch. The madness provoked me to pass him in the middle of the intersection.

The road in front of Stephanie's building was dark, no flashing lights, which meant Peter was in the clear. I turned onto the street, but he was nowhere in sight. I pulled over to the side of the road and opened the window. "Peter! Peter!"

A few minutes passed and I yelled again. Thinking he might have had to pee, I turned the car off and waited. I kept my eye on Stephanie's building hoping he'd come walking out from behind the bushes. When he didn't, I leaned back against the seat and dialed Peter's number. The center console rang. When I lifted the lid, I found Peter's cell phone and wallet.

Wild thoughts of Peter hitting his head on the sidewalk raced through my mind. He could be wandering around aimlessly with a brain full of amnesia. I took a deep breath and mentally talked myself back to reality. The more realistic picture appeared even dimmer. The police had probably arrested him, or worse, rushed him to the hospital.

In an emergency like this, I shouldn't have had a second thought about driving straight to the police station. My expertise in dealing with the men in blue had become a finely honed skill. But we weren't exactly near my police station.

I looked through every crevasse in my purse for Officer Storey's business card before I remembered I'd dropped it into the pocket of my blazer. I called the only person left to call.

"Hello," a woman said and then giggled.

Oh brother, that sucks. I hung up.

A few minutes later my phone rang. "Hello."

"Aspen, Let me expl—"

"I need your help." I didn't need or want to hear Jack's explanation.

"Okay, but I want you to know th—"

"Peter's missing."

"Missing? Where are you?"

"I'm on Lindell Boulevard. Peter asked me to circle around because the police were coming. When I got back he was gone. I think they may have taken him. Could you find out for me?"

"I'm not going to ask why you are involved with the police again, just swing by my house and pick me up."

"Can't you just call and then call me back?"

"Is it possible Peter might need a lawyer?"

"Maybe."

"Exactly what I thought. By the time you get here I'll have figured everything out."

I agreed to pick Jack up, but wasn't happy about it. I hadn't seen or talked to him since he slinked out of the hotel in Kansas City. My willpower had stayed strong by avoidance and I worried a single glance into his tequila gold eyes might screw it all up.

When I arrived at Jack's house, I sat for a minute to collect my thoughts. "You can do this, Aspen. You go girl!" I pushed myself out of the car and onto the walkway leading to his front door.

Step after step, affirmations flashed through my head like the Goodyear Blimp. Before I had a chance to knock, the front lights blinked on and the door opened. I tried catching a glimpse inside, but Jack was too quick. Within seconds, he closed the door behind him.

"It's good to see you again." He flashed his smile, chipping away at my willpower.

"Did you find out anything about Peter?"

"You didn't tell me he had no identification on him. That's why they took him to the station."

"Oh, thank God. I was worried they had taken him to a hospital. Guess there's no need for a lawyer so you don't need to come with me."

"Not exactly, the lack of ID wasn't the only reason. The officer I spoke with mentioned something about a dumpster."

Oh crap. I'd forgotten I was wearing my cat burglar sweats with a splash of eau de garbage. Semi-relief settled over me, as I realized not even the world's ugliest man would make a pass at me in this getup. My willpower would stay intact, at least for the night.

We'd barely driven a block when Jack spoke. "I apologize, Aspen."

"For what?"

"For not telling you I had a girlfriend. I should have told you we were in the process of breaking up."

"You were, but you aren't now?"

"No, we aren't in the process of breaking up. We've already broken up."

"Oh."

"I'd like for us to start over."

Silence in a car with another person usually triggered my mouth to open and words to come out, but I was too busy listening to my willpower cracking, despite my smelly attire. After a heated internal debate, the pro-Jack side claimed victory. "Okay."

Jack didn't say a word. He leaned over and placed his hand on top of my thigh. A zillion electric shocks pulsed through my body. My leg jerked and my right hand flew off the steering wheel, smacking Jack in the chest.

Once he finished coughing, he leaned back toward the passenger side door. "Guess we'll take it a little slower."

After that freaky display he'd probably never touch me again. "Sorry, just caught me by surprise."

"What about dinner Wednesday night?" He kept both of his hands planted firmly in his lap.

"That could work, but I have one question first."

"Sure."

"Who answered your phone earlier?"

"So you do want an explanation."

"Only if you want to go out on a date."

"That's my niece, Sandy. My sister and her daughter are visiting for a few days. They leave tomorrow. Take a left here."

I obeyed his instructions and approached a parking lot lined with police cars. I parked on the side of the road and turned off the ignition.

"I'll wait here."

"You sure? Might be a little while."

"In case you haven't noticed, I smell like garbage."

"Really?" He closed the door and walked toward the station entrance.

———

When the alarm went off it was like I was on a zero gravity carnival ride. My eyes were open but I couldn't move. I had stayed up until four o'clock in the morning, worrying about all my problems and resolving none. Today was going to require a lot of caffeine.

I skipped my morning shower since I'd practically washed myself down the drain last night trying to remove the stench. I threw some clothes on and headed down to Mrs. Rippetoe's place.

"Good morning, Hun." Her chirpiness was a little too much for me.

"Mr. P has to go home today."

"Sassy and I will miss her."

My irritability almost made its debut. I wanted to yell 'Dammit, it's Mister P', but I held in my bitchy words. "Maybe I can bring Mr. P over for a visit again soon."

"Oh my, would you? I'd, well, we'd both love that. Mrs. P is such a delight."

"Sure thing. Sorry I can't stay." I fastened the lead to his collar and walked him outside to do his duty before we got in the car. He turned around and around and around and then looked up at me pitifully, so I covered my eyes to give him privacy.

Mr. P and I trudged off to the Fuglymobile. He nestled his head in my lap. I rubbed his ears as I drove, hoping I'd relax. My encounter with Mr. Q would be challenging. Even though he apologized, I was tired and I was still ticked off. We hadn't spoken since he divulged his deception.

I stopped scratching Mr. P to make a quick call to Mirella.

"Sorry to wake you, but I need to know if we can meet today. Around eleven at the student center?"

Mirella yawned. "Sure."

"I'll be at the same table where we first met. Bye."

Mr. P jumped off my lap and into the passenger side seat. The speed of his tail proved he knew he'd be home soon. By the time I parked I thought his tail might break off and fly across the yard.

Mr. Q didn't answer my knock on the door and the familiar heart palpitations returned. One more dead or injured client and I'd be doing something more serious than thinking about leaving town. I'd probably shoot myself. A second knock didn't produce results either, so I used my key to let myself in. "Hello?"

No one returned my greeting. I put Mr. P down and went into the kitchen to start the espresso machine. I needed a cup of cappuccino with a capital C.

Assuming Mrs. Rippetoe hadn't had time to feed Mr. P, I fixed him a breakfast rivaling the buffets of the Las Vegas casinos. The speed at which he ate made it almost impossible for him to have tasted a thing, but the swing in his tail nullified that thought. He was a happy boy.

I unlocked the dog door leading from the porch to the yard and Mr. P trotted outside. I headed back to the kitchen and discovered an envelope on the side table by the door, addressed to me. Panic struck with incredible force. I ran outside to make sure Mr. P. hadn't been napped again. He barked and I relaxed.

With my cappuccino in hand, I moved into the living room, sat down and opened the envelope. I took a sip as I unfolded the letter. The froth in my cup got sucked into my mouth when I gasped.

The enveloped contained a check in the amount of five thousand dollars. Thirty-five hundred more than what had been spelled out in the contract. Crapola, how could I be mad at Mr. Q while I held a huge check in my hand?

A letter was attached. Mr. Q had personally written a note to apologize for his antics and to rave about my service. In addition to paying for the hotel and time we spent hunting down Mr. P, he was doubling my rate for being a good sport. The best part was him committing to signing a three year contract with Moore Time.

I was energized. A three-year contract was an amazing deal for my company. So amazing I could give serious thought to hiring an assistant.

"Yeah, Mr. P! You're going to see a lot of me." I ran outside to the porch. He came running through the doggie door barking and bouncing. We chased each other back and forth around the house. When we stopped, I scratched his ears and tummy to settle him down.

He followed me back into the kitchen and watched while I cleaned up both our dishes. When I finished I picked up my bag and headed out the door. "Be a good boy."

———

When I arrived at the bank, I put my signed check into the capsule and pressed the button transporting it directly to the teller inside the bank. My day was packed and I didn't want to chance losing the largest check I'd received since starting my business.

I drove to the post office to pick up Brackford's mail, smiling at the sight of a beautiful new window. My big check and the pristine window had to mean something. They were like a sign of renewal and I hoped it would carry through to my love life too.

Jack and I had experienced a false start, but tomorrow night would be our second chance. One I hoped would evolve into something more than the type of relationship I had with Peter.

Thoughts of Jack continued to invade my mind as I walked up to Thomas Brackford's front door. I worked diligently to stack those thoughts nicely in my brain's storage unit so I could focus on the task at hand.

"Aspen?"

"Oh. You startled me."

Brackford had become a lot more social of late.

"I was lost in thought." I handed over his mail since he had extended his hands.

"I hope you were thinking about what you were going to help me cook up tomorrow night."

"Tomorrow night?"

"Yeah, don't you remember? You said you'd help me fix a special dinner to serve the lady coming over."

"Now I remember, yes, one of the nurses from the hospital."

"That's right."

I had to think of something quick. Thomas Brackford inviting a woman to his house was a big deal, a much bigger deal than my date with Jack. The smile on his face told me all I needed to know.

"What if I come back over tonight and we cook everything ahead of time?"

"I'm not sure. Wouldn't everything be spoiled?"

"Absolutely not. I have an idea for a recipe. The longer the dish sits, the herbs and spices are absorbed and the flavors are enhanced." I was more of a sucker for somebody else's romance than for my own, but at least this way we'd both be able to keep our dates.

"I guess tonight would be okay. If you're not here she might think I can cook."

"Forgot your boxes." I ran back to the car and retrieved them. "I'll see you around six."

———

The heebie-jeebies took hold as I exited the car. Though Samuel Martin said he was calling off his goon, he could have changed his mind. I shook off the feeling and continued on to the student center.

I spotted Mirella easily, her big head of curly hair a beacon. "Have you been waiting long?"

"No. I got a late start. I was trying to convince Sara to stay another night. She wants to go home. I think you should give me the box to take back to her. She needs to go through the contents. You know, face her demons."

"What demons?"

"Sara obviously still has issues with the death of her husband. Her going through the box might help." Mirella sounded more like a therapist than a student.

"What makes you think her husband is dead?"

"He's been gone a long time and she says he wasn't the type of man to walk out on her."

I pulled out a chair and sat down. "Mirella? Can I ask you about your relationship with Max?"

"Maybe later."

She clearly wanted to avoid the topic. I decided I'd broach the subject again after discussing the note I'd found. "There was something interesting in the box Sara gave me."

Mirella leaned on the table and popped her bubble gum with her tongue. "Oh yeah, Nick told me."

"Might not be anything." I directed her attention to the index card on the table.

She picked it up. "What does it mean?"

"I was hoping you or Sara might know. I searched on the Internet and came up empty. Can you try?"

"Sure." Mirella stood up with the card in hand.

"I'll write down the info for you on a piece of paper."

"Why don't I just take the card?"

"I think I better hold on to it."

"Ridiculous. What do you think I'm going to do, lose the thing?"

I grabbed the card out of her hands.

"What the hell did you do that for?'

"I asked you to give it back." Her attitude bothered me. I'd taken her word on the nature of her relationship with Max, but now wondered if she'd been his friend or his foe. Once again I was back to not being sure who I could trust. I wrote down part of the information incorrectly and hoped she wouldn't notice.

"For the record, you didn't ask me to give the card back to you."

"Mirella, let's not argue about this. Can you figure out what the words mean?"

"I'm working a short shift answering phones in the registration office, so I can't start until after I finish."

"Fine. I'll call Sara and ask her to stay at least until you get back. I'm heading to Clayton to the property records department."

I left Mirella at the student center and walked back to the parking lot. As I neared the car the heebie-jeebies returned and I wondered if Fugly had begun to resent me. I hoped he wasn't turning into Stephen King's Christine.

I called my office to retrieve my messages, but someone answered the phone.

"Peter? Is that you?"

"Yes."

"How did you get in my office?"

"What makes you think I'm at your office?"

"I called my office."

"I called you," he said.

"I didn't even hear the phone ring."

"Because, you were too busy punching numbers. I think you gave me Tinnitus."

"Tinnitus isn't catching."

"Neither is what I had last night. Sorry about the commotion. I get these cramps at the oddest times then they just go away," Peter explained.

"IBS."

"BS? What's that supposed to mean?"

"No IBS. Means you ought to go to the doctor."

"Real men don't need doctors."

"Uh huh."

"I didn't call to talk about my stomach. I called to ask if you were free for dinner tomorrow night."

Geez, what was it about tomorrow night? "Sorry. I can't."

"Got a hot date or something?"

If he hadn't spoken so sarcastically I might have let it slide. "As a matter of fact, I have a date with Jack."

We were at a standoff. No one was speaking. I tried hard not to be the first to crack, but there was dead air to be filled. "So what do you think about that?"

21

SOME QUESTIONS ARE BETTER LEFT unanswered. In a way, I was glad Peter had abruptly said goodbye and hung up the phone. It beat having some big, long conversation about the dangers of Jack Arbon.

I squeezed Fugly into a tight parking space all the while wishing I had my Jeep. The only thing I admired about Fugly was the ability to eat anything I wanted inside of him without worrying. I dug change out of my purse, plopped a few quarters into the parking meter, and threw the rest into my briefcase.

A horrible sense of panic hit me as I set off toward the building carrying my mysterious red briefcase. What if the briefcase had been intended as some sort of identifier making me a walking target for a hit man?

The panic subsided when I made my way through the doors of the building without having to dodge a single bullet. An older woman behind the counter looked up briefly when I reached the records department.

"Where can I find information about the Marston Place planned community?"

"Depends. What are you trying to find?"

"Let me start with the subdivision plats."

"Against that wall." She pointed behind me.

I flipped through the oversized books until I found the two subdivision plats, Marston View and Marston Reserve. I jotted the numbers down and handed the paper to the woman behind the desk.

She returned with an even larger book and laid it on the desk. I carefully turned each page until I found the one I needed. "Can you make a copy of this one for me?"

"Sure. That'll be two dollars."

My wallet held a dollar. I scrounged around the bottom of my briefcase. The result was not pretty, but the change was correct. I handed the lady the dollar bill piled high with nickels and dimes.

When she returned with the copy, I shoved it into my briefcase and kept a watchful eye as I made my way back to my car. My inability to trust was causing my paranoia or perhaps it was my paranoia that was making me unable to trust. Either way, I took it out on Mirella and I had to fix it because I needed her help.

I gave her a call when I got into the car. "Hey, I'm sorry I was short with you earlier," I said when Mirella answered the phone.

"Apology accepted. Dealing with Max's death has been hard on a lot of people."

"In my rush earlier I think I left out some information. What did I write down?"

"Cream Boulder Flip 89127. I think it might relate to Nevada because of the Las Vegas zip codes, which is in close proximity to Boulder City, Nevada. Not sure about the Cream Flip though."

"I definitely wrote the information down wrong. You got a pen?"

"Sure."

"Creek Boulder Flat 86927. Show that to Sara. I mentioned the phrase to her but maybe seeing the words might trigger something."

"If you find anything, call me right away."

"Will do."

A sigh escaped as I found myself lamenting my old life and loathing my new. How had I arrived at this destination? My plethora of problems was overwhelming and I tuned in talk radio to listen to someone else's for a while. A pig-headed guy complained about a local politician for a few minutes. The host cut him off to break for commercial. A grocery store spot reminded me I still had to buy the ingredients for Thomas Brackford's big date.

When I'd told Brackford I had an idea for a dish, I wasn't lying. I had an idea. I just didn't have a recipe. It was a small dilemma though because luckily my Aunt Jenny, the chef of our family, made a hobby out of sharing all her recipes with the world, over the Internet.

I headed back to my office to search for a recipe. The closest open parking space ended up being right in front of Peter's shop. I tried not to peer through his window when I got out of the car, but it was like trying to stop myself from looking at a train wreck.

When I glanced inside, he was standing next to the window staring back at me. I waved and kept on walking. After all, I had important work to do.

The blinking light on my answering machine caught my eye. I'd forgotten to retrieve my messages after the confusion of Peter's call. I pushed the power button on my computer, pressed the button on the answering machine, and sat back in my chair, exhausted. My physical exhaustion seemed secondary to my mental exhaustion which had reached levels double the recommended daily allowance.

"Ms. Moore. It's Harry Corbitt. I really think we should meet."

I erased the message. He was extremely persistent. I didn't want to call him back, for two reasons. He was creepy and they hadn't booked a place for the reception. At this late date, I might have to tell Harry Corbitt he'd be throwing the garter at Bango's Biker Bar.

"What are you thinking about?"

I glanced away from the computer. Peter stood next to the door with his arms folded across his chest.

"I'm thinking I need to hire an assistant," I said.

"Do you have that much work?"

"Not too much, just too much for me."

A small smile formed on his face. He walked toward me. "Don't let things get you down, Aspen. I'm sure everything will get better soon."

Peter sat in the chair in front of my desk. Two friends chatting like nothing had happened. He had been upset with me earlier, but clearly he had chosen to move on. I assumed his earlier irritation was out of concern for my well being and not out of jealousy because he had Madeline. She was tall and beautiful with long dark hair that glistened even under fluorescent lights.

"Sometimes it's hard to believe things will get better," I said.

"You look like you could use some cheering up. Want to get a bite to eat tonight?"

"I can't. I'm cooking some dishes for Thomas Brackford. He has a date coming over tomorrow night."

"No kidding? Good for him."

"Yeah. I'm making something he can just heat up."

"Why don't I come over to your place and help you?"

"Actually, I'm cooking everything over at his house." I felt bad for Peter. I'd rejected him twice in one day.

"No problem. The more help the sooner you'll be done. Call him and let him know he'll have two cooks in the kitchen and we'll make dinner for all of us tonight as well."

I rolled the idea around in my head. "Gosh, I don't know. It is business."

"Regardless of what people might say, it is okay to mix business with pleasure. Necessary, at times."

"I'll try. He doesn't like to have people in his house much. I'll call you when I finish at the store and let you know then."

"Great. I'll pick you up at six." He was serious.

"Peter. I can't promise you he'll say okay."

"See you at six," he said and walked out the door.

He could be pleasantly stubborn at times.

Turning back to my computer, I typed in my aunt's website. Aunt Jenny wasn't any master chef. She was an organized master chef. She had recipes with links to corresponding menus, which in turn had links to recipes for all the other dishes listed on the menu. And the best part was the link she provided to a shopping list. Her website held valuable lessons on how to be user friendly.

I printed everything I needed and then popped over to her blog. I ached while I read her recent entry about recipes for family celebrations. I wanted to tell her I craved her cooking and yearned for our monthly shopping sprees that always ended with a glass of wine over lunch. Most of all I wanted to tell her I missed her and I loved her, but I knew making a comment on her blog would be dangerous.

Going against the marshal's directions was risky. Each time I communicated with my mom over a pay-as-you-go mobile phone I endangered myself and my family. An additional indiscretion would only increase my chance of being found by the bad guys. My love for my aunt would have to be conveyed through my mom.

I grabbed the recipes and shopping list off the printer and closed up shop so I could go to the grocery store.

On the way I called Thomas Brackford. "Hello, Mr. Brackford, it's Aspen."

"What time you coming over?"

"That's why I'm calling. My friend Peter offered to help me cook the food for your guest and suggested the three of us have dinner tonight."

"Never heard of him. I don't need any strangers around here," he grumbled.

"I can vouch for him. He's a good person and an excellent cook."

"I thought you were an excellent cook?"

I tried to remember if I'd ever spouted anything off about the level of my cooking skills and hoped I hadn't fibbed when he interviewed me. "I'm a good cook, but Peter, well he is excellent."

"I want the dinner to be perfect, so if you think he would be the best person, then I guess you can let him come over. Just tell him he can't get near my trains. What time?"

"Six." I hung up the phone and said a silent prayer that Peter really could cook.

Each new item I placed in the shopping cart caused saliva to flow toward my lips. I grabbed a couple of free samples in the bakery section and popped them in my mouth to soak it up.

Being single and busy, I hadn't cooked an entire menu from scratch in years. By the time I made my way to the dairy section the cart was full and I was worried the menu might be a little more complicated than I'd anticipated.

I picked up the marinated mozzarella balls, which reminded me that I still needed to pick up prosciutto. I also needed to get toothpicks to hold the prosciutto around the cheese balls once they were wrapped.

Like a kid lost in the woods, I circled the grocery store twice before I found the toothpicks by the paper plates. I splurged and picked the ones with the colorful plastic frilly stuff on the end.

A package of bright matching napkins caught my eye, so I scooped them up along with a medium sized candle in a red glass container. I had a feeling Thomas Brackford was going to need a little something extra to make tomorrow night's dinner special.

My phone rang just as I placed the last bag in the back of Fugly. I saw Sara's name and closed the hatch.

"Hold on a sec okay?" I opened the driver side door and settled myself inside the car. "Is everything okay?"

"I figured out what the words on the card are referring to," Sara said.

"What?"

"I think they are referring to one of Mitch's paintings."

"A painting? What about the numbers? Is it paint-by-number?"

Sara laughed.

Her laugh brought a sense of relief, but at the same time made me cringe. I must have sounded stupid suggesting paint by numbers.

"Of course not. I'm not quite sure what the numbers mean," Sara said after she stopped laughing.

"What makes you think it's the painting?" I asked.

"Mirella was here asking me a ton of questions hoping to trigger something in my mind. After she left I realized Mitch must have been referencing a painting hanging in his work studio."

"In the house?"

"No, behind the house. Mitch was an artist. I haven't touched a thing in his studio since he went missing. I always hoped he'd return home."

"I can't go with you tonight. Why don't we go to your house first thing in the morning?"

"I really want to go tonight."

"I can't and I think it would be safer in the daylight and if there were more than two of us at your home. Please be patient. Let's plan to meet at the studio tomorrow morning, nine sharp."

"I'm not real happy waiting. I'm not sure how well you know Mirella and Nick, but I'm uncomfortable here."

"Not all that well. What's going on?"

"They seem overly interested in the box I gave you and keep asking me all kinds of questions. Maybe I'm just homesick."

"Mirella probably wants to complete whatever she had been working on for Max. Anyway, if we go in the morning and everything seems safe, you can stay home."

"Good. Mitchell is getting restless away from his room and toys. Oh and Mirella mentioned you were doing some research of your own. Did you find anything?"

"There's an interesting piece of land in one of the subdivisions in Marston Place. I'll check it out with Mirella once we finish at your house tomorrow."

Mitchell started crying again and Sara cut our conversation short.

I had to be at Thomas Brackford's place in an hour and a half, so I placed a call to Peter. "I know you said you would pick me up at six, but—"

"So he said no, did he?"

"No, he said yes."

"Oh yeah. Am I good or what?"

"Helloooo Mr. Egoooo."

"You're just jealous I'm so smart. What time should I pick you up?"

"Five-thirty. See you're not that smart, you said six!"

"Okay, Tonto. I give."

———

The first thing Peter did when we entered Thomas Brackford's house was shake Brackford's hand. The second thing he did was pull a pristine Lionel train in its original box out from under his arm.

Thomas Brackford's eyes widened and his jaw dropped. "Where did you get that?"

"I wondered if you could tell me a little about the car."

"You bet I can. Where'd you get it?"

"My dad purchased the train car for me the day I was born. He came across it cleaning out the basement and gave it to me when I went back for Christmas last year," Peter said.

"Come with me. I want to show you something." Thomas Brackford wheeled his chair around and Peter followed.

"Ah, ah, ah. Haven't you forgotten something?"

The two turned around and looked at me like two little boys in trouble. I pointed at the bags on the hall table. Peter sulked his way back.

"You're ruining the fun," he said after we entered the kitchen.

"You're the one who volunteered to come help me cook. Now I discover the real reason." I glanced at the train box under his arm.

"No, *this* was an afterthought. You were my main thought."

"Oh."

"You know what I mean. I'll be back to help in a minute." With that, he vanished from the kitchen.

My attention turned to the food. I rolled each piece of prosciutto into a log before slicing the ham into even strips. I pulled a mozzarella ball out of the marinade, wrapped the prosciutto around the ball then stuck in a toothpick. When I finished all of them, it resembled a party.

Knowing all good cooks taste their dishes, I grabbed a ball by its toothpick and popped it into my mouth. Peter entered the room while the frilly red plastic hung from my lips.

"What's in there?"

"I'm...pre...tending...to be a good cook." I tossed the toothpick in the trash.

"Unlike you, I don't need to pretend." He grabbed a mozzarella ball off the plate.

"I hope so because you're in charge of tonight's dinner."

I turned back toward the counter and began layering noodles, spinach, cheese, sausage, and tomato sauce into a baking dish, following the "Uncooked Noodle" lasagna recipe to the tee. I pre-heated the oven and set the dish aside.

"My turn at the counter." Peter brushed up against my back as he worked his way around me.

A tingle ran up my spine and I stiffened. My body had reacted the same way the night before and I was beginning to worry there was something wrong with me. Sure I found Peter sexy, but he was my friend. He wasn't a man I should be tingling with.

"Why so tense?"

"Just nervous about cooking."

"Relax." He placed his hands on my shoulders and massaged them a few times.

The more he massaged, the stiffer I became.

"You need to go to your friend Stephanie and get another massage. You're so stiff."

"Can you pass me the sponge cake?" I pulled my shoulder from underneath his hand and pointed to the bag on the table.

I popped the chocolate chips into the microwave. When they were melted, I coated the indented part of each sponge cake. As soon as they hardened I'd put in some raspberries and drizzle them with melted chocolate.

"You do your thing and I'll go check on Mr. Brackford." I cleaned off my hands and threw the dishtowel onto the counter.

"Tom said to come get him when everything is ready."

"Tom? You've known him all of five minutes and you're on a first name basis?"

"Why is that so odd?"

"I've been working for him for months and he's never asked me to call him Tom."

"You never really asked, now have you?" Thomas Brackford said as he wheeled himself into the kitchen.

"No. I guess not."

"You need to loosen up. You're so stiff," he said.

"So, should I call you Tom?"

"I prefer Mr. Brackford."

I was stunned.

"See what I mean? Relax. Yes, call me Tom." Brackford smiled and then looked over at Peter.

Peter nodded and smiled back.

Their first meeting and they were already trading inside jokes. I ignored both of them and began setting the table. When I finished, Peter sent us into the living room with a bottle of wine so he could finish getting dinner ready.

I poured Brackford a glass of wine. "So, Tom."

"Yes."

"Do you know anything about this nurse you're having over for dinner?"

"She's a good nurse."

Not exactly the answer I was looking for, but a start. "Has she ever been married?"

"How should I know? She's just my nurse."

"Oh. I thought this was a date tomorrow night."

By the time he finished laughing, my glass of wine was finished and I poured myself another.

"Dinner's served." Peter placed the food on the table. "I offer you my famous Petertalian spaghetti."

If there was any Italian in Peter it was probably a speck and nothing more.

"Looks and smells like a fine Italian meal," Brackford said as he positioned himself at the table.

"Did I miss anything?" Peter asked.

The question caused Thomas Brackford to erupt into another fit of laughter. "She thought I was having a date tomorrow night."

"You're not?" Peter asked.

"No. I am just having her over for dinner to thank her for treating me so well. She's a sweet woman. Without her I don't think I would have made it out of the hospital."

Peter shot a glance my way, which I returned. My eyes sent a clear message to change the subject or risk a most unpleasant ride home.

"Did Tom tell you about my train?"

"No." I stuffed a piece of garlic bread in my mouth.

"An excellent specimen. Those are his exact words. Right, Tom?"

"You bet. The car would fetch well over two thousand dollars from a collector."

"That's amazing." All of a sudden I had a greater appreciation for toy trains.

We talked current events, politics, and even touched upon religion. I learned more about Thomas Brackford over dinner than I had since I'd started working for him. I also learned a few things about Peter too, like he wasn't extremely religious. We all held different positions on politics. Thomas Brackford fell to the left and Peter to the right, with me holding steady in the middle.

"I've got Spumoni," Peter announced as he gathered the plates.

"Real Spumoni?" I asked.

"Actually, I have Neapolitan ice cream, but we can pretend, can't we?"

"Sure."

While Peter served up the ice cream and coffee, I loaded the dishwasher and went over the notes for tomorrow night's dinner with Brackford.

"You can scratch the part about lighting the candle." I handed him the pen.

"No. I think candles might be pleasant."

The twinkle in his eyes suggested he secretly wished it were a date. And if he did, I hoped tomorrow's dinner turned into the best date of his life.

I took a few sips of coffee and was about to dig into my ice cream when I heard my phone beep. I quietly retrieved the phone from my pocket and read Sara's text. Thinking I'd had too much wine, I rubbed my eyes and read the text a second time. The message was clear – 911.

22

"SO WHAT'S THE EMERGENCY?" Peter asked as we pulled away from Thomas Brackford's house.

"Sara just sent me another text message with her address."

"And the emergency?"

"I'm not sure. I don't think I should call her because if she could talk she would have called."

"Then we're off to... What's the address?"

I showed Peter the text message. We weren't far from her house. The gravity of the situation set in and I felt responsible and helpless at the same time. I'd never forgive myself if something happened to Sara and little Mitchell. And I definitely would never forgive Max's killer; the person who triggered the fall of this disastrous line of dominoes.

We drove past Sara Obermier's house. The Jaguar was in the driveway, but all the lights inside were off. A light glow came from somewhere in the back yard. Peter parked down the street allowing us to be discreet and approach unnoticed.

Peter opened his door. "Stay here."

"No way." I opened my door and got out.

"Seriously, Aspen. We might be walking into a dangerous situation."

"Right. Hold on." I ducked back into the car and snatched my pepper spray from my purse.

Peter frowned. "Stay behind me and keep quiet. I know that's hard for you."

I smacked him on the arm. "Are we going in the front?"

"Shhh." He grabbed my hand and led me off to the side of Sara's house.

With one hand tightly clasped to Peter's and my other on the pepper spray, I let myself be led into an unknown situation. I kept my thumb steady on the pepper spray's lever while my heart commanded me to retreat. If someone jumped out of the dark, I'd pee my pants.

Peter stopped and leaned toward me. "A light's on in the shed out back."

"That's not a—" I obeyed Peter's index finger when he raised it to his mouth.

We avoided the sidewalk, staying on the grass as we inched our way toward the small building in back of the house. We crouched down as we neared the window. He pointed to himself and then to the window above us. I nodded, but hoped he would change his mind and we'd run the other way.

Peter peered through the window. "I only see two women."

"Two? What do they look like?"

"One with short gray hair and one with long black hair like a curly mop."

"Crap. That's Sara and Mirella." I jumped up and barged through the door.

Peter had somehow propelled himself in front of me. "Jesus, Aspen! What if someone had been hiding in here with a gun or something?"

"You scared the hell out of me, Sara!" I screamed.

"I didn't mean to. I texted you because I didn't know if you would answer the phone in the middle of your dinner. I thought you'd want to know that Mirella and I came to the studio."

I stopped talking and surveyed the room. Paintings covered the walls top to bottom and an unfinished work sat on an easel in the corner.

"These are beautiful." I moved next to Sara so I could view the painting she held in her hands. It was about the size of hardback book, a forest scene, with a deer and her fawn.

Light reflected off a tear in Sara's eye. "Mitch's photo-realistic style was breathtaking. He'd been scheduled for a show at a gallery in the city before he disappeared."

"You think this painting relates to the note?" I asked.

"It has to. But I'm not sure what he is trying to tell us."

"Here, let me take a look."

She handed the painting to me and I walked over to a brass floor lamp on the other side of the room. Peter followed and we spent time going over every inch. The front, the back, we even turned off the light to determine if he used glow in the dark paint.

"Nothing on the painting seems unusual." Peter turned toward Sara. "Are you sure this is the one?"

"Yes. I can't think of any other flat boulder. When we came back from the Appalachian Trail in Maine, he painted the Piazza Rock to commemorate our first hiking trip together. The painting had always been my favorite."

The life-like painting drew the viewer in. I'd been silly for thinking he did paint by numbers. His works were truly art.

"Do you think the numbers are a location around the rock?" Mirella asked.

"Wait. Where did you take the painting down from?" I asked.

"Hanging on the wall, over there." Sara pointed to a blank spot above a credenza.

"Where's the note?" Peter asked.

Mirella reached in her jean pocket and pulled out the paper I'd given her earlier. "It's kind of scribbled on since Aspen didn't initially trust me with the real information."

I glared at Mirella as I gently took the note from her hand. "Maybe it's a code number to a file or something."

I slid open the doors to the credenza, which revealed brushes and tubes of oil paints. I squatted for a better view inside. "I see a book in the back. Perhaps page numbers?"

The book turned out to be a box and I opened it once I stood. "Oh. I..." Closing the lid, I handed the box to Sara.

"What is it?" she asked.

"Something personal. I'm sorry I should have given it to you to open. Perhaps we should step outside, so you can open the box in private or you might want to wait until we leave."

"No."

"Are you sure?" Peter asked.

Sara didn't bother to answer. She opened the box, laughing and crying at the same time. "It's beautiful."

She held up the box, displaying its content. A small oval-shape gold pendant housing a hand-painted miniature of Sara in the nude, dangled from a gold necklace.

"Of course that was ten years and one baby ago." She blushed. "I remember the day he asked me to pose for him. I had no idea he'd planned to create a gift for me."

"The entire piece is stunning," Peter said.

"Where's little Mitchell?" I asked, suddenly aware of his absence.

"He's at my neighbor's house."

"Are you okay with continuing?" I asked. "I have one more idea."

Sara nodded. I turned back toward the credenza and tapped on the wall.

"A secret hiding place?" Mirella asked.

"You watch too much television," Peter said, but he started tapping too. "Doesn't sound hollow anywhere."

"Maybe something is behind the credenza," Sara suggested.

I peeked. "Nothing back here."

Mirella's phone rang.

"I'm busy. Can't it wait?" she snapped.

All of us turned our attention to Mirella. She lowered her voice and covered her mouth and phone with her hand. Her dark eyes grew larger as she argued with the caller and still seemed upset when she ended the call. "Sorry. Nick says he needs me. He's here to pick me up. I have to go."

"How'd he know you were here?" Sara asked.

"Oh, we've got that family tracking thing on our phone accounts. My mom wanted to make sure she could locate us at all times. Aspen, are we still on for tomorrow?"

"Yeah." I waved my hand at Mirella in a mixed motion of see-you-later and just-go-we're-busy.

After Mirella left, I gave the credenza a shove. "Damn this is heavy. Can you help Peter? We need to get the thing farther away from the wall."

On the count of three Peter and I pushed. When the credenza moved more easily than I'd expected I lost my balance and landed on my rear behind the credenza.

"Hoool-ly cow. Check this out." I got on my knees and ran my hand over the front of a safe tucked inside the back of the credenza. "No wonder this sucker weighed so much."

"The numbers. Try the numbers," Peter said, sounding like a kid on a treasure hunt.

"Sara? The safe is yours. Do you want to try the numbers?" I asked.

"No. You go ahead."

"Are you sure? I mean with the necklace and all." I didn't want her to feel like I was taking away her privacy.

"After the box, I'm not sure I'm ready to find out what's inside the safe." The sadness in her eyes appeared to weigh heavily, causing her head to hang.

I fumbled with the tumbler. The second time I tried a combination of numbers from the paper, the door opened.

"You should be a safecracker," Peter teased.

"Just luck. I had no idea what I was doing." I pulled out a large manila envelope, a bundle of cash, and then stopped. "Peter? Can you get this?"

He knelt down and his eyes lit up. He reached inside and grabbed the gun. "This is a forty-four magnum and one expensive gun."

"Something was definitely wrong. Mitch would never have had a gun without a reason." Sara's forehead wrinkled and her brows furrowed. I had to work to ease her worry.

"Do you want me to open this up?" I asked Sara.

She nodded. I sat in the chair next to the brass floor lamp, took a deep breath then opened the envelope.

"He was on to something. This is a log of some sort." I handed the papers to Peter.

"Who's Kyle?" he asked.

"Mitch's little brother." A hint of hope crept back into Sara's voice as if she might still have a chance of finding Mitch alive. "What kind of log?"

"He was documenting his brother's meetings with Samuel Martin. He also has some comments about bank withdrawals." Peter flipped the pages.

While they discussed the log, I pulled out a second set of papers. I scanned the pages and caught several references to Samuel Martin. "Wow."

"What?" Peter grabbed the papers from me.

"Post-it note label says 'dad's notes' and many of the words are not nice." I paused to watch Peter as he registered what was written on the pages then I pulled the last set of papers from the envelope.

Peter glanced over at Sara. "Looks like Samuel Martin was threatening your father-in-law after he refused to sell his land."

"Mitch was clearly collecting evidence. Did he tell you about any of this?" I asked.

Sara fidgeted as Peter and I stared. "No. I knew Mitch had been upset because he wanted to keep the land in the family and Kyle kept pestering him to sell so he could get half the money. But Mitch never mentioned anything to me about papers from his father."

I returned my attention to the papers I held in my hands. "These are your father-in-law's death and medical records. The notes indicate Mitch had concerns regarding his father's cause of death. Here, Peter."

Sara's eyes dulled and the skin beneath had become puffed like bread dough. I was afraid she was on the verge of collapsing.

"Come on, let's count the money. Once we're done you should go rest," I said.

Sara and I sat on the floor while Peter continued going through the papers. We counted the money three times before our amounts finally matched. A testament to how tired we both were.

"Twenty-thousand dollars." I banded the bills together.

"That's a whole bunch of Benjamins," Peter said.

I handed the bundle to him. "Can you put this in the safe?"

"The safe is no longer safe. Multiple people know the combination. Sara, do you have a safe deposit box?"

"Mitch got one when we first opened our account."

"Put the cash in there as soon as you can. Don't deposit it. Anything over ten grand and the bank will report it. We need to keep this quiet, to buy us some time. It may take us a little bit to figure out what's going on." Peter took the cash, extended his other hand toward me and helped me up.

"Here, let me help you." I reached over to pull Sara up and she broke down in tears.

"I just don't understand why he didn't talk to me. We'd been through so much. We could have figured this out together."

The hurt in her voice drew me closer. I hugged her tight. "He didn't tell you because he loved you."

Unfortunately, my attempt to comfort her only made her sob. Ten years had passed since Sara's husband went

262

missing and now she had to live the nightmare all over again.

When Sara finished sobbing, Peter stopped pacing and took his hands out of his pockets. He'd been ready to leave from the minute her first tear had escaped. My propensity to prattle never surfaced as we drove home in silence. I'd sensed Peter's need to reflect on our evening.

He dropped me off in front of our building and waited for me to go through the door. I waved when I was safely inside. He pulled away, heading to Madeline's place. I headed upstairs to pass out from exhaustion.

The door to my apartment was cracked open. The urge to run down the road after Peter's car was strong, but a closer look at my door showed no signs of forced entry. I was sure I had checked my lock multiple times before I left, but my days had started to meld together and perhaps the lock checking had happened another day. I retrieved my pepper spray and inched my way forward.

I collected myself and pushed the door open. "Get back! I have a weapon!"

No one was inside my living room or kitchen. I kept my pepper spray in hand as I walked through my apartment. The place was vacant and all my stuff appeared in order. I walked into the kitchen to check my mad cash jar. All the money was gone.

The only person who had access to my place was Mrs. Rippetoe, unless Toby kept a key when he replaced the lock. If he'd needed to borrow money he should have asked and if he borrowed it without asking he should have at least locked my door when he left.

I trotted the few steps over to Toby's and knocked. I shoved my key ring with my pepper spray into my pocket because I was mad and accidents happen. Probably a good thing he didn't answer.

23

"I THOUGHT YOU WERE GOING to pick me up at nine," Mirella said after opening up the passenger side door. "Is this your car?"

"Why?"

"Just figured since you owned a business you'd have something a little nicer."

I smiled at her. "My Jeep's in the shop."

Mirella's shoulders relaxed and the muscles in her face followed suit. "So how come you're late?"

"I had to do some shopping. Home Depot and Radio Shack."

"You left me waiting while you went shopping? That's not nice."

"I had to get equipment for our treasure hunt," I said.

"Like what? A shovel?"

"Exactly."

"You are serious about this. We have to dig? I thought we were only going to check out the property by driving by," Mirella said, obviously not as excited by the hunt as I was.

"Picked up a metal detector too. If anything is buried there they probably put it inside a box. Could be money."

I didn't know what I was looking for but I believed Samuel Martin hid a large sum of money, a gun, or something he wanted to keep hidden until he needed it. I glanced down as Mirella scratched her foot. "Did you bring other shoes?"

"No."

"I hope the place isn't muddy. Are you going to be able to run in high-heeled boots?" I asked.

"You didn't say anything about running."

"We're not, but you never know."

Marston Place hid its sinister past well. The masquerade of stone fountains and park benches told a much happier story than the truth.

"Can you direct me to lot 48?" I handed Mirella the plat map. "We're at the Marston Lane entrance."

"Take a right, a left, a right, a right, and a left."

"Whoa, Einstein. Not everyone's as smart as you."

"Sorry. Take a right."

I turned right and followed her instructions until we ended up at a large wooded corner lot in Marston Reserve. The neighborhood was an exclusive subdivision of million dollar homes, inside Marston Place. Each one built on no less than three acres. The houses set back from the street with trees and gates protecting their entrances. The level of privacy meant we didn't have to worry about a homeowner spotting us through a front window and calling the police.

"Hey, I've been here before with my Uncle B. I think he owns one of these lots. My Uncle B's property holdings are what got me interested in writing a paper on the development."

"What does the B stand for?"

"Benedetto. He's my dad's brother."

"Does he own this lot?"

"I don't think so, but I'm not sure. I used to come here a lot as a kid before they built all the houses. I didn't go much into the details of who owned what lots."

"Is he friends with the Martins?"

"Not really. He said he only met them a couple of times."

"Did you bring a jacket?"

Her blank stare gave away her answer before she opened her mouth. "The weather's been warm lately."

"But the woods are thick and we should protect our arms. I think my blazer's in the back so you can wear this jacket." I tossed her my Eddie Bauer parka.

I handed Mirella a shovel and took out the metal detector before closing the Fairmont's tailgate. "Let's start on the left side and work our way back and forth."

In the first hour the detector didn't emit a single beep and we'd covered one length of the five-acre lot. Mirella had already taken the parka off and tied the jacket around her waist with the sleeves. I chose to bear with my blazer instead of dealing with dangling clothing, even though I had started to sweat.

"This may take a couple of days." I took a break and leaned against a tree admiring the autumn leaves.

"I don't think I can come out here tomorrow."

"Maybe I should do wider swings so we can cover more ground. What do you think?"

"Anything to avoid making another trip through these woods."

My swings became wider the longer we walked. I couldn't hold the detector much longer. I needed something to distract me from the pain. "Want to play twenty questions?"

"Sure," Mirella said.

"Okay. You think of something first." I always preferred to be the one to start off asking the questions.

"Are you dating Peter?"

"That's not how you play the game. You're supposed to pick an animal, vegetable, or mineral and then I ask you questions."

"My version's more fun. So are you?"

"Why would you even ask that?"

"Because I think you are. I can tell by the way his eyes followed you last night."

"And what are you? All of twenty-two? It takes more years than that to know what a man is saying with his eyes."

"I'm twenty-four and it doesn't take that many years when you take a class on love."

"Don't tell me you got credit."

"As a matter of fact, I did. The class covered everything from infatuation, sexuality, fidelity, and even body language. We got to study hundreds of men and the way they responded to women they loved. And I'm telling you, Peter has that look."

I was about to challenge Mirella's remark when the detector went off. "Finally."

"I'll dig." Mirella scooped up a pile of dirt with the shovel.

Each time she removed dirt, I put the detector over the hole to check if anything still registered. Three piles later, the hole became noiseless.

"Hold this over the pile while I spread the dirt." I continued digging until I touched something hard.

"What is it?" Mirella seemed impatient.

I held up a set of car keys. "Wonder who lost these?"

"You think that's what they buried?"

"No. Probably belongs to some teenager." I pointed to beer cans scattered beside a log.

"Haven't you noticed the way he looks at you?"

"Can we skip talking about Peter? He'd be ticked at both of us if he knew we were doing this."

"You didn't tell him?"

"No. Why should I?"

"Did you tell anyone where you were going?

"No."

"My mother always says you should tell someone just in case."

"In case of what?" I asked.

"In case they need to find you or in case you never come back."

I fondled my phone. "If someone wants to find me they can just call my cell. Did you tell anyone?"

"I forgot. My mom would kill me."

"I'm sorry, nothing against your mom, but isn't that a little fatalistic?"

"No. Her advice is smart and I should have followed her rule and told Nick where I was going."

"I thought he could find you with the special GPS thingy."

"He can if my phone is on, but I forgot to charge it last night so I'm conserving."

"Well go ahead and call him."

Mirella turned her phone on and punched a couple of numbers. "Hey Nick. I'm out by Uncle B's lot in Marston

269

with Aspen. No, I'm not going to leave. No. I am not coming home right now."

Mirella turned the phone off and shoved it back in her pocket.

"Everything okay?"

"Yeah. Nick's just an ass."

"Shhh."

"What?"

"I thought I heard something."

"You're just trying to avoid calling Pe—"

"Seriously, be quiet."

Half the hairs on my neck stood up while the lazy ones laid there waiting for proof of danger. All I heard was our breathing and a few birds chirping as they fluttered in the brush.

"Probably the birds. Sorry. Where were we?"

"You should call Peter."

Two steps forward and the highest pitch on the detector went off. I moved away and the beep grew faint. I moved back and the sound grew louder.

"That's the sound of gold. Maybe that's what they were hiding. My arms hurt from holding the detector for two hours. Do you want to dig first?"

Mirella started digging. Each time she placed a pile of dirt outside the hole, I ran the detector over the mound to make sure we didn't miss anything. The hole was pretty deep and we still hadn't come across whatever had set off the detector.

"I have to stop." Mirella sat down on the ground.

I grabbed the shovel and started digging. The pile of dirt continued getting higher and the hole deeper, but still the sound of gold triggered each time I moved the detector over the hole.

"We could go faster if we both were digging. Why don't you go back to the car and get the other shovel?" I laid down the one I'd been using.

"You brought another shovel?"

Reading her body language wasn't necessary because Mirella's tone said it all. "I didn't think we would need it," I defended.

"Fine. But if you find anything while I'm gone, don't open it up until I get back."

"Deal."

Without Mirella, checking the hole each time I removed dirt was more difficult, but I continued to dig and monitor. Almost three feet down something glistened. I knelt down and brushed away the dirt.

The object was gold. There was something white underneath glass. It looked like it might be a watch. I dug around it with my hands, until I saw the bones.

———

An earthquake shook me awake or so I thought until I realized I wasn't at home in my bed. It was dark and every few minutes my body involuntarily rolled from side to side.

"Shit." I hit my head when I tried to sit up. I swept my hands on either side of my body and felt rough carpet. Thank God the space wasn't coffin sized. My hand brushed against something cold and hard and I ran my fingers along its contour, easing my fingertips into the octagonal hole of a tire iron.

A car honked. Panic engulfed me as my brain processed my surroundings and spit out my location like a ticket dispenser. The trembling began in my hands, shot up my arms and into my chest. I couldn't breathe. I desperately tried to remember how I had gotten here, but all I could recall was standing up after seeing the bones and then smelling some funky sweet odor.

"Focus, Amelia." The sound of my real name coming from my own lips jarred me. I closed my eyes and took deep breaths through my nose and exhaled letting the fear exit my mouth. I pulled my phone from my blazer pocket. The car jerked forward and I lost control of the phone as the driver made a hard turn. Who the hell was driving this car?

The phone's light blinked off. I used the tire iron to extend my reach and maneuver the phone closer to me. I ran my hand along the carpet like a blind person in a strange surrounding. By the time I held the phone again, I was sobbing.

I pressed the number nine then the phone rang. "Help me," I screamed.

"Hey girlie, what do you need help with?"

"Stephanie. Someone's kidnapped me."

"You are soooooo funny. No way you can yank my chain though."

"I'm serious. Call the police."

"You are kidding aren't you?"

"No. Call someone for help okay?" I ran my hand across my face wiping away the tears. "Stephanie? Stephanie?"

She didn't answer and I could only hope she had hung up to call for help. A heaviness settled in the pit of my stomach and my chest began to constrict once again when I realized the car had come to a stop and the cellular service had faded. No digital bars, not a single one.

The sound of a car door slamming cut short my sobs and kicked in my adrenalin. I slid the ring button to vibrate and glimpsed a single vertical bar before I pushed the button to darken the screen. One tiny little bar filled me with hope. I slid the phone into a hidden pocket on the inside of my blazer and then shoved the tire iron up the right sleeve.

"Come on. Get out."

Sunlight bore down on my face challenging my vision. A fuzzy outline of a big body finally appeared and caused me to doubt my planned escape, but if I didn't act quickly I might not have another chance. "What did you say?"

"I said get out."

I pulled myself up into a sitting position.

"Jump out and don't even think about running. You're in the middle of no place."

Even if he was telling me the truth, I chose not to believe him. I had one bar on my phone and that was enough to keep my hope from fading.

"Aaaaaargggggghhhh." I swung my right arm with the tire iron against the jerk's head, praying I'd see it crack open like a rotten egg. Instead, I heard a crack and a woman scream. My breath escaped me. When I hit the ground and the screaming stopped, I realized it had been me who'd let out the awful scream. Pain radiated from my arm.

"You stupid bitch." He let out a deep, guttural laugh followed by an unexpected high-pitched snort.

He grabbed my broken arm. I screamed and shoved my foot between his legs right before I threw up. He doubled over for only a minute then stood upright.

"That's it, you little slut." He leaned over, grabbed me by my hair and started dragging me.

"Jerk off. Leave her alone," someone said.

The jerk let go of my hair and stepped back. I looked up through my sobs, thankful someone had come to my rescue. When I realized it was Rocco I was confused. How could I be happy to see the man who'd been stalking me?

"Here, let me help you." He extended his hand. I grabbed it with my good arm and he pulled me up off the ground.

"I need a doctor." I held my right arm.

"Sure. Follow me."

I surveyed my surroundings trying to get a bearing on exactly where I might be. A thick forest of trees stood off to my left. An even denser grouping of trees bordered my right.

My nerve endings had gone on retreat because I no longer hurt. I'd read about people overcoming great pain when amputating their own limb to save their life. I thanked God for only giving me a broken bone.

"You're walking too slow." The jerk pushed me. I stumbled and woke up my nerve endings causing a throbbing pain to grab my attention.

"I'm really in pain you guys."

"Shut your trap," the jerk said.

We were in a row on a dirt path. He was behind me and Rocco in front. Rocco's cell phone rang and almost sent me into tears of happiness. If his cell worked then mine might work too.

"Yeah. Got her right here." Rocco hung up the phone.

I followed him over a small bridge. Looking down at the running water below took my attention away from the pain and focused it on my level of hope. It was growing. The creek had to lead someplace and I planned to follow it to freedom once I formulated my plan of escape.

274

"Keep moving," the jerk said, shoving me forward again and causing the pain to take center stage one more time.

I let my eyes wander in hopes of finding something to take my mind off the pain. Ahead was a log cabin. The yellow and orange leaves on the trees near the cabin reminded me of apple cider. The pasture to the right of the cabin brought back memories of touch football at college, but I was sure they didn't bring me here to play games.

Rocco opened the door to the cabin and the jerk followed me inside. The place was surprisingly nice and somehow calmed me. A big overstuffed leather chair sat comfortably near the fireplace and I longed to curl up in its embrace. To fall asleep in front of the fireplace and wake up only after the nightmare ended.

"Sit here," Rocco demanded.

He sounded meaner than he had outside. I sat down in a wooden chair at the kitchen table.

"Glad you could make it." Samuel Martin moved out of the hallway and into the kitchen, sitting down in a chair across the table from me.

I propped up my arm on the table wincing in pain. "Do you have some aspirin?" My question sounded stupid when I asked it, but I'd settle for anything that might help take the pain away.

"Got something even better. Get some ice Rocco." Samuel Martin got up and walked over toward the kitchen sink and opened a cabinet. He pulled out a glass and a bottle of Jack Daniels.

Rocco brought a small ice bucket to the table. Samuel Martin threw a couple of cubes into a glass and poured whiskey halfway to the rim. "Here, this should take the edge off."

Desperate, I grabbed the glass and chugged. I slammed the empty glass down on the table. After I finished coughing and gagging, I reached for the second round that Samuel had poured.

"Slow down. Better sip the next one." Rocco put some ice in a bag and handed it to me.

"Can you call an ambulance?" I asked after placing the bag on my arm. When none of the three men in the room responded, not even with a laugh, I took it as a bad sign.

I downed my second drink. I had to find the balance between deadening the pain and staying alert enough to make my escape. Samuel Martin poured a third.

"Ms. Moore. I need to know what you were working on for Max Vanderbur." Samuel Martin set the bottle of Jack on the table.

"Ah, I didn't do much. Just a little research for him." I felt tipsy, but the pain continued so I poured the third glass of whiskey down my throat hoping my adrenaline would keep me from getting sloppy drunk.

"How much research?"

As my head became woozy, the pain began to subside. I sipped on a fourth glass of Jack in case I had to crawl out a window to escape or God forbid they killed me.

"Are you worried I got something on you?"

"I think your information's wrong."

"Oh. So you think I'd be wrong if I said you killed Max Vanderbur or had him killed?" My words were slurred, which should have made them easier to stop as they worked their way out of my mouth.

"I have no idea who killed Max Vanderbur. For all I know you killed him."

"Why would I kill him? You and Mrs. Vanderbur are the ones with the motives."

I rubbed my eyes as both Samuel Martins shifted in their chairs. The ice cubes clinked and echoed through my head. I slid my glass across the table for a refill.

The whiskey was a great pain reliever and courage enhancer. "Either you killed him because of Marston Place or you both killed him because of your affair."

His eyes bugged out. A sure sign he had no idea how I knew about his affair and that knowledge made me smile. Who cared if I was in a secluded cabin with three men and way past the point of making a good grade on a breathalyzer test? The most important thing was that I believed I had the upper hand.

"Ms. Moore, I don't know—"

"Oh come on, Sammy, admit it. You're not a real estate developer you're a killer. You killed Max Vanderbur and Mitch Obermier, and you probably killed Mitch's father too. So why don't you just come clean."

I wasn't sure who was talking. I mean I knew it was my voice, but it sounded off a bit, like some tough broad in a movie. Whatever I said was working because through the slits of my eyes I noticed Samuel Martin's face twitching.

"The Obermier family had a chance to become millionaires. They were simple people who didn't understand progress," Samuel said.

"So you killed all of them?"

"You think I'm going to tell you I whacked someone? You're just as much of an idiot as the Obermier's were. Kyle Obermier got rid of his own father. He was stupid. Had no idea he wasn't going to be able to sell the land."

"What about Max Vanderbur?"

"His death was a gift. I don't know who killed him, but God was looking out for me."

Ice clinked in my glass again. "I'll have s'more." I laughed and snorted. "S'more...did you hear that? Hah. Got marshmallows? Let's light the fire. Got any graham crackers or chocolate? Mmmm, doesn't that sound good?"

"Why don't you have another one and then tell me where the professor's information is being kept." A full glass of Jack Daniels appeared like magic. I probably wasn't getting out of here alive. Drinking myself to death sounded much better than being murdered.

"Don't you want to have another one of these too?" I raised my glass for a toast.

When nobody else raised a glass, I realized I'd been the only one drinking. I stood up. "I gotta pee."

"Rocco. Take her to the bathroom. Don't let her out of your sight."

Rocco walked me down the hall. "The window's painted shut and if you try to break it I'll be in here before you even stick your head outside."

I locked the door behind me. As I walked toward the window, I caught a glimpse of myself in the mirror. The reflection didn't resemble me. It looked small and frail. I opened the medicine cabinet hoping to find pills so I could end it all now and avoid suffering a torturous death. Instead I found a few razor blades and an idea.

I grabbed a blade and sliced the edges of the window. When I finished both sides I worked on the bottom until I became nauseated.

I bent over the toilet. "Huuuhaaaaaaaarrrggggg."

Most of the vomit hit the wall and floor, except for the part that came out my nose.

"Jesus. That's disgusting," Rocco said from the other side of the door.

The bathroom contained no tissues, so I tore off some toilet paper from the roll and wiped my eyes and nose. At least I knew Rocco was still outside the door.

I returned to slicing through the paint on the bottom of the window. I worried he might get suspicious if it took much longer.

"Huuuhaaaarggggg." I made vomiting sounds as I attempted to open the window. A second nudge and it started to open.

"Hurry up or I'll break the door down."

"Let me puking finish, I mean Pinish fuking. Crap. Just let me finish."

Two large bath towels hung on the wall. I knotted one together, fashioning it into an arm sling. "Huuuuhaaarrrggg. Ptha. Ptha." I continued pretending to throw up.

The window opened just enough for me to climb through. I turned the faucets on, flushed the toilet, grabbed my makeshift sling and started climbing out the window. I wanted to hurl obscenities of the most horrible kind at Rocco as the pain in my arm caused me to grit my teeth. I held back my tears, flopped onto the porch and ended up ten times sober than I had been.

I scanned the woods for the best escape route and caught sight of someone standing by the side of a tree. I was doomed. On the verge of becoming hysterical I squinted trying to stop the tears. My squinting revealed that the person in the woods was Nick. He motioned for me to come to him. I scrambled to my feet and never looked back.

24

NICK DRAGGED ME behind him. "Where are we going?"

"The car's about a mile through the trees that way."

"A mile?"

"If you want I can leave you here."

I picked up my pace. "No way, you are not leaving me. I've been through hell and I'm not about to let my ride to freedom take off without me."

Bugs in all makes and models landed on my face and I swatted with abandon. I felt as though I were running a marathon, teetering between exhaustion and exhilaration. With each step the alcohol oozed its way out of my body leaving behind the pain it had been so skillfully masking.

"The car's up ahead." Nick pointed.

My joy was expressed through tears. I had never before been so happy to set my eyes on Fugly. "Where's Mirella?"

"She took the Volkswagen and went home. Too dangerous."

"How did you find me?"

"I drove to the lot. Mirella told me you had disappeared. A car with two guys inside drove by at the same time, so I followed it. I wasn't sure you were in the car. I took a—"

"I don't know how to thank you, Nick."

"No need. Get in."

We drove for a while in silence, partly because my hangover had started, but mostly because I'd end up screaming in agony if I opened my mouth for any reason. My arm was on fire.

Nick finally broke the silence. "What happened back there?"

"Samuel Martin wanted to know what kind of information I had on the Marston development. He also wanted me to tell him where I hid my notes."

"He broke your arm?"

"No. I did. Long story for another time."

"Did he say anything about my uncle?"

"No. Why?"

"Just wondering."

Nick took a left turn onto a gravel road. I realized he had been heading away from the city all along. "Where are we going?"

"Somewhere safe."

"Nick, I want to go home."

"Can't do that, Aspen."

"Why? Is something wrong with my place?"

"You're what's wrong."

The young innocent Nick I'd talked to about fraternities and college classes had disappeared. The new Nick's face muscles tightened and his eyes darkened.

"What's a matter? What did I do?"

"You couldn't just leave things alone. Mirella tried to get the box from you and send Sara Obermier home, but you had to stick your nose in where it didn't belong."

"Mirella helped investigate too."

"I told her to stop. I told her she needed to get the box back and not ask any questions. She had no idea what she was getting ready to expose."

"I'm confused. What are you talking about?"

"I'm talking about you not being able to drop your research after Max died. I'm talking about the body of Mitch Obermier you dug up in Marston."

I didn't like this side of Nick. "How do you know whose body was buried on that lot?"

"The night Mitch got killed I watched my uncle and Sam Martin open the trunk and drag something into the woods. My uncle is like a father to me. Whenever my dad goes off on drunken binges, my uncle steps in. I can't let anyone destroy his life. I had to stop Max and now I have to stop you."

"Max? Stop me?"

I jumped when my phone rang. I reached for it.

Nick pulled a gun from his jacket and aimed the barrel at my forehead. "Answer it and you're a dead woman."

"What's it matter? You're going to kill me anyway, right? Isn't that what you meant by stop me?" I held the phone in my hand, thinking. I'd escaped once already. Was I crazy to think a second break for freedom in the same day would end in success?

"Answer the thing. Fine by me."

I stared as the phone stopped ringing and Stephanie's name turned into a missed call. The phone went dark. "Are you at least going to let me call my family before you kill me?"

"Hey. I realize you're not a bad person. Family's important and if you don't cause me any trouble I'll let you make a call once we stop."

"Where are you taking me?"

"A little place near the Meramec River."

Great. He planned to dump me in the river. I'd end up a floater, bloated and unidentifiable. I picked my purse up off the floorboard where I'd left it when Mirella and I went digging.

"What are you doing? Put that down."

"I want a mint. My mouth tastes like a distillery."

"If anything remotely looking like a gun comes out, you're dead."

I opened my purse and rummaged around for my wallet. I slid my driver's license out and hid it behind the tin of Altoids as I removed them from my purse. "You want one?"

Nick didn't answer. I figured he didn't hear me or he was dreaming about how to end my life. I slipped the license into the front pocket of my jeans, so I wouldn't end up a Jane Doe.

"Sure you don't want a mint?" I held the tin out.

Again he didn't answer. He'd disconnected. That was a bad sign. I wasn't ready to die. I could grab the wheel and run us off the road, but he might shoot me before I had a chance to crash the car.

As I dropped the Altoids back inside my purse, I touched another metal object. My heart palpitated. I'd forgotten I'd hidden a spare pepper spray. Cupping the canister, I removed it as I placed my purse back on the floorboard.

Up ahead, off to the right, stood an old farmhouse. It was probably my last chance before we hit the river. As we approached I awkwardly positioned my left hand thumb over the pepper spray button and yelled, "Hey, Nick!"

He screamed and his hands flew off the steering wheel as the spray peppered his face. I continued to push the button over and over with the desperation of passenger in an out of control car. I didn't attempt to grab the wheel. The time had come to let go and trust Fugly.

We ran into a ditch, flipped over twice, then landed right side up. I'd had the sense to buckle up when I'd gotten into the car, but Nick had not. He was no longer next to me in the driver's seat.

My body was pain free. I was in shock or I was dead. The pepper spray remained lodged in my hand. I lowered my arm and dropped the spray into my pocket. Miraculously my phone had remained in my blazer where I had dropped it. I released my seatbelt and scrambled around until I found my purse.

The sound of Nick calling my name floated through the busted car windows. I froze. Without his seatbelt, how could he have survived the crash? I caught sight of his body on top of a bale of hay. If he was uninjured he'd already be after me. I opened the car door and ambled my way toward the farmhouse.

———

I woke up to the smell of barn animals. Two horses, a cow, a pig, and three cats stared at me like I'd walked right out of a scene from Night of the Living Dead.

I wasn't sure how long I'd been passed out. I remembered my knock on the farmhouse door had gone unanswered, but my memory of how I'd made my way back to the barn and into a soft but itchy pile of hay was lost.

I flinched when my cell phone rang.

"Hello?"

"Hey, girlie, where are you?"

I was relieved to hear Stephanie's voice. "I'm at some farmhouse. I need yo—"

"I know, but whereabouts?"

"How would you know that?" I wasn't sure who to trust anymore. What if Stephanie had somehow become involved in Nick's agenda?

"Dummy, you called me."

"I don't think so. I'll call you back." I ended the call and browsed my call log.

A flicker of hope returned when I saw the last outgoing call was to Stephanie. My defensiveness melted away and I called her back. "Stephanie?"

"What is going on Aspen? First you call me up mumbling about pigs and cows and needing me to come get you. You didn't know the address and I had to pull your location out of you between sobs. You didn't even say goodbye. You just burped and hung up."

"Where are you?"

"I'm outside the stupid farmhouse. I couldn't get right through because there was an accident up the road."

"Was anyone hurt?"

"They were taking somebody away in an ambulance. Where are you?"

"I'm in the barn. Are you outside?"

"I'm pulling back to the barn right now."

I made sure I closed the barn door before running full force with my arms wide open. "Thank you for saving me Stephanie."

She leaned away. "Damn. What the hell happened to you?"

———

Stephanie pulled up to the hospital and let me out at the emergency room entrance. My entire body hurt as I got out of her car and made my way inside to the check-in desk. I couldn't tell the truth about what happened so I told the triage nurse I'd fallen down a hill by the river.

The speed at which they placed me on a gurney in the emergency room corridor made me whisper a little thank you to whatever Supreme Being might be watching over me. The nurse handed me a hospital gown. "Everything off and this should open from the back."

"Uhm."

"Right. Hold on one sec and I'll help, if you like."

I nodded.

By the time we got my clothes off I discovered my broken arm was not my only problem. I had a two inch long gash on the outside of my thigh.

"That's a little deep. What happened there?"

"I'm not sure. Probably stabbed by a branch." I thought back to the car accident and vaguely remembered hearing a gun shot. A bullet from Nick's gun must have ricocheted inside the car while we rolled. I hoped it wasn't lodged in my flesh because a bullet didn't fit with my story.

"The doc'll take a look. I need to get some information from you." The nurse tapped away on the laptop keys as I answered questions about medications, allergies, and pain levels. When she was finished she took some blood and inserted an I.V. just in case.

Eternity would have felt shorter than the time it took for a doctor to stroll into the room. "I hear you want something for the pain." Once she raised her head and observed me, she added, "Let me get that order going right away." The doctor left.

"I must look horrible," I said to no one.

The doctor re-entered a few minutes later with a nurse. "Your blood alcohol is not as high as the smell would lead one to believe, so you're clear for pain medication." She nodded at the nurse who shot some stuff into my I.V. line.

"We know you've been drinking, but did you eat today?"

The odor wafting from my skin must have been the reason the triage nurse didn't blink when I told her I fell down a hill. "Yes. I ate something this morning."

"We're going to keep you overnight so we'll operate on your arm tomorrow morning. The alcohol must be deadening the pain because that is one extremely broken arm, not to mention the gouge on your leg."

The pain killers had kicked in and I had no worries. They could admit me to the hospital, slice my arm open, even shave my head as long as they kept feeding me drugs.

I asked the nurse for my phone before she left the room and I called Stephanie. "Hey. They're going to keep me overnight so you don't need to wait."

"I just dropped you off and left. I'm having a few drinks with my co-workers."

Again, I questioned Stephanie's friendship that she would leave me in the emergency room by myself and run off to happy hour. At least she had rescued me from a barn, so I couldn't be too upset. I ended the call and closed my eyes.

"Hello. Ms. Moore."

I opened one eye to see U. S. Marshal Anthony Cutter standing by my bed.

"Want to tell me what's going on?"

"Nuffin." I licked my dry lips to loosen them. "Nothing," I repeated.

"Doesn't appear like nothing."

"How'd you know I was here?"

"You don't remember calling me?"

Oh no. Why the hell did I call him and what did I say? I was screwed. He probably already packed my bags. "Sorry. I'd been drinking with some friends and had a little too much."

"That's not exactly the story you told over the phone right before you begged to be taken to the emergency room."

"Wait. I'd remember if I talked to you because I couldn't have drunk dialed you. By the time we were on our way to the hospital I was no longer drunk. If someone's telling a story it's you. Are you following me?"

"No, you butt dialed me."

"Very funny trying to convince me I called you on purpose. Were you trying to trick me, thinking I had something to confess?"

"No. I was thinking you might be in some trouble and need some help."

"Nothing I can't handle. I don't want you to move me."

"We're in the business of keeping people safe. It cost a lot of money to relocate someone, so I can guarantee you if you haven't been outed, then you're here to stay."

"Good. I'm starting to create a life—."

"But if you end up in more trouble and there's no logical answer we may need to reconsider, so keep your nose clean."

"My nose is clean, well I'm sure it's dirty right now, but nothing a shower can't fix."

"You need to acknowledge you understand what I mean, Aspen."

Geez. He was all business. "Yes, Cutter, I understand and thanks for looking out for me."

Cutter bid me farewell and I knew I'd remain a resident of St. Louis for at least one more day.

25

A MILD ALLERGIC REACTION to the anesthesia caused me to spend a second night in the hospital. My leg wound turned out to be minor, with no sign of a bullet. My arm ended up a major event, with a cast from my hand all the way to under my arm pit.

The doctor had cleared me. I was dressed and ready to go. I supported my arm on a pillow while I waited for the nurse to bring in my discharge instructions. I tried to keep myself from thinking about the frustration to come. Having my dominant hand restrained meant my life would be far from normal. Forks, toilet paper, bras, and all the other things I used each day would require ninja like skills to maneuver.

The number of arrangements I needed to make mounted in my head. Someone to help me with my customers, someone to help me with my own care, but the biggest arrangement was for the arrest of Nick Russo.

I grabbed the business card out of my jacket pocket. "Officer Storey? I mean, Eli?"

"Yes. Who's this?"

"Aspen Moore. I'm the one—"

"I know who you are."

"Is that bad? Because I could really use your help."

"No. I meant what I said. Any time you need something you can give me a call. That's why I gave you my cell number."

"I'm so relieved because I'm getting ready to ask you for a big favor."

I explained about the car accident and what Nick had said to me about Max. Eli didn't ask any questions because I had asked him not to. He just said he'd be at the hospital in twenty minutes.

I called Peter and left him a message asking if he could pick me up in a few hours. He'd obviously been by to check on me at some point, evidenced by the words 'Peter was here' and a smiley face scrawled sideways across my cast. Not seeing an autograph from Jack had been a relief because it was hard to keep an air of mystery while in a hospital gown.

Still thinking of Jack, I was stunned when he entered my room. "Getting ready to go?"

"What are you doing here?" I self-consciously adjusted my hair and tried holding my head down and at an angle to camouflage the dark circles beneath my eyes.

"I thought I'd stop by on my way out of town. Wow, you did take a nasty fall."

"I'm sorry I couldn't make dinner the other night, but—"

Jack laughed. "Don't apologize. I'm just happy we'll be able to reschedule. Though I might need to cook and feed you too." Jack ran his hand over the cast.

"I'm definitely facing a challenge. Where are you going?"

"I'm off to Virginia for the weekend to visit family. When I get back I'll make you anything you want."

"Sounds wonderful. Jack? I uh." I tried to figure out how to tell him about Fugly. "Your car—"

"I was worried you had been in the accident, but the police said a man was driving. I figured you loaned the car to someone. Guess you should be glad you only fell down a hill."

The nurse walked into my room. "Here are your papers. I need to go over these with you."

"I'm glad you're doing okay. I'll call you when I get back in town." Jack leaned over and gave me a small peck on the lips.

Tears began trickling down my cheeks. My entire escapade had been dangerous and irresponsible. Had I died, my mother would have been devastated. The thought of not seeing her again opened the spigot allowing my tears to flow freely. I had to talk to Cutter about arranging a meeting with my mother or if necessary, arrange one myself. "I'm sorry. I think the pain medications are getting the best of me."

"I understand."

I decided against telling Jack I hadn't loaned out the car. "I'd like some sort of comfort food."

"So is that a definite yes for dinner?"

"It is."

He smiled and walked out the door.

The nurse went over my discharge instructions and gave me the doctor's prescriptions. I assured her I wouldn't be driving since I had no car at the hospital.

My phone rang right after the nurse left.

"Hello?"

"Ms. Moore?"

I recognized his voice and wasn't sure if I should speak to him or end the call.

"Ms. Moore? It's John Martin."

"I know who you are."

"I called to find out if you received the red briefcase and if you still planned on attending the Black and White Ball."

Was he crazy? "I guess you didn't hear. My arm's in a cast and your father's a murderer."

"I know."

"How do you know about the cast?"

"I didn't know you had a cast. I knew my father had been accused of murder. The story is all over the news."

"Really?"

"Yes. You are too."

"I'm not accused of murder."

"No, you're on the news."

He had to be lying. If my face had been plastered all over the news, Cutter would be here with my suitcases. Plus Jack would have said something. I clicked on the television right as the intro montage to the noon news finished.

"Did you say you gave me a red briefcase?"

"Yes. Did you like it?"

"Is something wrong with you? Why would I like a briefcase that you used to practically kill me?"

"What are you talking about?"

"The envelope. The note you put in the side pocket that lured me to Tower Grove Park where someone attacked me."

"Why would I do that? The case was a gift. A peace offering. You said you would attend the ball and I wanted to make sure you had good things to say about me when you talked to the patrons. The only envelope I put in the box held an apology. You weren't home so I set the box at your door."

If he was telling the truth, I had to talk to Toby again about what happened when the person dropped off the briefcase. The newscaster mentioned my name. "I need to go. Sorry I won't be going to the ball."

The coverage could have been worse had my photograph been displayed across the screen. The only good fallout from the bad situation had been the mention of my business. How they knew I dug up a body was a mystery to me.

"Nothing, huh?"

I looked up as Cutter walked into my room. "Please don't make me move. Please," I begged.

"I'm not here to move you. I do need you to be honest with me though. If I ask you what's going on, don't tell me nothing when in fact you have been digging up a skeleton."

"Sorry Cutter, but I was trying to handle things on my own."

"You're lucky they didn't plaster a photograph of you all over the city. And what if the story goes national? You need to keep yourself better hidden while I do a little damage control to keep your face from hitting the newspapers. Is there anything else you should share with me that you don't want to?"

"Maybe one more thing. I didn't actually fall down a river bank. My injuries resulted from a car accident. The driver's here in the hospital and he killed Max Vanderbur.

I called Officer Storey and he is going to come over and help me get the guy to confess."

Cutter didn't say a word.

For once, I stayed silent.

"Smart choice not to talk right now." Cutter paced the length of my hospital bed.

Thank goodness Eli entered the room. "Hi, Ms. Moore."

"Officer Storey?" Cutter asked presenting his hand to Eli.

"Yes sir."

"I'm Marshal Anthony Cutter. Can I speak with you for a moment?"

Cutter motioned somewhere outside of my room. I didn't like Cutter talking to Eli without me present, but challenging him at this point was suicidal.

I turned off the television and waited.

"Looks like we have an understanding," Cutter announced as he and Eli walked back into the room.

"What kind of understanding?"

"I told Marshal Cutter everything you told me and he informed me that you are a special lady he would like me to help him keep an eye on."

"So you're going to be tag teaming me?"

They both laughed. I didn't see the humor.

"Aspen, it's always good to have a friend on the force. I feel comfortable with you reaching out to Officer Storey if you're in a bind and can't get a hold of me."

Eli had a smile on his face that made his laugh lines stand up with pride.

"Are we still going to make sure Nick Russo gets what he deserves?" I asked.

"Sure. Let's get you in a wheelchair." Cutter pressed my nurses call button and asked for a chair.

We discussed our plan until the nurse entered. I limped over and sat down in the wheelchair.

"So are we all on the same page?" Cutter asked.

"Yes. As soon as Aspen says the code phrase, I am clear to arrest Nick," Eli said.

"What's the code phrase, Aspen?"

"Book him, Danno."

Cutter furrowed his brow. "Aspen, come on, this is serious. I need to make sure we all understand the code phrase."

"Fine. The code phrase is, I'm tired."

The four of us made our way to the elevator and rode down three floors. The nurse wheeled me into Nick's room near his bed by the window. She closed the curtain and left.

"See what you get for messing with me, Nick?"

"I didn't mess with you. You messed with me. You wrecked the car and took off making the police think I had been the driver."

Nick's words threw me. "Are you trying to blame me?"

"I'm just telling the truth."

"Doesn't matter what you say now, because I recorded everything you said then."

"Right."

His arrogance pissed me off. "You're a stupid kid."

"I'm a lot smarter than you think. You probably didn't have a recorder before, but I bet you do now."

"Where? No pockets. Oh right, I'm crazy and stuffed it down my cast. You are an idiot."

His face became visibly warm. "If I'm an idiot how did I get Max to hang himself so it looked like a suicide? I even fooled the police."

Eli, Cutter and I had agreed I would say the code phrase once I got a confession, but I wanted Nick to spill every ounce of incriminating evidence he had. I continued talking. "I guess that was smart but turning in your uncle and Samuel Martin when you were a kid would have been smarter."

"I should have turned in Sam Martin is what I should have done. He killed Mitch Obermier, not my uncle, but my uncle taught me to be loyal. He was loyal to Sam Martin which meant I was too."

His mouth was starting to loosen up so I continued prompting. "How do you know who killed Mitch? Did you watch Sam do it?"

"Sure. Sam shot him and they stuck him in the trunk. I got tired of waiting in the car that night and walked up as Sam tossed the gun into the hole. While my uncle and Sam were rolling Mitch into the hole, I grabbed the gun. Same gun I was going to kill you with. Too bad you ruined my plan. You destroyed everything." The redness in Nick's face deepened and he started to get up out of his hospital bed.

"Boy, I'm tired."

Nick started coming at me.

"I said, I'm tired!"

I heard jingling and footsteps behind me.

"Nick Russo. You're under arrest," Eli said, grabbing Nick by the arm and pushing him back into the hospital bed. He cuffed his wrist to the bed rail.

"Didn't you hear me, Eli?"

He smiled at me before he answered. "Sorry, I was waiting for, Book him, Danno."

I said goodbye to Eli, then Cutter wheeled me back to my room. The little bit of interaction with Nick wore me out. I crawled into the bed to wait for Peter and I didn't have to wait long.

"Wake up sleepy-head."

"I'm not asleep," I said, turning my head toward the door. Peter stood there with a hand full of balloons.

"What are you doing? Balloons for my ride home?"

"Don't you remember anything we talked about during my visit?"

"I don't even remember seeing you. Only evidence was my arm," I said pointing to his name on my cast.

He grinned.

I stuck my finger into the top of the cast attempting to scratch an itch. "What did we talk about?"

"Somebody passed by your room with balloons and you went on about how happy balloons made you."

"That's all we talked about?"

"You said a few more things. Like how you are so lucky to have me."

"Did I?" Tiny fragments of our conversation were coming back slowly. I was slightly embarrassed by my adulation toward Peter while under the influence. But my biggest concern was on whether I had let my real identity slip. "Did I say anything else?"

"No. After you told me how lucky you were to have me, you fell back asleep, so I left."

"You're enjoying repeating what I said, aren't you?"

"Did I say that you said, you were lucky to have me? I meant you said you were really, really, really lucky to have me." Peter winked.

"It's true."

"Why don't we get your things and get you out of here. I'm taking you back to Madeline's place."

"I don't think I'm up for talking with Madeline. I'd just like to go home."

"Trust me. You want to come to Madeline's place. Besides, she isn't there. She had to stay an extra day in L.A."

———

I did a double-take when we pulled up in front of Madeline's house. "Is...Is that mine?"

"Sure is."

Parked in the driveway was my beauty. The dark blue skin flawless and the platinum trim as shiny as the day I first drove the Jeep. "Excellent. I'll drive myself home."

"Hold on Tonto. I'm going to feed you some lunch then I'll drive around with you for a little bit until you get the hang of this big boy."

"That's just plain stupid."

"Did you forget your leg is messed up and your arm's in a cast?"

I gave in and agreed to lunch. Afterward, Peter and I headed out to my Jeep. "I didn't tell Jack about being in his car. He thinks I loaned the Fairmont to Nick. Was the thing a total loss?"

"Never mind."

"Oh God, it was a total loss wasn't it?"

"Don't worry. He should have dumped the heap a long time ago. You did him a favor."

Regardless of what Peter said, I felt terrible for destroying part of Jack's past. "Maybe I better tell him about being in the car."

"Probably a good move. Otherwise you'll have to keep lying to him."

Even if I told Jack about me being in the car, I still had to keep lying to him and Peter too. And anyone else who came into my life. "You're right."

"Damn right. I'm always right."

"I better get going Peter."

"Be careful. And if you need me to do anything for you over the next several weeks, like feed you, draw more pictures on your cast, fasten your bra just give me a call."

I laughed.

Stepping up into the Jeep was difficult and challenging with my arm in a cast. Peter helped me. I inserted the key into the ignition and turned it with my right hand, but had to shift into drive with my left.

"You sure you don't want me to drive you?"

"Nope. You can't be my chauffeur for six weeks."

———

I made my way to my street without any problems. Parking was another matter. After a fifty-five point turn I backed myself into a space a block away from my apartment. A drizzle fell as I hurried down the block in an attempt to keep my cast dry.

Mrs. Rippetoe watched me out the window and opened the door as soon as I hit the front steps. "Toby's gone."

Inside the warm foyer, my skin tingled as the damp spots began to evaporate. "I'm sure he'll be back.

300

Remember last week when you thought he had gone missing and he showed up later?"

"No, this time he's really gone. I was going to walk down the street and get a soda pop, but when I went to get the money out of my secret money jar the money was all gone. I must of had five hundred dollars"

"What does your money jar have to do with Toby?"

"Did I tell you about my money jar?" she asked.

"No."

"I told Toby once. Opened the jar today and found an unsigned IOU inside. I went upstairs to talk to him and the door was parted, so I pushed it open and everything's gone from his apartment."

"Oh, Mrs. Rippetoe, I'm sorry. Are you going to be okay?"

"I'm a strong woman. I expect I'll never lay eyes on the money again. Took me a long time to save up that much. But listen to me going on this way. What happened to your arm?"

"I fell down a hill."

"Your face is a mess too."

She didn't hold back. I hadn't looked in a mirror yet. None of the men in my life had been brave enough to mention anything about my tragic face. "Yes, I had quite the fall."

"Let me know if you need anything, Hon."

"I sure will." The difficulties involved with being a landlord at her age were greater than for someone younger and I promised myself to check in on her more often.

Toby sneaking away would have been hard to believe had it not been for the empty apartment. My suspicion of Toby being the culprit who drained my less bountiful money jar deepened. I walked into the kitchen. I took the lid off my money jar and looked inside just in case Toby had robbed Mrs. Rippetoe to pay me back. There was no money, but there was a piece of paper, most likely an IOU.

I unfolded it and found a complete letter. He apologized for taking my money and Mrs. Rippetoe's money without asking, but promised when he made it big in California he'd pay us back. One paragraph captured my attention. His confession that he'd been paid by a lady to put an envelope in my briefcase. With Toby gone I'd never find out who lured me to the park or who attacked me.

Stephanie's name popped up on my phone and I answered.

"How are you?" she asked.

"Got a gigantic cast on my arm, but I'm alive."

"You need some help?"

I didn't know how to answer the question. Stephanie wasn't the right candidate, but who else could I get? "I could use a little help."

"Great. I generally make more than this, but for you I will accept a wage of twenty dollars an hour."

"Oh. I thought you were offering to help around my house or something."

"I got fired! They found out about my clients coming to my house. I'm really desperate for a job. I think they blacklisted me because none of my old clients want to come to my house."

Stephanie wasn't my first pick to help me at my office, but I didn't have much of a choice. "You're hired."

"Oh thank you. Thank you. Thank you. You won't be disappointed. I promise I won't take anything from anybody."

I knew she meant to reassure me, but the statement actually raised my anxiety level. "Thank you. I am counting on you. Hey, did you talk to the police the other day after you picked me up from the barn?"

"No. Should I have?"

"No. Everything is fine. I was wondering because of the story on the news."

"Oh. I don't watch television. I don't even own one."

I learned more about Stephanie every time I talked to her. Television had become my necessary escape. "How do you go without watching television?"

"I have more important things to attend to."

Ouch. "I'll see you in my office first thing Monday morning."

The only person other than Stephanie or me who could have told the police anything was Mirella, but why would she turn in her own uncle? I knew I would eventually have to call her.

———

After taking a few days off, I was glad to be getting back to work. When I pulled up in front of my office, I didn't recognize the place. Wooden blinds hung in the window and the walls had been painted a misty blue. I walked through the door and found Mirella behind a new reception desk. "How did you get in here?"

"I talked to Peter and he had the building's owner let us in. Do you like what we did?"

I glanced around hoping Peter was here too. Sweat began forming on my forehead, my heart pounded, making me wish I had my pepper spray. If Mirella turned out to be even half as crazy as her twin Nick I would need it.

Peter was nowhere in my office. "I think you better leave."

When the phone rang, Mirella answered the call. "Moore Time, how can I help you? Sure I will have a concierge call you today."

She wrote down some information and hung up the phone.

"What are you doing?"

"I hope you don't mind. I figured I had to do something to help you while you were in the hospital."

"I'm grateful, but I'm not sure you should be here, with Nick and all."

"Nick called me after the accident. I'm so sorry about what happened. I had no idea what was going on with him. All I knew is he kept yelling at me. He scared me when he drove off in your car like a wild man. I figured something was wrong, so I called the police and told them everything."

"What did you tell them?"

"All about us digging up the body. I know you're upset, so I'll go now."

"Wait. How's Sara?"

"She is doin—"

The phone rang. Mirella took the call. "Moore Time, how can I help you?"

She sounded professional as she answered the phone. Had her brother not tried to kill me I might have considered employing her instead of Stephanie. Each time Mirella tried to answer my question about Sara, the phone rang. If I counted correctly, five calls had come in since I'd walked through the door.

"What's going on?" I asked.

"It's been like this all day because of the story on the news," Mirella said. "Oh, and Sara and little Mitchell are doing great. When the police arrested her brother-in-law

Kyle for murdering his father, she decided to take Mitchell to Maine to visit the Piazza Rock."

The phone rang again. "Can you stay a little longer and answer the calls?"

Mirella nodded. I let her get the phone and I walked around my office. A new coffee machine sat in the entry near a waiting area that included two chairs, a table, and stack of magazines.

The place felt alive. For the first time since I discovered Max Vanderbur swinging from his rafters, a sense of rightness settled over me.

"By the way, Mr. Corbitt called and asked if you could cancel his wedding plans. Seems the fiancée was out of town with a business partner and they weren't exactly conducting business."

I cringed. I knew exactly what Mr. Corbitt had gone through. He was creepy, but nobody deserved to go through that. I felt bad for him, but in a small way I was relieved I wouldn't be putting on a wedding.

"Anything else before I head back to my desk?"

"Oh, yes, I almost forgot. Someone named Stephanie called and said something came up and she wouldn't be able to start until tomorrow."

Of course, she did. I thanked Mirella and poured myself a coffee before heading back to my desk, which they'd left in the rear of the office. A Plexiglas divider had been added, giving me more privacy, but still providing easy access to the back door.

My eyes lit up at the sight of a Lucky Bamboo plant in a red vase. It sat on the corner of my desk next to a box of Hostess Ding Dongs. I reached for the small envelope tucked in the plant and opened it.

Tonto,
Luck has nothing to do with it.
- Peter

THE END

ACKNOWLEDGEMENTS

Inspiration is such an important component when it comes to believing in your dream. I received mine compliments of my late mother-in-law Mary. While her children were at school, she typed away on her typewriter, completed her novel and mailed it to the publisher. With each rejection, she continued to write more novels, sending those off too. The inspiration did not come from her getting her novels published, because she never did. The inspiration came from her sheer determination and commitment. The satisfaction derived from penning the final page of a novel is tremendous and I have Mary to thank for that.

Many others are also responsible for guiding me through to completion. I must thank my husband, Bill, for reading and re-reading the extremely rough drafts, with never a yawn, and being supportive of the time I spend writing. I must also thank Kim, my wonderful sister and an avid reader, for tackling version one and still offering encouragement. And for my entire family, I give you a big hug for being my biggest fans.

When it comes to crafting, I must give a big shout out to Lisa Bork, Teresa Inge, Shelley Shearer, and Kathy Whalen (aka The Ladysleuths) for being the best online critique group in the Universe. They read page after page, looking for typos and grammar faux pas, offering wonderful suggestions and loads of encouragement. And lastly, I would like to thank Al Gore for inventing the Internet, without which I would not have been able to breathe life into my novel.

ABOUT THE AUTHOR

A geographic mutt, Kelly Cochran has lived on the East Coast, the West Coast, and in many places in between. During her childhood, she attended thirteen different schools, in twelve years, all before going off to college at the age of seventeen. To her surprise, she turned out somewhat normal and went on to have a 20-year career in information technology.

Currently she lives in St. Louis, Missouri with her husband and three dogs. Her son lives in the Washington, D.C. area where he never tires of Kelly's efforts to get him to move closer.

When she isn't writing, she divides her time between managing Internet-based retail businesses, talking to her mother, using her high-tech cell phone to play Wordsmith and Tap Fish, and wondering why she doesn't have enough time to finish writing her next novel.

Kelly is a member of Sisters in Crime. Find out more at www.KellyCochran.com

Made in the USA
Charleston, SC
22 August 2012